THE DECEIVING

LAURIE HARRISON

Visit my website at www.laurieharrisonauthor.com

Cover Designer: Tim Barber, Dissect Designs, www.dissectdesigns.com
Editor and Interior Designer: Jovana Shirley, Unforeseen Editing, www.unforeseenediting.com

ISBN-13: 978-1-7332859-3-3

Library of Congress Control Number: 2020918344

Emerald Rain Publishing LLC
7643 Gate Parkway, Ste. 104-156
Jacksonville, FL 32256

For my husband, Dran.

ONE

NATALIE

I stared down at the phone in my hand, failing to push away an overwhelming sense of guilt. I'd always hated lying, but over the past three months, I'd become good at it.

As part of our daily routine, my boyfriend, Michael, had just called to make sure I'd made it to work safely. I'd lied and said I had, but the truth was, I wasn't really at work.

I'm not trying to deceive Michael, I justified to myself. There was nothing for me to gain by lying to him. I was actually lying to protect him, to keep him safe.

I slid the phone back into my purse as the doors to the elevator opened, and I stepped off. A woman at the reception desk greeted me with a wide smile, exposing her perfectly straight, pearly teeth.

"Hi there," she said. "Can I have your name, please?"

"Natalie—" I started and then hesitated.

They hadn't asked for my last name when I made the appointment.

Should I use my real last name or the fake one I created when we moved to San Antonio?

The woman looked at me expectantly.

"Clark," I added, deciding to use my real name.

"Okay. You can go on in." The receptionist nodded toward an office to her right. A shiny gold nameplate that read *Wayne Cartwright, Private Investigator* hung outside the door.

"Thank you."

Before I reached the door to his office, a stocky man with a stubby gray beard appeared in the doorway. He was wearing a pale blue button-down dress shirt with the sleeves rolled up to just below his elbows.

"Hi, I'm Wayne Cartwright," he introduced himself as he firmly shook my hand.

"I appreciate you meeting with me on such short notice."

"Sure. Come on in." Wayne stepped to the side to let me walk past him and into the office.

He shut the door as I sat in a black leather chair in front of his desk.

I glanced around as he took his seat behind the desk. His office was immaculate. There wasn't a folder or piece of paper out in the open, which told me he was serious about keeping his clients' confidentiality. That was exactly what I needed. We were still being hunted, so one slipup from him, and we could all end up dead.

"How can I help you, Miss Clark?" he asked, folding his hands on the desk in front of him.

I opened my purse and retrieved a manila envelope that contained everything I needed for the appointment. I reached into the envelope and pulled out a photo of Chad Henley.

"I need you to find this man and tell me where he is," I said, passing him the photo.

He nodded as he looked it over. "Chad Henley of C. Henley Labs Incorporated. I've heard of him. They have an office in Austin."

I stiffened. "How do you know that?"

A smile tugged at the corner of his lips. "It's my job to know."

"But you don't know him personally?"

"No," he replied, looking me square in the eye.

I studied him for a minute and decided that he was telling the truth. I had been born with a keen sense of intuition, and I would've detected if he were lying.

I could've just read his mind, but I used that ability as sparingly as possible. First of all, it wasn't something that I enjoyed doing, and second, it was a huge violation of privacy. I reserved it only for extreme circumstances when I couldn't rely on just my intuition.

I removed another photo and a sheet of paper from the manila envelope.

"Here is a list of all of his known office locations," I said, handing the sheet of paper that listed every location I could find on the internet. "But it's possible he has more that aren't advertised."

He leaned back in his chair as he looked over the list. "Okay, so I'll find out where he's spending his time and take photographs for confirmation. Is there anything else you'd like me to look into?"

I looked down at the photograph in my hand and choked back a lump that had formed in my throat. I held back the photo, unsure of whether or not I was willing to part with it.

I took a deep breath and reluctantly passed it to him. "You might not see her, but I need you to tell me if you spot this girl. Her name is Becca Clark. She is my sister."

He took her photo and studied it. "Did she run off with Chad Henley or something?"

"Something like that," I lied.

The truth was, Henley had been holding her prisoner for almost five years. Becca had the same sense of intuition that I did, and Henley was forcing her to help him try to find Michael and his sister, Raina. I'd realized only three months ago that Henley was holding Becca captive.

Wayne flashed me a confident smile. "It's half up front and then half when I provide Chad Henley's location. How would you like to pay?"

"Cash." I pulled the money out of the envelope and gave it to him. I'd already read about his fees online, and I had the exact amount ready. "I'll pay the entire fee in full now." There wouldn't be time to settle the debt later. If Wayne were to locate Henley, I would immediately leave town to go rescue Becca.

He quickly counted the cash and then stood up. "I'll be in touch soon."

He shook my hand one more time before I left his office.

"Have a lovely day," the receptionist said cheerfully as I walked past her desk.

I forced a smile back but didn't respond. My day was going to be anything but lovely.

I stepped onto the sidewalk outside his office building and nervously pulled my long auburn hair into a bun. This arrangement with Wayne had to work out. I needed him to find Henley, so I could find Becca. There was no telling what was happening to her now that Henley knew about my abilities.

Henley would do anything to find Michael, Raina, and me. Aside from the fact that Henley believed Michael and Raina were his property because he had been responsible for creating them, we had the powers he needed. Henley wanted to study our special talents, so he could re-create them, bottle them up, and sell them to other people who also wanted to possess them.

Michael had the ability to heal other people, and Raina could move objects with her mind. I had both of those skills; plus, I had unusually strong intuition, and I could read people's minds and visit people in their dreams. I also had the one talent that Henley coveted above all of the others—the capability to heal myself.

As I walked the three blocks from Wayne's office to the building where I worked, I kept an eye out for any suspicious vehicles. Henley could find us at any moment, so we had to be vigilant at all times. If I did spot Henley, I would need to send a group text to Michael, Raina, and their parents, Alexander and Lorena, to warn them. Our protocol was to drop everything and meet at a safe house that Alexander had set up, so we could leave town.

We'd had to activate this protocol four times over the past three months, and I had activated them all. Each time, I'd gotten a familiar knot in my stomach—the one that warned me when something wasn't right. I had known that we were in danger, and luckily, we'd been able to escape in time.

Michael didn't like the fact that I'd taken a job in downtown San Antonio instead of one closer to home. It was about a thirty-minute commute each way. Aside from the fact that he didn't exactly trust my driving skills, if we had to activate the protocol, it would put me at a much greater risk of being discovered by Henley on my way to the safe house. Everyone else could be there in less than ten minutes if they left from their jobs.

I knew that working so far away was risky, but I also had an ulterior motive for choosing this particular job—one that I couldn't share with Michael. Once I got what I needed, I intended to quit and find something closer to home.

I briskly walked past the parking garage, where I'd parked my car, and made my way into the office building of Araragi Medical Solutions.

I worked there as an assistant to Todd Nelson, the vice president of sales.

As I took my seat at the cubicle outside of Todd's office, I peeked to see if he was in there. Unfortunately, he was. I hid the disappointment on my face as he looked up and caught me watching him. I just smiled politely and waved, as if I were just letting him know that I had arrived.

I had hoped today would be the day, but no such luck.

Wanting to discourage Todd from coming out to make small talk, I turned my attention to my computer monitor and opened up Todd's calendar. He was supposed to be in Dallas, visiting a client, but apparently, the client had rescheduled for the following day. Todd's calendar was now filled with back-to-back conference calls, so there would be zero chance of him leaving his office long enough for me to find what I needed. I wished he had waited for me to get in and plan his day for him. I would've conveniently scheduled all of his conference calls for the end of the week and encouraged him to visit a different client today.

Resolving myself to the fact that today would be another wasted day where I failed to save Becca, I eagerly poured myself into my work.

With Todd preoccupied in meetings, I handled all of his phone calls for him throughout the day. I resolved the ones I could and carefully took notes for the ones that required him to call back.

At the end of the day, I compiled all of my notes into a single email and sent it to Todd. He was on his last conference call of the day, but he gave me a thumbs-up from his office to let me know he'd received it.

I shut off my computer and pulled my phone out of my purse. I sent Michael a text to let him know I was leaving work.

He instantly replied back.

Michael: Drive safe. At your place, making dinner.

Michael lived in the apartment below mine, and Raina lived in the apartment across from Michael's. We all had modest one-bedroom apartments, but I didn't mind. It was still larger than the one I'd had in St. Augustine, Florida, and I loved that Michael lived so close by.

Aside from it being safer that we lived near each other, it was nice to see him every day. Of course, it also meant that I saw Raina more often. Even though she didn't seem to hate my existence anymore, she and I were by no means best friends.

After fighting rush-hour traffic to get home, I was pleasantly surprised when I entered my apartment and found only Michael waiting on me. There was no sign of Raina, and Michael was in the kitchen, flipping slices of bread in a skillet.

"French toast?" I asked, getting a whiff of cinnamon in the air.

I couldn't help but let out a small laugh. Of course he would be making something sweet for dinner.

He turned to me and smiled. "It's almost done. How was your day?"

"Uneventful," I replied with a shrug. That was mostly true, thanks to Todd's off-site meeting cancellation, but deep down, I knew that not telling Michael about the private investigator was still technically lying.

It's better if he doesn't know. It's safer this way.

Not only had Michael spent the majority of his childhood living at Henley, but he'd also been captured again three months ago.

While at Henley, Michael had been subjected to unimaginable suffering in the name of medical testing and scientific research. Fortunately, Alexander had broken Michael and Raina out of there when they were kids, and then we'd managed to rescue him after he was recaptured.

The night of Michael's rescue was the same night I'd realized Henley was holding Becca captive. When I first came to this realization, I wanted to tell Michael. In fact, I went into his bedroom in the middle of the night to wake him up and tell him. But when I got there, he was having a nightmare. I had no doubt that his nightmare was about his ordeal at Henley. I'd ended up waking him up to give him relief from whatever anguish he had been replaying in his mind and decided it wasn't the right time to tell him about Becca.

Hiding the truth just snowballed from there. It never felt like the right time, and the longer I waited, the harder it was to tell him. The dark circles that had set under Michael's eyes told me that he was continuing to have nightmares. Although I'd asked him about it numerous times, he continued to reassure me that he was okay.

I grabbed the butter, syrup, and a basket of blueberries out of the fridge. I placed them on the round four-seater dining table as Michael plated our French toast.

He sat across from me, and I watched with a smile as he put syrup on his French toast. He used almost half the bottle.

"What?" he asked, oblivious.

I laughed. "You could just take the lid off the syrup and drink it straight."

"Don't tempt me."

I loved how his blue eyes sparkled when I bantered with him, but I noticed that the shadows under his eyes had gotten even darker. I felt the smile leave my lips.

"What's the matter?" he asked, noticing my shift in mood.

"You look tired. Still not sleeping?"

He took a big bite of his gooey French toast and shook his head. While he could admit that he wasn't sleeping well and that he was stressed out about Henley, he wouldn't go into detail about what his dreams were about.

Although I had the ability to visit him in his dreams and find out for myself, he trusted that I wouldn't do that without his permission. And as much as I wanted to know what was bothering him so I could help, I wouldn't violate his privacy that way.

He put down his fork and reached across the table for my hand, which I gladly placed in his.

"I promise I'm okay," he said, giving my hand a reassuring squeeze. "Going back to Henley was tough, and then with everything that happened … I just need a little time to process it all."

I knew exactly what he was referring to. My best friend, Seth, and I had been the ones to break into the Henley facility to rescue Michael. We were caught during the rescue, and Henley planned to kill both me and Seth. Henley had the gun aimed right at Seth, but I made the choice to use my abilities to pull the gun away from Seth and toward myself. I was shot and would've died, except I was able to heal myself. Prior to that, no one had known it was an ability that I possessed—not even me.

We were all still trying to come to terms with everything that had happened. We'd been through so much, even before Michael was captured by Henley and I was shot.

Henley had been hot on our trail right after Michael saved me from a fatal car accident. Michael was able to easily tap into his adrenaline and used it to rip the door off my mangled car and pull me out. Then, he used his healing abilities to save my life.

What Michael hadn't known at the time was that I naturally had these same abilities, plus some. When he saved me, it essentially unlocked them in my brain. After sleeping for days, I awoke with my newfound powers, but I didn't understand them at first, and they were out of control. I'd accidentally caused a power outage that Henley was able to detect, and it'd ultimately led him to find us.

I was grateful that Michael had chosen to save my life, but I also regretted the consequences he was forced to live with now. Michael and his family had been experts at eluding Henley, and if it hadn't been for me, Henley probably wouldn't have caught him. Still, I was selfishly glad that Michael had come into my life and trusted me with his secret because it had brought us together. I couldn't imagine my life without him.

"Okay, your turn," he said, running his thumb across the back of my hand.

"What do you mean?"

"What's been bothering you? I can tell something has been on your mind." His eyes were filled with concern.

He knew me too well.

I had to look away from him.

I really wanted to tell him the truth, but how could I do that, knowing he was still haunted by what had happened at Henley? If I received information on where Becca was being held, I would have to go rescue her. There was no way Michael would let me go by myself, and I couldn't put him through that. I refused to be the reason he went back to Henley again.

"Same. Freaked out about what happened at Henley." I hated myself as the words came out of my mouth.

I gently pulled my hand back and took a sip of water.

When we were finished with dinner, he helped me load the dishes into the dishwasher.

I was about to ask him if he wanted to stay and watch a movie, but his phone chimed. It was Raina, asking if he could come over and help her figure out why her washing machine wouldn't turn on.

"Sorry, I have to go," he said. "I don't know how long this will take. There's no telling what she's done to it."

In the short time since I'd known Raina, she'd managed to break almost every appliance in every apartment she lived in. The worst was the microwave—when she'd left a metal spoon in her soup bowl and set it on fire.

"That's okay. Rain check for tomorrow night?"

Michael smiled as he wrapped his arms around my waist. "Definitely."

He softly kissed me on the lips, and as he started to step back, I grabbed him. I pulled him back and kissed him again. It was only in these moments that I could block out the reality of what was really going on. I could forget the danger and pressure of finding Becca and just get lost in his kiss.

His phone chimed again, and he groaned against my lips. This time, I let him pull away.

He glanced down at his phone and shook his head. From the expression on his face, I knew it was Raina nagging him to hurry up.

"She so owes me," he said.

"Go ahead," I told him. "I'll see you tomorrow."

He started to walk away and then stopped at the kitchen entrance and turned toward me. "I know running from Henley is scary, but I meant what I said back in Charlotte," he said. "We'll face whatever happens together. I love you."

"I love you too." *And I will do anything to keep you safe.*

Two

Natalie

"Seriously? Come on!" I whined as I tightened my grip on the steering wheel.

Traffic was bumper-to-bumper, and a car had just cut me off, only for the driver to promptly slam on its brakes.

I forced myself to take a deep breath. My frustration wasn't really about the car or the traffic; it was about Becca. I'd had another sleepless night, hoping that she'd contact me in my dreams, but she hadn't.

In fact, it had been months since I dreamed of Becca. The last time was when I'd figured out that Henley was holding her captive. This worried me because, up until then, she'd been appearing regularly. I feared her absence meant that Henley had hurt her. Or worse.

Although I had the ability to visit people in their dreams, I had never been able to reach Becca. Every time I tried, I was met with an empty feeling of darkness. I hadn't been able to connect with Michael when he was captured by Henley either, and I believed it was because of the sedatives that Henley had given him. Despite the fact that I was never successful, I continued to try to visit Becca's dreams every night, hoping that maybe Henley's sedatives would wear off long enough for me to connect with her.

I sighed to myself as I thought about how I'd come pretty close to telling Michael about Becca this morning. When I'd walked out to my car to leave for work, I could see the light on in Michael's apartment. I knew he was awake, getting ready for work. I got the sudden urge to confess everything to him just so I could feel his strong arms around me as he told me that everything would be okay. I'd taken two steps toward his apartment, but when I'd come to my senses and remembered why I was keeping the secret from him in the first place, I'd turned around and gone back to my car.

I have to protect Michael, no matter what.

I pulled into the parking space at work, and as soon as I shut the car off, my phone rang. It was Michael.

As much as I wanted to talk to him, to hear his voice and feel comforted, I let the call go to voice mail. If he heard my voice right now, he'd know that I was a wreck, and that would just lead me to lie to him even more than I already had.

Not wanting him to worry about why I hadn't answered, I decided to send him a text.

Me: Sorry. Just got to work.

I tossed my phone into my purse and hurried into the office. Despite the traffic, I had made it there with one minute to spare.

My phone was already ringing when I reached my desk. It was Todd.

"I'm not going to be in the office today," he said.

I perked up.

He must still be planning to visit his client in Dallas.

"Can you handle a couple of things for me?" he asked.

"Of course." I grabbed a pen and took a breath.

I didn't want to sound overly enthusiastic. I couldn't risk him getting suspicious and deciding to pop in to check up on me today. This was the opportunity I had been waiting for, and I didn't know when I'd get another chance like this.

As Todd rattled off his instructions, I did my best to focus and capture everything accurately. I repeated my notes back to him, hoping he felt at ease. It was crucial that Todd believed I had my tasks under control, so he would stay away.

"All right, good," he said, sounding satisfied. "Just call my cell if anything comes up and you need me."

"Will do."

After we hung up, I stood up and casually surveyed my surroundings. There was only one other lady in the office, and she was on the other side, deep in thought on whatever she was typing at her desk. Todd was a bit of an early bird, which meant I needed to be in the office early, too, but everyone else usually came in later in the morning. This could be my only chance. The office would only get more crowded from here on out.

Stealing one last glimpse around, I strolled into Todd's office. It wouldn't be unusual for an assistant to be in their boss's office, unsupervised, but I needed to seem completely normal, just in case that lady took an interest in what I was doing.

I calmly walked over to Todd's desk and opened the top drawer. A framed photograph of his twin five-year-old boys stared at me as I pulled a key out from inside the drawer. I discreetly glanced through the window at the other lady in the office. She was still focused on her work and oblivious to what I was doing.

With the key in my hand, I walked over to a row of filing cabinets in the far-right corner of Todd's office. Luckily for me, Todd still hung on to paper files for his clients despite the company's desire to go paperless.

On my second day, Todd had asked me to come into his office to file. While completing the task, I saw a file for C. Henley Labs Incorporated. I wasn't surprised to find it. In fact, I'd known all along it would be there. I just couldn't open it at the time because Todd had been in his office, working. He would've caught me for sure.

Prior to moving to San Antonio, I'd researched everything I could find on the internet about Chad Henley. In my search, I stumbled upon a sales presentation for Araragi Medical Solutions, which listed C. Henley Labs Incorporated as a client. The second I found out we were relocating to San Antonio, I sent Araragi Medical Solutions my résumé. Lucky for me, Todd had been hiring.

I unlocked the cabinet and went straight for the file. The file wasn't as thick as some of the others, but I hoped it contained something useful.

I opened the file and laid it down on top of the open drawer of the filing cabinet.

The first page in the file didn't provide any helpful information. It was just some basic facts about the company, which I'd already known. I noticed the office address listed was one I'd retrieved from the internet and given to Wayne.

The next page was interesting but not valuable. It was a log of interactions between Todd and Chad Henley. It showed every visit, every call. It looked like their first interaction had occurred three years ago. In that time frame, Todd had visited Henley at his main office location in Chicago, and then every other interaction was outside of a Henley facility. They'd met for lunch several times and even played golf twice.

I was sure Henley was careful to keep outsiders as far away from the nightmares occurring at his facilities as possible. Even though he kept them secure, he couldn't risk people finding out the truth about what they were really up to.

Their last face-to-face interaction had been almost nine months ago at a restaurant in Austin. I had been hoping for something more recent to give me an indication of where Henley was now.

I flipped the page, and my heart stopped. It was a list of Henley's delivery locations. This was exactly what I had been hoping to find. I'd memorized every address that I'd given to Wayne, so I carefully scanned the list to see if there were any new ones.

There was a total of three additional locations that I hadn't previously had. One was in Rapid City, South Dakota; another in Evanston, Illinois; and the last was in Flagstaff, Arizona.

The remaining pages in the file were details about their medical supply orders. The last order had been sent to the Charlotte location, around the same time Henley had taken Michael captive.

I grabbed the list of addresses and headed down the hall to the copy room. I made a copy and placed it on my desk. I brought the original paper back to Todd's office and returned it to the file.

I noticed that two additional people had arrived in the office, but thankfully, neither of them paid me any attention. I carefully put the file away and placed the key back in Todd's drawer.

Before leaving his office, I took one last look around to make sure there was no trace of me ever being in there. I didn't want to draw any suspicions from Todd.

Sooner or later, Todd would probably need to pay Henley a visit to ensure he was satisfied with his products. That was what Todd did with all of his major clients. When he did, I planned to follow him there.

I returned to my desk and slipped the list of addresses into my purse. As much as I didn't want to get my hopes up, these new addresses could be promising. It was possible that Becca was being held at one of these locations. I just needed Wayne to verify it, and the second he did, I would be on a plane to rescue her.

I'd played out the rescue scenario a million times in my head. In some of those fantasies, Henley would willingly give her up, aware of the destruction I was capable of with my powers. In the more extreme scenarios, I'd blast out every wall of his facility to break her free. Either scenario was acceptable to me as long as I got her back.

Although I did my best to focus on completing the tasks Todd had requested, I couldn't help but watch the clock for the next three hours. The second the clock hit noon and I could take my lunch break, I was out the door and briskly walking to Wayne's office.

"Miss Clark," the same receptionist greeted me when I arrived. I was surprised that she'd remembered my name. "Is Wayne expecting you?"

"No, but I have some updated information that I need to give him."

"Take a seat, and I'll see if he can meet with you," she replied.

"Thank you." As I sat down, I realized that I had a death grip on the paper that contained the additional addresses. I tried to relax as I smoothed the wrinkles out of it.

A few minutes later, Wayne emerged from his office. "Come on back."

I followed him into his office but didn't sit down. Instead, I just handed him the list. "I was able to get some extra addresses." The words flew out of my mouth, as I was eager for him to start researching the locations.

He raised an eyebrow and took the paper from me. He raised the other eyebrow as he scanned the list.

"Are you sure you need me?" he asked, sounding amused by my efforts. "This is good. I'll check these out as well. I sent one of my best guys to the headquarters in Chicago because I know he can be discreet, but he confirmed about an hour ago that Chad Henley is definitely not there. He wasn't at his condo either."

"He's probably going to be at one of these lesser known locations, if I had to guess."

Wayne eyed me for a second. "Good to know. We'll keep looking, and I'll let you know as soon as we find him."

"It's extremely important that we find him quickly." I made a conscious effort to keep my hands from shaking as I pulled another two hundred dollars in cash from my purse and handed it to him.

Wayne nodded. "We'll check these locations out today, and I'll call you tonight with an update."

I felt a small sense of victory as I made my way back to work. I hadn't found Henley or Becca yet, but this was more than I'd been able to uncover in months. Despite the fact that Henley had been aggressively pursuing us, he was also taking great care to make sure we couldn't find him first. He knew what I was capable of and wanted to guarantee capturing us was within his control.

Henley was so obsessed with being in control that a part of me almost half-expected him to let me find Becca. He had to know that I would come for her, and at the end of the day, he was really after me. The only reason he even had Becca in the first place was so she could help him track down Michael and Raina. Now that Henley knew of my ability to heal, he no longer needed them. I had become his number one target.

As determined as I was to find Becca, I knew getting her out of there was going to be tricky. When I'd rescued Michael, I'd been able to sneak into the facility where they were holding him. At the time, it worked because Henley didn't know about my abilities. Henley hadn't been prepared for it, and he had been taken off guard. Rescuing Becca wasn't going to be so simple. Without a doubt, Henley was prepared this time and ready for me to make my move.

When I returned to work, I jotted down all the voice mails that had been left for Todd. There wasn't anything urgent that would require me to interrupt his client visit, so I just compiled them into an email and hit Send. He'd call me if he needed me to take any action on his behalf.

With all of my tasks finished, Todd out of the office, and my Henley snooping mission completed, I had nothing left to do. I looked at the clock and still had another three hours before I could leave for the day. I dreaded the thought of having to sit there for the next several hours, obsessing over whether or not Wayne was making any progress.

I spent the next thirty minutes wandering around the office, asking various people if they needed my help with anything. I was eager to tackle any project anyone was willing to give me in order to pass the time, but no one had anything they were willing to part with.

Desperate for a distraction, I returned to my desk and opened up the internet search browser. My fingers lingered on the keys as I pondered what would keep my mind off of Becca. I had no idea what I wanted to look up. Nothing felt important compared to finding my sister.

I was about to mindlessly read the news when I got an idea. I typed *Jen Walsh* into the search bar.

Jen had been my closest friend when I lived in St. Augustine. Before I left, she'd been interning at a news station in Jacksonville, so there had to be footage of her news stories.

I hadn't seen Jen since she and Seth left us in Charlotte. They'd gone to Hawaii for a long vacation in an attempt to lay low and get out from under Henley's radar. Surely, they were home now and back to their normal lives.

Over the past several months, I'd missed them both terribly and often thought of contacting them. The realization that it would put them in danger prevented me from actually doing it. Henley could very well be keeping an eye on them, and if he believed they knew of my whereabouts, he would go after them for information.

If I couldn't see them in real life, watching Jen's news footage would have to be the next best thing.

Several news stories popped up in the search results. It looked like she was getting a lot of airtime, which I knew had to be making her happy. As I scrolled through the list of stories, I noticed there was one that had been posted earlier today, so I popped in my earbuds and clicked on it.

Jen appeared on my computer screen, standing outside of a hospital in Jacksonville. Her expression was sad and serious, likely because of the story she was covering, but overall, she looked good. Her blonde bob had grown out some and was now grazing the top of her shoulders.

"This is Jen Walsh, reporting to you from Jacksonville Children's Hospital, where six local second-grade students are being treated for third-degree burns. The students were traveling to Orlando this morning for a class field trip when their bus was struck head-on by a vehicle, which was mistakenly traveling north in the southbound lane."

She paused but remained composed. Someone who didn't know her well would think she was just pausing for dramatic effect, but I knew her better than that. She was having a hard time reporting on such an upsetting story.

"The bus, which was carrying a total of twenty-five students and two chaperones, caught fire, leaving several students trapped inside. Firefighters were able to rescue all of the victims. I spoke with Dr. Ken Langford, who has been treating the children, and he described their condition as serious but stable," she said.

The video cut to Dr. Langford, but I stopped it before I could hear any more. I'd wanted a distraction, but this wasn't what I'd had in mind.

Those poor kids.

I scanned the rest of the videos on the list and found another one that looked harmless. It was from a week ago, and Jen had been reporting from the county fair.

In this video, Jen's bubbly personality shone as she interviewed families about what they enjoyed most about the fair.

"Which ride was your favorite?" she asked a boy who appeared to be about ten years old.

"Um …" The boy contemplated. "The Ferris wheel!"

"Mine too!" she agreed, shifting her microphone from her right hand to her left hand.

I gasped and paused the video.

Is that what I think it is?

I leaned in closer to my monitor.

Sure enough, sitting on her left ring finger was a dazzling emerald cut diamond ring. I'd seen this ring before. It had belonged to Seth's grandmother. It was an *engagement* ring.

She and Seth had been dating for about six months now, and it had been love at first sight for them. Still, I hadn't expected Seth to propose so soon.

He doesn't know Becca is alive.

I raked my fingers through my hair. Although I was happy for Jen and Seth, I couldn't ignore the fact that Seth had been in love with Becca his entire life before she disappeared.

Have I made a major mistake in not telling him that I know Becca is alive? Is it fair for Seth and Jen to get engaged without knowing all of the facts?

I had kept the truth from Seth for the same reason I'd kept it from Michael—to protect him. If I told Seth that Becca was alive and Henley was holding her captive, he would figure out that his father was the one who had taken her. It was bad enough that Seth had learned his father had been secretly working with Henley, but this new revelation would break his heart.

In addition to trying to protect Seth from the pain of what his father had done, I also didn't want Seth risking himself to save Becca. If I told him where Becca was being held, he'd be more than willing to lead the charge to rescue her. He had almost died once at the hands of Henley. I would never allow that to happen again.

THREE

NATALIE

A school bus passed me on my drive home, and I couldn't help but think about the kids who had been in the accident in Jacksonville. Although I hadn't finished watching the story, my intuition told me the prognosis wasn't good.

It was hard, having this newfound ability to heal and not be able to use it. As much as I wanted to head straight to Jacksonville and help those kids, I knew that would set off Henley's radar and put him right on our trail. If he were able to get there quickly enough, he could follow me back home. I couldn't risk leading him straight to Michael.

I parked in my usual spot at our apartment complex and headed to Michael's apartment instead of my own. It was my turn to make dinner. Michael and I usually traded off, but sometimes, it varied, depending on our schedules.

I let myself into his apartment, which had the exact same layout as mine, only with different furniture and decor. All of the apartments in the building were furnished, which had been a deciding factor in choosing this particular complex. With Henley so hot on our heels the past several months, it was just easier to have everything move-in ready.

Since I hadn't stopped to actually eat lunch today, my stomach began to rumble. I went into Michael's kitchen and began rummaging through the cabinets and fridge, trying to figure out what to make for dinner.

No, Michael, we cannot have cookies for dinner, I thought with a smile.

I moved three different variations of cookies out of the way in the cabinet as I searched for something more substantial. His sweet tooth was the craziest I'd ever seen. Raina's was pretty intense too. Once, I'd made Alexander check Michael's glucose to make sure he wasn't diabetic from all of the sugar consumption, but it was in the healthy range. Perfect even. I'd joked with Michael that consuming unlimited quantities of sugar was another one of his superpowers. He'd responded by rolling his eyes, as he always did when I compared him to a superhero.

After assessing everything in his cabinets and fridge, I realized I had all of the right ingredients to make his favorite kind of spaghetti. Michael hadn't been a big fan of spaghetti, but after remembering how much he liked pineapple on his pizza, I'd experimented with adding pineapple to the sauce the last time I made it. Once he'd tried it like that, it had become one of his favorite dinners. I wasn't a fan of the pineapple, but it was easy enough to pick out.

I pulled my cell phone out of my purse and placed it on the counter beside me. I wanted to keep it in earshot, just in case Wayne called with an update.

As I boiled the noodles, I contemplated what I would do if Wayne were to call me with confirmation that he'd located Henley. Without a doubt, I would go, but would I tell Michael? I mean, I couldn't just leave without a reason. I couldn't think of an explanation that would result in Michael being okay with me going by myself. He was protective of me—and rightfully so. We both knew that Henley would jump at the chance to capture me.

Telling Michael the truth was going to be difficult, but it was the right thing to do. He was going to be mad at me for hiding it from him for so long, and I couldn't blame him for that. The longer I waited though, the angrier he was going to be.

I browned the ground beef on the stove, and when it was done, I added the chunks of pineapple to the pan. Then, I poured a jar of spaghetti sauce on top to heat it up. As the sauce hit the pan, drops of sauce splattered up, setting two red stains into my green blouse.

"Oh no," I groaned, grabbing a paper towel. I attempted to wipe them off, but the stains just smeared further into my shirt.

"Don't rub it in," Michael said, hurrying across the kitchen toward me.

I hadn't heard him come home.

He grabbed a clean paper towel and ran it under the faucet. "The trick is to use cold water."

He walked back over to me and carefully blotted the first spot, which was up by my collarbone.

I watched in anticipation as he moved on to the next stain, which was at the bottom of my shirt. He held the wet paper towel to it, soaking the stain, and then rubbed the paper towel against it until the stain disappeared.

As I gazed at him, I allowed myself to fantasize about how normal our life could be. For a moment, I could almost pretend we were this ordinary couple who didn't have all of the challenges of unique abilities and being hunted by a madman.

In that world, I wasn't a liar who was hiding the fact that I knew my sister was alive while secretly trying to find her. In this fantasy, we were safe, and our biggest problem was deciding on which TV show to watch that night.

Despite the fact that our lives weren't normal, there was no denying that our relationship was extraordinary. We'd been through so much together, and we had somehow managed to survive it all. Every day, I found myself falling more and more in love with him. I'd never met anyone like him before—and it wasn't just because of his abilities.

He looked down at me, noticing for the first time that I was watching him. His hand lightly grazed my stomach as he let go of my shirt. At his touch, my skin tingled, as it always did.

I tensed as he lowered his head toward mine. He needed to know the truth. Now.

He deserves to know.

"Michael," I whispered, "I need to tell—"

There was a knock at the door. Michael reflexively jerked away. Despite how many times I'd told him that Henley wouldn't be polite enough to knock, his first instinct was to always assume the worst. I wasn't worried at all though. If Henley were this close, my intuition would be trying to warn me. I didn't sense any danger at all.

"I'll get it. Stay here," he said before walking to the front door.

I lingered in the doorway to the kitchen as Michael looked through the peephole before opening the door.

It was Alexander and Raina.

"Oh good, you are here too," Alexander said as he looked over Michael's shoulder and spotted me.

Raina huffed. "I told you so. Where else would she be?"

Michael let them inside, and I pulled out four plates from the cabinet, ignoring Raina's comment.

"Would you like to stay for dinner?" I asked. "We're having spaghetti."

"With pineapple?" Michael asked, his eyes hopeful.

I smiled back at him. "Of course. Who in their right mind eats spaghetti *without* pineapple?"

Michael returned the smile, knowing that I was teasing him. He opened his mouth to respond, but Raina huffed again. She hated it when we flirted with each other in front of her.

"No, thanks," Alexander replied. "Lorena is making dinner now. I just wanted to stop by for a quick chat."

"Sure, have a seat." Michael motioned to the kitchen table.

"Raina?" I held a plate up to see if she wanted dinner. I was determined to be nice to her whether she liked me or not.

"No," she said, and then she followed it with an awkward, "Thank you." It wasn't much, but at least she was being polite.

I put the plates on the counter and sat at the table with them. We could wait to eat until after they left. Whatever Alexander wanted to chat about sounded important, and I wanted to give him my full attention.

"What's going on?" Michael asked, not hiding the apprehension in his voice.

"Do you remember a few months ago when we talked about Henley having a raven?" Alexander asked.

I stiffened.

"Yeah," Michael replied. "Why? Has the raven made contact?" His eyes shifted nervously to Raina.

Alexander held up a hand to stop Michael from jumping to conclusions. "No, not yet, but we have to be prepared in case it does."

Michael visibly relaxed, and I reached over to him, reassuringly rubbing his back. If Alexander had arrived five minutes later, I would have told Michael the truth, and he'd already know there was nothing to worry about. Becca was the raven, but she wasn't a spy. I couldn't tell him right now though, not in front of Alexander and Raina. I would have to wait until after they left.

"Dad's come up with a dream blocker, and he wants to test it out tonight," Raina said, cutting to the chase.

Alexander reached into his pocket and pulled out a brown pill bottle. He gave it a quick rattle before placing it down on the table.

Michael and I sat back in our chairs at the same time. I was the only one between the three of us who could visit someone else's dreams, so he needed Michael or Raina to agree to let me invade their privacy.

"I could let Natalie test it on me, but I think you'd both have more natural defenses against it," Alexander said. "If we want to see if it really works, I think we'd have to try it on one of you at some point anyway."

Even though I knew Becca didn't pose a threat to us, it was still a good idea to figure out how to block Henley. I wouldn't put it past Henley to find another spy, especially now that he knew Becca was my sister.

Please, God, don't let him hurt her because he knows she is my sister.

Michael and Raina stared at each other. It was like they were having a conversation that no one else could hear. If I didn't know better, I would've thought that they could read each other's minds.

"I'll do it," Raina blurted out.

She ran her hand through her hair, tossing it from one side to the other. She'd recently chopped it off into a chin-length style and dyed it a blue-black shade. Not a lot of people could pull it off, but I had to admit, it suited her.

I gaped at her. I'd visited her dream once before in order to find out where she and her parents were, so I could help them rescue Michael. Although I believed she understood why I had done it, she'd also made it very clear over the past several months that I was not welcome to do it again. I'd assured her I wouldn't.

I looked over at Michael. He opened his mouth to say something, but Raina interjected.

"It's fine," she said, not looking happy about it at all. "I don't want to argue about it."

Alexander gave the pill bottle to Raina and instructed her to take them at bedtime. One of the pills was the dream blocker, and the other was something to help her sleep. We agreed that Raina would take them around ten p.m., and then I would go to bed shortly after to try to make contact.

"I'll call you tomorrow to see how it went," Alexander said to me as Michael and I walked them out.

Once they were gone, I fixed plates of spaghetti for Michael and me. We sat back down at the table and ate in silence.

Now that we were alone again, it was my opportunity to finally tell Michael the truth.

As I picked out a piece of pineapple and moved it to the side of my plate, I couldn't seem to find the words. *Where do I even begin?*

The longer I sat there, the more I reminded myself of the reasons I'd kept the truth from Michael in the first place. If Raina had volunteered to let me visit her dreams, it could only mean it was because Michael didn't want me in his. He didn't want me to know how bad his nightmares really were because he didn't want me to worry about him.

If I told him the truth, I wouldn't be protecting him. It would be to ease my own guilt for lying. His nightmares would surely intensify if he knew there was no choice but to go back to Henley to rescue Becca. I couldn't do that to him.

After dinner, Michael insisted on doing the dishes, but I remained in the kitchen with him.

"Why did Raina volunteer?" I decided to ask.

Deep down, I was hoping he'd say something that would convince me that it was safe to tell him the truth.

"She just wants to help." He rinsed the soap off his hands and dried them off on a hand towel before turning to me.

I waited to see if he would elaborate on his own, but he didn't.

"Is it because you don't want me in your head?" I probably should have thought of a better way to phrase the question, but I was desperate for answers.

He sighed and placed the hand towel on top of the counter. "It's not a trust thing, if that's what you're worried about."

"Then, tell me, what is it? Is it Henley?"

"Yes," he confirmed. "Sometimes, my nightmares can be … disturbing. I don't want to put you through that."

I'd been right. In his dreams, he was reliving the torturous nightmare he'd endured when he was captured by Henley.

My cell phone rang, startling me. I practically leaped across the kitchen to pick it up. I noticed right away that it was Wayne's number.

"This is work," I lied. "I'll just be a sec."

I took the phone into Michael's bedroom and closed the door behind me. With a shaking hand, I answered the call.

"Hi, Wayne. Any updates?" I asked eagerly, hoping he had good news.

Wayne let out an audible sigh, and my heart sank. "I'm afraid not, Miss Clark. We haven't been able to locate Chad Henley."

"Did you check the addresses I gave you?" I made a conscious effort to keep my voice low.

"Yes, we did. Chad Henley hasn't visited the Rapid City or Flagstaff locations in months. We even checked out all of the hotels in that area, and there's no recent record of him having stayed at any of them."

"What about the Evanston location?"

"I have a guy on his way there now. I should know by noon tomorrow," he replied. "I'll be in touch shortly after."

"Okay, thanks." I sounded as defeated as I felt.

When I hung up the call with Wayne, I fought the urge to burst into tears. I needed to hold it together—for Michael. If I cried, he would push me to tell him what was wrong, and I just couldn't involve him in this.

Michael was sitting on the couch, watching TV, when I emerged from the bedroom. He looked up at me expectantly. It wasn't typical for me to get a work phone call in the evening.

"Everything okay?" he asked.

"Yeah." I avoided his eyes. "Todd just wanted to update me on his visit today with a client."

"Oh."

Instead of sitting on the couch with Michael, I sat in a separate armchair. If Michael thought it was odd, he didn't say so.

I pretended to watch TV, but I couldn't focus. Instead, my mind was racing. *What am I going to do?* Wayne was the best private investigator in the state of Texas. I'd researched them all. *If Wayne can't find Henley, what chance do I have?*

"Nervous?" Michael asked, interrupting my thoughts.

I stared back at him, confused. *Does he know?*

"About testing the dream blocker?" he prompted.

Oh, that.

I shook my head. "No. It's just an awkward encounter with your sister. I get those on a daily basis anyway."

He smiled, but his eyes lingered on me for a second. I was worried that he could tell something was wrong and he would ask me about it. I didn't want to lie to him again. All of the lying was exhausting.

I stood up and stretched my arms, pretending to be more tired than I actually felt. I wanted to leave before he started asking me more questions.

"I'm going to go home and get ready for the dream visit with Raina," I told him. Before he could stand up to say a proper good-bye, I walked over and gave him a quick peck on the lips. "I'll see you tomorrow."

I was almost to the door when Michael called behind me, "Hey."

I turned around to face him.

"It's going to be okay. The dream blocker is going to work."

"I know. Good night," I replied, forcing a smile.

I let myself out and headed upstairs to my apartment.

I opened the door, stepped inside, and quickly closed it behind me. I let out a breath and just stood in the darkness for a moment, my back against the door.

I felt helpless, much like I had the night Becca was kidnapped. Despite my best attempts to convince myself that it wasn't my fault, that I wasn't responsible for what had happened, I still felt guilty. And now, I was in the situation all over again. She was in trouble, and I was failing to save her.

It was only eight thirty, so I had another hour and a half before Raina would be in bed. Peeling myself away from the door, I decided to take a hot bath and try to relax. It would be bad to be so worked up that I couldn't fall asleep to test the dream blocker.

We needed this dream blocker to work. It was important to have another safeguard against Henley being able to find us. Henley was a threat to us all.

Surrounded by a few lit scented candles, I attempted to focus on the smell of lavender and the soothing, warm water as I soaked in the tiny bathtub. My mind, however, refused to cooperate and kept wandering back to Becca.

I could only imagine what she must be going through. The fact that she hadn't made contact with me in months meant one of two things. Either she couldn't or she wouldn't, and both of those scenarios equally terrified me. If Henley pushed her to make contact and she refused in order to protect me, he would make her pay dearly for it—potentially with her life.

I reached for a candle at the edge of the bathtub and blew it out. It was silly to think that I could relax at a time like this. I could, however, feel the emotional exhaustion begin to shift into physical exhaustion, and that gave me hope that I'd be able to test the dream blocker after all.

I finished blowing out the rest of the candles, and then I climbed out of the tub, dried off, and put on my pajamas. By the time I brushed my teeth and crawled into bed, it was a quarter after ten.

Yawning, I turned off the lamp on my nightstand and settled under the covers.

The carousel was just as I remembered it. It was beautiful with brightly colored horses held in place with brass poles beneath a red-and-white metal canopy. The only time I'd seen it in person was the day after Michael told me the truth about who he was. It was the first time I could recall feeling like myself after Becca disappeared.

I stood in perfectly manicured green grass, admiring how the colors of the carousel contrasted beautifully with the clear blue sky in the background. The carousel cheerfully played music as it turned around and around.

As the reality that I was dreaming set in, I recalled that I needed to test the dream blocker on Raina. Too bad I couldn't bring her into my dream. Michael had told me this was where she went to clear her head when we lived in St. Augustine. It had the same effect on me—I was happy and more carefree here.

Dream visitation was fairly easy, like melting from one imaginary world into another. All I had to do was find the connection, and the transition would be seamless.

I focused on Raina and willed myself to connect with her.

As I searched for her, all I found was emptiness. It felt like she didn't exist. I cringed at the familiarity of it but reminded myself that she was at home and safe. In this case, not being able to connect with her was a good thing because it meant that the dream blocker was working. Our dreams would be safe from whatever new tactics Henley was cooking up to try to locate us.

I relaxed and turned my attention back to the carousel in my own dream. Now that testing the dream blocker was out of the way, I could just allow myself to enjoy this escape from my own reality.

Thunder rumbled in the distance. Within seconds, clouds covered the sun, blocking out all of the light. It was now nighttime. I fought for control of my dream and tried to force the sun to come back out, but the clouds stubbornly stayed.

The carousel continued to turn as a chill set in the air. From the other side of the carousel, I could see the shadow of a person sitting on one of the horses.

I tensed.

There was no telling who it could be.

A loud squawk belted out from behind me, and I jumped. Instinctively, I turned around, searching in the darkness for the culprit, although I already knew what it was.

Sure enough, a raven was perched on the branch of a large oak tree.

The music from the carousel turned into a series of sour notes as the carousel came to a stop. I turned back around to face it and noticed that the person had gotten off their horse and was walking toward me. The shadow was a familiar, petite shape.

I stood there, frozen, as the shadow grew closer and closer. I held my breath as the person behind the shadow emerged.

It was Becca.

"Is it really you?" I asked, just above a whisper.

Is she really here, or am I just wishing it were her?

She didn't respond, and I began to wonder whether or not she could hear me. Although we were face-to-face, she wasn't making eye contact. It was as if she were looking through me instead of at me.

I resisted the impulse to throw my arms around her. For some reason, I felt like the gesture might frighten her. Something in her demeanor made me believe that she wasn't well. She didn't seem like herself.

"Becca, can you hear me?" I gently asked her.

She nodded but still didn't look at me.

My heart felt like it would beat its way out of my chest, and I desperately struggled to get it under control. I needed to calm down before I woke myself up. This might be my only opportunity to get answers from her. I didn't know when I would get another chance, if ever.

"Do you have any idea where Henley is keeping you?"

Becca shook her head.

"Are you okay? Are you hurt?" I instantly regretted asking the question. Of course she wasn't okay.

"Michael and Raina are in danger," she said. Her tone was flat, but the words cut through me like a sharp knife.

"Does Henley know where we are? Is he here?" I fought the urge to panic. Is that the real reason I couldn't connect with Raina earlier?

Becca sighed, but her reaction was delayed. "Not yet."

I shook my head, confused. If Henley doesn't know where we are, what is the danger?

"But Michael and Raina are in danger of being captured?" I needed her to be more specific about what the threat was.

Despite the fact that I was desperate to talk to Becca, I would have to force myself awake if Henley were on his way here. I would need to warn Michael.

Becca slowly shifted her eyes to mine, but she still seemed distant, almost detached. "Not captured. Killed.*"*

"Killed?" I could barely say the word. "What are you talking about?"

"You already know it's true. Henley is only interested in you. He doesn't need them anymore."

This came as a surprise to me, although it shouldn't have. We all knew that Henley wanted to study my ability to self-heal. I'd just always assumed though that he would still want to bring Michael and Raina back into captivity. I hadn't considered the possibility of him actually wanting them dead.

I didn't respond, and even in her trancelike state, Becca must have noticed. "They are just a liability to him now. You've made their value to Henley obsolete."

"I … I don't know what to do," I said, trying to process it all.

Becca took a step closer and put her hands on the sides of my arms. Her motions seemed forced, like she had to put great effort into making them happen.

"You have to leave them," she said.

Leave them? No. *I couldn't do that. Michael and I had agreed to face the future together regardless of how uncertain it was.*

"I can't do that to Michael. I love him." I remembered how I'd felt when Michael left me to keep me safe. My heart had broken into a million pieces.

"You will if you care about them at all." Becca removed her hands and placed them back at her sides. "Could you live with yourself if Michael died because you were too selfish to do the right thing?"

Her words were harsh, not at all like Becca, but she was also right. I would never be able to live with myself if I was the reason Michael died.

"I haven't told Michael, but I am trying to hunt Henley down," I told her. "If I could just have a little more time, I can figure this out. I know I can. I will find you."

"How are you going to do that?"

"I've hired a private investigator. He's looking everywhere."

Becca's eyes snapped to mine. She seemed suddenly alert. "How close are you?"

I didn't want to tell her that we'd come up empty-handed. She needed to have hope, so I padded the truth. "We're getting closer. I can feel it. Just hang in there a little longer. I promise I will come for you."

Becca eyed me for a second, considering what I'd told her. "If you are going to come for me, you need to do it now.*"*

"I know ..."

"No, you don't know."

I could feel my heart pounding harder, and I willed myself to stay asleep.

"I'm in here because of you," she said.

I fought back tears. "I'm so sorry—"

She cut me off, not wanting to hear my weak apology for failing to save her the night she had been kidnapped. "Now that Henley knows about your abilities, you've made me obsolete as well."

It was what I'd feared from the moment that I knew Henley had her. I felt like screaming, but I knew that would jolt me awake.

"You have three days. That's the time frame Henley has given me to locate you and turn you in."

"What if you refuse?" I knew what she was going to say, but I needed her to confirm it.

She didn't respond.

"What happens in three days, Becca?"

She looked up, drilling her eyes into mine. "Henley is going to kill me."

FOUR

NATALIE

"H*enley is going to kill me."*

Those six words echoed over and over in my mind until my alarm clock finally went off.

I climbed out of bed and forced myself to go through the motions of getting ready for work even though I didn't want to go. Instead, I wanted to go to the facility where Henley was keeping my sister, blast out all of the windows and doors, and finish what I should have done when I'd had the chance. I should have killed Henley.

I would do it now, if I had to. I was willing to do anything to save Becca and keep Michael safe. The only problem was, I still had no idea where Henley was keeping her.

I slammed my hairbrush down on the bathroom counter in frustration. There had to be a way to find them. I just needed to figure it out.

Without bothering to put on any makeup, I grabbed my purse and walked out to my car.

Just as I was about to get into the car, my phone rang. It was Alexander. Reluctantly, I answered it.

"How did it go?" he asked.

"The dream blocker worked," I told him as I slid into the driver's seat.

"Fantastic. I was hoping you were going to say that. I spoke with Raina a few minutes ago, and she didn't remember you visiting her dreams last night."

"I wasn't able to contact her, so I took that as a good sign."

"At least we'll be a little safer now."

They would be safer without me.

"Traffic is terrible this morning, so let me run," I lied.

"Okay, drive safe."

I hung up with Alexander and drove to work in a daze. In two separate instances, I got honked at for sitting at a light after it already turned green.

I'd been hoping to gain some clarity on my predicament during my commute to work, but that didn't happen. I was stuck in a no-win situation. I only had three days to find Henley and Becca before he forced her locate me in order to survive. Locating me meant that Henley would also find and kill Michael and Raina.

In three days, either Becca would be dead or Michael would. I couldn't let that happen.

How could I ever choose between them?

As soon as I pulled into the parking garage at work, Michael called me to make sure I'd made it to work safely.

"Good morning," I greeted him, trying my best to sound cheerful despite the hoarseness in my voice.

"You sound tired," he said, instantly picking up on it.

"A little, but good news: the dream blocker worked."

"Yeah, Alexander just told me. That's a relief."

There was a long pause, and I worried that he could sense something was wrong with me.

"So, I was thinking," he finally said, his voice shifting to a lighter tone. "Your birthday is tomorrow, and I think we should celebrate."

"You don't have to do that," I told him, and I meant it. I had completely forgotten about my birthday, and with everything going on, the last thing I felt like doing was celebrating.

I could almost hear Michael rolling his eyes on the other end of the line. "I know I don't *have* to, but I *want* to. You only turn nineteen once. We should make it special."

"You'd better not take me to one of those restaurants where people sing to you," I warned. "Just remember your birthday is in July, so I have more than two months to plot my revenge."

Michael laughed. "It's nothing like that, I promise," he replied. "I want it to be something you'll actually enjoy."

I glanced at the clock on my dashboard and realized I was a few minutes late. "Crap, I've got to go. I'll call you later when I leave work. Love you."

I hung up the phone and dashed up the stairs to the office.

I sat down at my desk, and within a minute, Todd called to let me know he'd be out of the office again. He had decided to visit a different client today.

He gave me a long list of assignments to complete, but the majority of them were mundane. This would leave me with plenty of time to contemplate what I was going to do about saving both Becca and Michael.

I spent the first couple of hours of my workday calling clients to confirm the following week's appointments. Then, I headed to the copier to make copies of meeting materials for Todd. He had a meeting the following day, and I needed to make sure everything was prepared before he returned to the office.

As I waited on endless sheets of paper to print, my mind replayed my dream over and over in a continuous loop. As disturbing as Becca's message had been, I was grateful to at least know that she was still alive. It had been torture, not hearing from her for months and imagining the worst.

The worst is yet to come though, I reminded myself.

I could warn Michael, and we could leave, but I knew that Henley would kill Becca for failing to locate us.

What if I don't figure this out and end up losing them both?

If I was going to get ahead of this, I needed the Evanston location to pan out. I glanced at the clock, and it was almost noon. Wayne should have an answer for me soon on whether or not he'd spotted Henley there. If he had, I wouldn't waste any time. I would leave work and hop on the first plane that would get me there.

I would go alone. Although I had debated back and forth on what to tell Michael, I was now more inclined than ever to keep him out of this. I knew he would insist on coming with me to rescue Becca, and after hearing about Henley's plan to kill Michael, I couldn't let him go anywhere near a Henley facility. I couldn't risk something happening to him.

When all of the copies finished printing, I brought them back to my desk to begin binding them together. I was about to start when I realized it was one minute past noon.

I pulled out my cell phone and dialed Wayne's number, growing more and more anxious with each ring.

"Thank you for calling Wayne Cartwright's office. How may I help you?" the perky receptionist answered.

"Hi," I replied. "This is Natalie ..." I paused, realizing that I'd almost said my real last name aloud for others to hear. That would have been a mistake because all of my coworkers knew me as Natalie *Rowland.*

Luckily, she recognized me without my last name. "Hi, Natalie! I'll transfer you right over."

A second later, Wayne picked up the line. "Hello, Miss Clark. I was just about to call you."

"Any updates?" I asked eagerly.

Wayne sighed, as he had the night before, and I knew the answer.

"I'm afraid not," he replied. "I sent a guy out to that location in Evanston, and it seems that address belongs to a completely different company called G.G. Armand Designs. Have you ever heard of it?"

"No." I could feel my hope deflating.

"We're checking to see if there are any connections to Henley, but that could take a little while."

"What do we do now?" I fought back a lump as it formed in my throat.

There was a long pause.

"Unfortunately, we just wait," Wayne replied. "Henley will turn up eventually, and I assure you that my guys will alert me when he does."

I sat there, dumbfounded. *Wait?* I couldn't just wait around. *Becca can't wait.*

When I hung up the phone, I buried my head in my hands. *What am I going to do?*

Every minute I spent here continued to put Michael and his family in imminent danger. And on top of that, there was a ticking clock on my sister's life. I only had three days to find her, or someone I loved was going to die.

"Henley is going to kill me," Becca's voice screamed at me in my head.

"Everything okay, Natalie?" a woman's voice asked.

I looked up, startled. I had forgotten where I was for a second.

One of the women who worked in my office was standing over my desk, peering over her eyeglasses at me with concern.

"Can you believe I totally forgot to reschedule one of Todd's meetings?" I lied.

She gave me a sympathetic look. "It happens, hon. Try not to let it ruin your day."

I nodded, hoping she would leave me alone.

"I've known Todd for a long time," she whispered. "He's not as scary as he seems."

"Thanks," I replied, amazed that anyone would find Todd scary. I knew what scary looked like, and trust me, he wasn't it.

The woman turned and walked away.

I needed to pull myself together. I couldn't have a meltdown here in the office. It would draw too much unwanted attention. Plus, I had to keep my emotions in check at all times. Despite the fact that I'd gotten better at controlling my abilities, they sometimes came out when my emotions got out of hand.

The last thing I needed was to set off an alarm bell to Henley that would lead him right to us before I had a chance to figure a way out of this mess.

I debated on just leaving the office and going home, but what would I do differently there? I didn't have any answers. There was nothing I could do here or there that would lead me to Becca in time.

I took a deep breath and focused on binding the meeting materials together. The task was monotonous but required just enough concentration to keep my mind occupied. At least it made the time go by a little faster.

When all of the binding was finished, I took it upon myself to clean up Todd's office. I dusted all of his furniture, including the blinds. I knew the company paid a cleaning crew to come in at night, but aside from emptying out the trash cans, there was never evidence that they had actually been there.

At five p.m., Todd's office was immaculate, and I was ready to go home. Feeling emotionally drained, I yawned as I gathered my things.

My apartment was empty when I arrived home.

I glanced down at my phone and realized that I had a text message from Michael, letting me know he was working a little late. Tired, I plopped down on the couch.

I lay down and closed my eyes.

What if Henley doesn't wait the three full days? What if he decides he wants to come for us sooner?

I tried to focus on Becca and where she was. Even though I'd tried this a million times since she disappeared and it never worked, I hoped that maybe this time would be different. Maybe, if I could catch her when she wasn't so heavily sedated, I could get in. I wanted to connect with her, confirming she was still alive, and reassure her that I was working to find her.

I nodded off and searched for her in the darkness, but once again, my intuition failed me. I felt absolutely no connection to her whatsoever.

What good is having this so-called intuitive gift if I can't use it when it really matters?

Tears of frustration began to pour out of me, waking me up. I pounded my fist into the couch, wishing Henley could somehow feel the pain from it.

My front door opened, and Michael stepped inside.

He stopped in his tracks when he saw me. "What's wrong?"

I quickly sat up, wiping away the tears from my cheeks. I shook my head and attempted to smile.

He didn't buy it though and came and sat down beside me.

"What is it?" he pleaded, rubbing my shoulder.

I gathered the courage to look at him. He watched me with so much love and concern that I couldn't look him in the eye. He deserved so much better than a girl who lied to him and constantly put him in grave danger.

"Just a bad day at work," I said. "I'll be fine."

He stiffened. "What happened?"

It wasn't like me to come home and cry about something at work, so naturally, he would think it was something really, really bad.

I shook my head. "Nothing worth talking about. I'm just overreacting."

"Did something happen with Todd?" He asked the question calmly, but I could tell he was imagining the worst.

"No, nothing like that. I just forgot to reschedule an important meeting for him." *Apparently, this is my go-to lie today.*

He eyed me for a second, trying to understand why that was so upsetting. "Okay … was he a jerk about it?"

I forced out a little laugh to emphasize how "ridiculous" I was being. "He doesn't even know. I got it rescheduled before he found out."

My story was sounding more and more unbelievable. He looked confused, and I couldn't blame him.

I decided to change the subject. "Why don't you head down to your apartment and heat up some of the leftover spaghetti, and I'll be there in a minute?"

He nodded and stood up. He took a step toward the door but then stopped and turned back to face me. "Are you sure you're good?"

"I'm good," I replied in my most reassuring tone.

After Michael left, I went into the bathroom and washed my face. I needed to get a grip and appear normal. If I didn't, he would continue to press me for what was wrong, and sooner or later, I would cave and tell him everything.

You're doing this for him, to keep him safe, I reassured my reflection in the mirror.

When I finally pulled myself together, I headed down to Michael's apartment.

Raina was there, already diving into a plate of spaghetti. She didn't say anything to me when I walked in, but she did watch me as I made my way to the kitchen.

Did Michael tell her I'd been crying?

Michael was standing in the kitchen with two plates of spaghetti in front of him. He was carefully picking pineapple out of mine with a fork.

I walked up behind him and wrapped my arms around his waist. I laid my cheek against his back and closed my eyes. He straightened up when he felt me, and then he turned around to face me. He pulled me against him, engulfing me in his arms. I stayed there for a minute, allowing myself to feel safe. He kissed the top of my head.

"Eww," Raina said. "Can't you guys wait until I leave before you get all mushy?"

Michael pulled back a little but didn't release me. "You know, you do have an apartment of your own," he told her.

Raina rolled her eyes and continued eating her dinner.

He looked down at me. "Sorry. I didn't know she was coming over," he whispered, pushing a wild strand of hair out of my face.

I shook my head. "It's okay."

He gave me a peck on the cheek and then handed me a plate of spaghetti.

I reluctantly sat across from Raina at the table. Michael sat in between us.

Although she looked at me a few times, Raina didn't engage me in conversation. I expected her to at least ask me questions about testing the dream blocker the night before, but she didn't.

When Raina finished eating, she promptly got up and loaded her plate into the dishwasher. "Thanks for dinner," she called over her shoulder before letting herself out.

Michael shook his head when she was gone. "She can be so aggravating."

I wasn't the biggest fan of Raina, but I couldn't ignore the fact that she was in danger as well. Becca's warning hadn't just been about Michael; it had been about Raina too. As much as I knew Raina could push his buttons and get on his nerves, I knew Michael loved his sister. If something happened to her, he would be devastated. Having gone through it with Becca, I would do everything in my power to keep Raina safe as well—for Michael.

I pushed the spaghetti around on my plate but didn't eat much of it.

"Not hungry?" he asked.

I shook my head in response.

I could feel his eyes on me as I stared down at my plate, but he didn't push me to eat. He probably assumed I was still upset about my silly made-up work problem.

When Michael finished the last bite of his dinner, I grabbed both of our plates and started cleaning up.

He yawned and stood up, stretching out his arms.

"I've got this," I told him when he came to the sink to help me. I nodded toward the living room. "Go ahead. I'll be there in a sec."

He gave my back a quick rub of appreciation, and then he headed into the living room and turned on the TV. I washed the dishes while half-listening to the documentary on sharks that he was watching.

Once the dishes were done, I decided to wipe down the counters and sweep the floor as well. For some reason, cleaning always made me feel a little better when I was really upset. It was almost as if I could somehow scrub the problem away. That was never the case, of course, but at least it helped me take my mind off the real problem for a little while.

About twenty minutes later, Michael's kitchen was spotless, and I headed into the living room to join him.

Michael was lying down on the couch, sound asleep. He didn't move as I grabbed a blanket off the back of the couch and covered him. It was nice to see him sleeping peacefully.

Instead of going straight home, I sat down in the armchair, feeling paralyzed by this whole situation.

I was running out of time.

As I sat there, watching him take deep, relaxed breaths, I knew I wouldn't change my mind about telling him the truth. I would never intentionally put him in danger, especially to save someone he didn't even know. I needed to do something drastic to find Becca and keep Henley far away from Michael. Although I didn't yet know what that something was going to be, I was certain of one thing.

I was going to do it completely and utterly alone.

FIVE

MICHAEL

"Will you please stop? You're driving me crazy," Raina snapped as I rearranged the silverware on the table for the hundredth time.

Does the fork go on the left side or right side of the plate?

I placed the fork on the left. "Does this look right?" I asked, ignoring my sister's comment.

"It's fine. She's going to love it."

Today was Natalie's nineteenth birthday, and I wanted tonight to be perfect. It was the first birthday for us to celebrate since we'd started dating.

"I had no idea you were such a romantic," Raina said.

If I didn't know her so well, I would think she was impressed. But I knew better, and she was borderline making fun of me.

I'd gotten off work at two p.m. to start setting up the rooftop of our apartment building for the occasion. Raina had offered to come help. At first, I was adamant that she stay away. Then, after thinking it through, I decided even if Raina never let me live it down, the outcome would probably be better with a female's perspective. So, I'd caved and let her tag along. It was a decision I was quickly regretting.

On the rooftop, I'd set up a small table for two. The plan was to eat the dinner that I had arranged to pick up later from a new, eclectic restaurant that Natalie had been wanting to try. To add a touch of elegance to the table, Raina had brought a white tablecloth and a clear vase that normally sat on her own dining table. I wouldn't have thought to do that, but it looked nice. I planned to pick up some fresh roses to add to the vase while I was out, on my way back from the restaurant.

I wasn't much of a decorator, but to my credit, I had thought to buy some string lights to hang up. They'd had them at the restaurant I took Natalie to in Kentucky, and I remembered that she'd liked them.

I'd also brought some thick blankets and pillows, so we could do some stargazing after dinner. Raina laid them out and perfectly fluffed and arranged the pillows. It was something she referred to as *staging.* I had no clue what that was, and I had no desire to find out.

"This will look amazing at night," Raina reassured me.

I nodded despite suddenly feeling a little doubtful. *What if Natalie thinks it's over the top? It is kind of corny.*

I contemplated ripping up the blankets and bringing them back inside. Maybe stargazing was too cliché.

Raina rolled her eyes, as if she already knew what I was thinking. "It's *fine.* Are we almost done? Mom and I are going to get pedicures after she gets off work. I want to go home and take a shower first."

"You're the one who insisted on coming," I reminded her.

She smirked. "Well, you clearly needed the help."

"Let me just test the lights to make sure they come on, and we can go."

As I walked across the rooftop to flip the switch on the lights, my cell phone vibrated in my pocket. I pulled it out, thinking maybe it was Natalie. I frowned. It was a number I didn't recognize. Probably a spam caller.

I sent it to voice mail.

I flipped the light switch, and the lights came on.

"Okay, now, we can go," I told Raina.

My phone buzzed again, this time in my hand. I looked down at it, and it was the same number.

"Who is it?" Raina asked.

"Probably a telemarketer." I decided to just answer the call and decline whatever it was they were trying to sell, so they'd leave me alone. "Hello?" I answered.

"Hi. Is this Michael Somers?" a guy's voice asked on the other end.

I paused but only for a beat. Somers was my fake last name in San Antonio. "It is."

It was always hard, getting used to a new last name every time we moved. I'd lost count of how many I'd had over the years, but if I had to guess, it would be in the one hundred fifty to two hundred range.

"This is Todd Nelson at Araragi Medical Solutions."

Natalie's boss.

That's strange. Why is he calling me instead of Natalie?

"I have you down as Natalie Rowland's emergency contact," he said.

I stopped dead in my tracks. *Did he say* emergency*?*

"Is she okay?" I spoke so fast that I wondered if it was even audible.

"Well, I don't know," Todd replied slowly.

What does he mean, he doesn't know?

"Natalie never showed up for work today," he explained. "I've tried calling her, but I can't get ahold of her. It's not like her to be late, much less not show up at all."

My blood turned to ice as I realized that I'd never received a text message from Natalie to let me know she'd made it to work safely. I'd texted her when I first woke up to wish her a happy birthday, but she hadn't responded to that either. I had been so preoccupied with getting things prepared for tonight that it hadn't dawned on me until now.

Stop panicking, I told myself. *Maybe she decided to take off from work today and just forgot to tell me … and her boss. It wouldn't be unreasonable for her to want to take a day off. It is her birthday after all.*

"I appreciate the call," I said, trying to keep my voice even and controlled despite the fact that my heart felt like a heavyweight boxer trying to jab his way out of my chest.

In our years of running from Henley, Alexander had conditioned us to always appear calm. Showing too much emotion could draw unwanted attention.

"No problem. I hope everything's okay."

"I'm sure it is," I lied. "I'll check on her and have her contact you. Thanks for calling."

I hung up the phone and immediately dialed Natalie's number. Raina said something to me, but I wasn't listening.

Natalie's phone went straight to voice mail. *Huh. It didn't even ring.*

I tried again.

Voice mail.

Get a grip, Michael. Maybe her phone died.

I tried once more.

Voice mail.

"What's wrong?" Raina asked.

I didn't respond. Instead, I darted for the door leading back into the apartment building.

"Michael!" I heard Raina call behind me, but I didn't stop. I needed to figure out what was going on.

I flew down the stairs until I reached Natalie's apartment. I fumbled through my keys, looking for the right one. Without knocking, I unlocked the door and barged inside.

"Natalie?" I yelled, hearing the fear in my own voice.

There was no response.

"Natalie!" I tried again.

What if Henley has her? What if he captured her on her way to work? I shook my head, as if it could erase the thought. *I knew she shouldn't have taken a job so far away from home.*

Her apartment was vacant, quiet.

I rushed into her kitchen, half-expecting something to be out of place. I was looking for anything that would give me a clue as to what was going on, but everything was neat, organized, and in its usual spot. There were no dishes in the sink or even in the drainboard for that matter. It didn't look like she'd been home at all today.

"Natalie!" I called out once again, as if she could be hiding somewhere in the apartment, playing a cruel joke. It wasn't like her, but I was willing to hold out any hope that I could.

I looked out the window in her living room that overlooked the parking lot. Her car was gone.

I went into her bedroom. Her bed was neatly made, as it was every morning before she left for work.

Raina appeared in the bedroom doorway, trying to catch her breath. "Will you please tell me what's going on?" she asked.

I didn't respond.

"Michael!" she demanded impatiently.

"Natalie is missing," I muttered, throwing desperate glances around her room.

There had to be some sort of clue as to where she was. There had to be a logical explanation that didn't involve her being captured by that depraved maniac.

"What?"

Raina stood, dumbfounded, as I rushed past her, back into the living room.

I stopped when I saw a note sitting on top of the coffee table. It had my name on it.

Raina came up behind me. She was about to say something but stopped. She must have seen the note as well.

For a split second, I felt relieved. Natalie had probably decided to run some errands and left me a note, so I wouldn't worry. It could be a plausible story.

Perhaps Natalie took off work to celebrate her birthday but just forgot to mention it to anyone. Maybe she'd also forgotten to charge her phone, and it died while she was out.

That was the scenario I wanted to believe, but I couldn't deny that I was filled with dread as the note stared me in the face. Natalie was a planner. The scenario didn't actually fit her at all.

I snatched up the note.

> *Michael,*
>
> *I know we agreed to face whatever came our way together, but I believe that we are safer apart. This is what is best for both of us. I'm sorry that I didn't say this to you in person, but I knew that if I saw you, I wouldn't be able to do what I knew was right. Please don't try to find me. This is what I want, and I hope you will respect my wishes.*
>
> *Love always,*
>
> *Natalie*

I read it three times before crushing the note in my hand. I wanted to squeeze out every painful word. Natalie hadn't been kidnapped. She'd left me because she *wanted to.*

I stood there in disbelief. None of this made any sense. Natalie loved me, and she wanted to be with me. I was certain of it.

Did the stress of running from Henley finally get to her? Living a life on the run from Henley was a lot to take on. I knew that. I'd brought her into my crazy world, and maybe it had been unfair of me to expect her to want to stay in it.

Still, she never voiced any concerns about the pressure getting to her. She always insisted that we were in this together, like she'd promised.

What could've possibly happened to make her have a change of heart now?

I smoothed out the note and read it once again. This just didn't seem right.

I looked over at Raina.

"What?" she asked, concerned.

I hadn't read the note aloud, but she could tell by my reaction that whatever was in it wasn't good.

"Do you think Natalie wanted to break up with me?" I asked her.

Raina was the one person I could count on to always tell me the truth even if it would hurt my feelings. It was possible that Raina had picked up on something I had missed.

She looked surprised at my question. "No, I don't. Why?"

"What makes you so sure?"

She pondered it for a moment. "I mean … she almost *died* to save you."

I shook the note in my hand. "This says she thinks it's better if we're apart, and she specifically asks me not to try to find her."

"That doesn't make any sense."

As I contemplated the possibilities, I started to believe that I'd had it right the first time. I felt like I was going to be sick.

"What are you thinking?" she asked.

"I think Henley took her and forced her to write this note to throw us off."

It was the only logical explanation. Natalie wouldn't just bail on me. No way.

Raina tightened her lips into a thin line. It was the face she made when she disagreed with me but didn't want to argue. Not arguing was hard for her, so it was like she was forcing her mouth to remain shut.

"Think about it," I said. "After Henley saw what Natalie could do, why would he even need us?" The clarity set in further as I talked it through. "He made her write this note because he doesn't want us to try to find her."

If Henley had captured Natalie, the last thing he'd want was a big, elaborate rescue mission to save her. He'd planned this whole thing to make me think Natalie didn't love me anymore and that she'd left on her own. It was his way of ensuring I wouldn't try to find her.

"Assuming that's true," she replied, "why would Natalie agree to write that? She'd want to be rescued."

I sighed. It was so obvious. "It's Natalie we're talking about."

As much as I loved Natalie, she was protective to a fault. She often did things without thinking of the consequences. Jumping off a bridge to escape Henley, breaking into Henley's facility to rescue me—all of these were prime examples of Natalie disregarding her own safety to do what she believed was right. In both instances, she would have died if it hadn't been for her self-healing ability, which she hadn't even known she had at the time.

I took another look around her apartment. If Henley had come here and taken her captive, there would be some evidence of that. I was just missing it.

I went back into her bedroom. Raina trailed behind me.

"What are you looking for?" she asked as I opened the drawers in Natalie's dresser.

Natalie's clothes were neatly folded inside.

Without responding to Raina, I went into Natalie's bathroom. Her toothbrush sat in the holder, and her hairbrush was on the counter.

"I don't see any signs of a struggle," Raina said, standing in the doorway. "If Henley had been here, I'm sure Natalie would've put up a fight. I mean, think about what she did to Henley's office."

"But Henley could have cleaned up her apartment, knowing we'd come here, looking for her."

"Okay ... or maybe she just left for a few days to clear her head. Agreed, not the safest move, but it does sound more likely than what you're proposing."

"If Natalie left town because she wanted to, why wouldn't she pack any clothes?" I gestured toward the bathroom. "Why wouldn't she at least pack her toothbrush?"

There was no doubt in my mind. Natalie hadn't left by choice. She'd left because she was forced to.

I walked over to Natalie's closet and opened the door. All of her clothes still hung on their hangers. Her suitcase sat at the bottom of the closet.

"If Natalie planned to leave, she would have packed *something*," I insisted.

Raina looked around, her brow furrowed. She opened her mouth to say something but then stopped. Something had caught her eye, and she walked back over to the dresser.

She picked up Natalie's cell phone out of a round metal tray that sat on top of the dresser and handed it to me. I hadn't even noticed it there. I inspected the phone and realized the battery was dead, which explained why it was going right to voice mail.

"I know you don't want to hear this right now," she gently said, "but we need to activate the protocol. We need to leave town."

I adamantly shook my head. "No way." *I can't leave now.*

"Whether she left by choice or not, Natalie knows we'd have to activate the protocol," she insisted. "She knew that when she wrote the note."

"No," was my only response.

She sighed. "If Henley has her, then that means he knows where we are too. He could come back for us. We could all be in danger."

As much as I didn't want to admit it, she was right. Henley was capable of anything. Just because he didn't need me or Raina didn't mean that he wouldn't still try to seize us.

I could see Henley coming after us just out of spite even if he didn't need us anymore. Henley didn't like to lose, and I knew that it hurt his precious ego that we'd been able to evade him for as long as we had. It wasn't even just me and Raina we needed to worry about. He could just as easily come after Alexander and Lorena for their part in helping us avoid capture.

Reluctantly, I nodded in agreement. I couldn't put the entire family in jeopardy. We'd only dodged Henley in the past because we were diligent about the protocol. The protocol had to be used consistently in order for it to work.

Raina took a deep breath as she pulled her phone out of her pocket. She typed out our code word, *Found*, and looked at me one more time to make sure I was okay.

I nodded again, giving her permission to hit Send.

Six

Michael

"I don't think the answers you're looking for are in that note," Raina said from the driver's seat. "How many more times are you going to read it?"

I didn't take my eyes off of the paper. "If Natalie was forced to write a note, I think she would leave some sort of clue in it for me."

Raina drew her lips into a line but didn't respond. She knew better than to argue with me right now.

"I think we're here," she said a few minutes later.

For the first time in about an hour, I looked up from the passenger seat. Alexander and Lorena were in the car in front of us and were turning into the hotel we would be staying at for the night. We'd been driving all day and traveling off and on for days.

When we'd left San Antonio two days ago, we'd started out heading northwest toward New Mexico. But Lorena had thought she saw a suspicious car at a gas station in El Paso, so we'd turned around and started heading northeast. Eleven hours later, we were stopping for the night in Oklahoma City. It would be another full day of travel to get to our next destination—Cincinnati.

Raina pulled into a parking spot on the opposite end of the lot, away from Alexander and Lorena. This was a new trick of Alexander's that he'd implemented after we left Charlotte. Park on opposite sides of the hotel parking lot in case we needed to make a fast getaway. If Henley showed up and blocked us from getting to one vehicle, we'd have another option to escape.

Raina got out of the car, and I grudgingly followed. I didn't want to be here. I wanted to be doing something more productive to find Natalie, but I didn't know what to do. Alexander had no idea where they would have taken her.

On top of all that, I wasn't even sure my family was convinced that she'd been taken captive at all. I got the feeling that they all believed she'd left by choice.

Alexander went into the hotel lobby while we waited outside. A few minutes later, he emerged with two keys for adjoining rooms. I wasn't thrilled about rooming with Raina, although this had been our arrangement our entire lives. She felt safer with me around, and normally, it didn't bother me as much as it did right now. The truth was, I just wanted peace and quiet to think and try to figure out a solution. There was no way that was going to happen with Raina nearby.

Our rooms were on the ground floor, as always. We'd learned a long time ago that a ground-level hotel room made for a safer escape in the event we needed to exit through a window—and we'd done that more times than I could count.

I recalled one time in particular when Raina and I were about nine years old. Henley's men had found us at a hotel we were staying at. I remembered it had been around eight a.m., and Raina and I were sitting on the floor, eating stale cereal and watching cartoons. There was an urgent pounding on the door. Lorena froze in the chair she was sitting in as Alexander carefully checked the peephole.

It was Henley's men. They were dressed as hotel maintenance workers, but luckily, Alexander recognized one of the men before he opened the door. Alexander quietly ushered us toward the bathroom, where there was a window for us to escape.

Henley's men began trying to kick down the door. It seemed like the door would come crashing down with just one final kick. In a moment of pure fear and instinct, Raina had used her abilities to slide the dresser in front of the door to stop them while we climbed out through the bathroom window.

This hotel room reminded me of that room. It had the same type of layout with a window in the bathroom.

Raina tossed her suitcase on the bed farthest from the door, so I took the one closer to it. This was the usual routine because it made her feel safer. I used to joke with her about how quickly she was willing to sacrifice me to save herself. She always claimed it wasn't true, and of course I knew it wasn't, but she still never offered to take the other bed.

Lorena knocked on the adjoining door, and I opened it to let her in.

She smiled sympathetically at me and then turned to Raina. "Do you have a coffeemaker in your room?"

Raina looked around and frowned. She loved coffee with about ten tablespoons of sugar.

"No," she replied, clearly disappointed.

Lorena's smile widened. "We do, if you'd like to come make some."

Raina eagerly followed Lorena into the other room. Lorena gave me another small smile before closing the door behind them. She'd lured Raina out on purpose because she knew I wanted some privacy.

With Raina gone and the room to myself, I threw myself onto the bed. I flipped over onto my back, staring up at the ceiling.

I couldn't believe this was happening. I hadn't seen it coming at all. *How had I missed signs that Henley was so close by that he could snatch Natalie right from under my nose?* I hated myself for failing to protect her.

I closed my eyes, but I knew there was zero chance I would doze off. I hadn't had a decent night's sleep since before I was captured in Philadelphia, and as tired as I was, I knew there was still no chance I'd be able to sleep anytime soon.

"Michael ..." I heard Raina say from the other room.

She didn't yell it but said it just loud enough so I could hear. We never yelled each other's names in hotel rooms because you never knew who could be lurking nearby and hear it.

I chose to ignore her.

If she'd broken that coffee machine, there was no way I'd have enough patience to fix it right now. I'd probably just smash it into a hundred pieces. On second thought, that wasn't a bad idea.

The adjoining door swung open.

Raina barged through. "Michael!"

The urgency in her voice made me sit up. "What's wrong?"

Has Henley found us already?

"You need to see this," she said before bolting back into the other room.

I jumped off the bed and rushed after her. "What are you—" I started, but then my eyes landed on the TV, and I stopped. I didn't need an explanation.

There, on the screen, was a sketch of a woman who looked just like Natalie. The caption under it read, *Angel heals children at hospital in Jacksonville, Florida.*

The screen shifted to a man with thick-rimmed glasses and a wide nose standing outside of a hospital. Considering the fact that he had a microphone in his hand, I assumed he was a reporter.

Alexander turned the volume up, so we could hear what was going on.

"Hospital officials believe the incident happened between the hours of two and three a.m., Eastern Standard Time," the reporter said. "I had an opportunity to speak with one of the parents of the children who were involved, and they said their son described the woman as a beautiful angel with red hair."

I glanced at Raina. She looked back at me with wide eyes.

The reporter walked over to a young woman in scrubs that were covered in cartoon cats.

"This is Ana Prater, the nurse who was on duty last night," he said. "Ana, can you describe to us what happened?"

Ana nervously looked at the camera and then back at the reporter. "I looked in on the children to make sure their vitals were stable and that they were sleeping as comfortably as possible. Then, I went down the hall to see some other patients, and about two hours later, when I went to check on the children again, they were all sitting up in their beds. It was a miracle. They were all healed."

"Did you see anyone else in the room with the children?"

"No. There was no one. I have no idea how they all could have recovered so quickly. I mean, there wasn't one scar left on any of them."

"Did you speak to the children?"

"Yes," Ana replied. "One of the boys told me an angel with long red hair came to visit him."

The reporter held up a copy of the sketch of Natalie to show Ana. "Have you ever seen this woman before?"

Ana shook her head. "Never."

"Did the boy describe his interaction with this angel?" the reporter asked.

kind of pain anyway. Cutting me out of her life was the only way she felt in control of the hurt she suffered after losing Becca."

"So, if she left on her own, she must have perceived some kind of threat," I rationalized.

"Likely to someone other than herself," Seth said.

I nodded in agreement. *That* sounded like Natalie.

The front door opened, and Jen stepped inside. She let out a deep breath and pushed a rogue strand of hair out of her face. I'd never seen Jen this frazzled-looking before.

Jen reached into her purse and pulled out a flash drive. "I owe the security guard at the hospital a dozen doughnuts every Friday for the rest of the year and an autographed photo of Miss Florida, but I got it."

Seth gave her a peck on the cheek and then took the flash drive from her. He walked over to his laptop set up on the coffee table.

"Thank you," I told Jen.

She nodded and gave me a quick hug. "Of course," she replied as we parted. She looked at Raina.

"I don't hug," Raina blurted out before Jen could even take one step toward her. "No offense."

I gave Raina a look as Seth inserted the flash drive into the laptop.

Seth sat down on the couch. Jen and I joined him. Raina perched on the arm of the couch, next to me.

"Okay," Jen said when the footage started, "they believe the children were healed sometime between two and three a.m., so maybe fast-forward until we get to one thirty."

Seth obliged and stopped at one thirty.

The footage was pretty clear, and from the looks of it, the camera seemed to be mounted at an angle, facing outward from the hospital. From this viewpoint, we could see the front entrance and the patient drop-off circle. We could also see part of the parking lot toward the right side of the screen.

We watched the footage for what felt like forever. Because it had been so late at night and visiting hours were over, there was barely any activity at all. When the clock on the footage showed that it was two fifteen a.m., I started to worry that maybe this "angel" had decided to use a different entrance.

Then, she came into view.

"There," Seth said, pointing to the far-left corner of the screen.

The person who appeared on the screen was definitely a female with long, curly hair and a petite build, just like Natalie. They even walked the same.

The video was in black and white, so I couldn't tell the color of her hair, but she was wearing a pair of jeans and an oversize sweater. I was pretty sure I'd seen her wear that outfit before.

"It's her," I muttered as we watched her walk into the hospital.

Seth looked at me and nodded. He moved to stop the video.

"No. Not yet. Let's see what happens when she comes out," I said, although I didn't know what difference it would make. It wasn't like I would be able to see what direction she had gone and follow her now, but maybe there would be some clue as to what had happened to her after she left.

"What's to the left of the hospital? More parking lot?" I asked Jen.

"No. That's the street," she replied.

"How do you think she got there?" Raina asked.

"Probably public transit," Jen replied. "There is a city bus line that runs really late and stops in that same area that she came from."

We watched and waited. Raina reached out and lowered my hand from my mouth. I hadn't realized I was chewing on my thumbnail. It was now too short, and the exposed skin was raw.

"Here she comes," Jen said as Natalie walked back out of the hospital.

I leaned in closer, anxious to see which direction she would go. If she went the same way she had come, then we would know that she'd probably caught a bus to her next destination. Maybe I could figure out the route and piece together where she had gone.

The automatic sliding doors closed behind Natalie, but she just stood there. She closed her eyes and took a deep breath, as if she were just enjoying a nice, relaxing evening.

A minute or so later, she walked over to a bench on the left side of the screen and sat down.

"What is she doing?" Seth asked.

I shook my head. *I have no idea.*

"She's not waiting for the bus," Jen said. "She's too far away from the stop."

We watched for over an hour while Natalie just sat on the bench. Unsure of how much longer this would continue, Seth slowly sped up the video.

A little over the third-hour mark, we saw blurred movement.

"Back up," I told him.

Seth rewound the footage to just before the blurred movement started. Natalie was still sitting on the bench, alone.

A black van pulled up on the street behind her, and my stomach dropped to my feet.

It was Henley's men. Raina recognized the van, too, and put her hand on my shoulder.

Natalie seemed oblivious to the four men who emerged from the van, wearing ski masks. She sat perfectly still with her back to them as they slowly approached the bench where she sat.

Jen gasped as she realized who it was and what was about to happen.

Run! Why are you just sitting there? I had to stop myself from shouting at the TV.

Natalie suddenly stood up, but she still wasn't facing the men.

This is it. This is where she will fight back and get away.

But she didn't turn to face her attackers. She didn't try to run away or fight. Instead, she dropped down to her knees, giving up.

I stood up with my fists clenched, as if I could go into the video and fight them off for her.

Jen buried her face into her hands, unable to watch.

The men surrounded Natalie. One came up behind her and plunged something into her neck. From the way she quickly slumped down to the ground, it must have been a powerful sedative to knock her out and suppress her abilities.

One of the men picked Natalie up off the ground and calmly carried her unconscious body to the back of the van. Two of the men hopped into the back with her. They shut the door as the other two men got into the front and then quickly pulled away.

Seth and I had witnessed Natalie blow a hole in the wall of Henley's office in Charlotte. Taking out four of Henley's men should have been easy for her to handle. For the life of me, I couldn't understand why she hadn't fought to escape.

It didn't even make sense why she would hang around there after healing those kids anyway. She would have known healing them would set off Henley's radar and that they would come looking for her.

Once the van was out of view, Seth stopped the video. We looked at each other in stunned silence. There weren't words to describe what we had just witnessed.

For reasons we might never understand, we had just watched Natalie surrender to Henley *on purpose.*

Seth stood up and started angrily pacing around the room. Jen watched him with wide eyes as he walked over to the magazine rack and kicked it, sending pieces of wicker and metal flying across the room, the pile of magazines spilling out onto the floor.

When he stopped pacing, he turned and looked at me. He didn't need to say anything for me to know what he was thinking. His expression was the same as mine. Angry. Hurt. Terrified.

He and I both knew what this meant. Regardless of the reason why Natalie had allowed herself to be captured, we both loved her. We had no other choice but to find her and bring her home.

We were going back to Henley to save her.

SEVEN

NATALIE

My eyelids felt like they had weights attached to them, but I managed to open them a crack, just enough to allow the bright light to pierce into them. The attempt was too painful, and I closed them again.

I heard a faint rustling noise and sensed someone leaning over me. They weren't touching me, but I could feel the heat radiating off their body. I hadn't noticed until then, but I was cold.

The awareness of my situation set in, and a wave of panic crept over me. Henley had captured me.

Has he been watching me sleep?

Despite the pain, I forced my eyes open.

Another pair of eyes stared back at me. Blue eyes. They were familiar.

Michael?

I blinked until the person was clearly in focus.

I gasped when I realized it wasn't Michael after all. Although this stranger had the same shade of blue eyes as Michael, his were rounder. He appeared to be around the same age and height as Michael, but his hair was dark ash brown.

He frowned, and without saying a word, he backed away from me.

I quickly scanned the room and was confident I was at a Henley facility. The room was depressing and sterile, and the gray walls matched the ones in the Charlotte facility. There was no way I was in

Charlotte though. I was certain Henley wouldn't bring me back to that particular location.

The guy who had been watching me sleep was the only other person in the room with me. He was wearing a pair of blue scrubs, so I assumed he must be one of Henley's employees.

I tried to sit but hit resistance and slammed back down onto the metal table.

"Try not to struggle against it," the guy said to me quietly, as if he didn't want anyone else to hear. "It will only make it worse."

Before I could respond, the door to the room opened. The guy in scrubs moved to the corner of the room. He stood silently with his hands folded carefully in front of him. I couldn't see who'd entered the room from where I was lying, but I could sense who it was. I knew it was Henley.

I helplessly lay there as I waited for him to come into my view.

"It's nice to see you again," Henley said as he towered over me. A smug smile tugged at the corner of his thin lips. "I know this isn't the warmest welcome, but the last time you were in my presence, you blew up my office." There was a hint of amusement in his voice, although I was positive that he'd found that encounter anything but amusing.

I didn't respond. I just stared back at him with hatred.

I should've blown you up with it.

"If you promise to behave yourself, I'll untie you," he said.

I didn't want to give him the satisfaction of a reply, but there was no way I could escape with Becca if I spent my time here, strapped to a table.

I nodded slightly.

Henley gave a wave of his hand, and the guy moved from the corner to return to my side.

He began untying the straps that bound my wrists, waist, and ankles. He glanced down at me once, making eye contact, but I immediately looked away.

As soon as I was untied, he retreated back to the corner of the room.

I sat up on the table and looked down at my sore wrists. I rubbed the red welts that stretched all the way around them.

I was no longer wearing the clothes that I had been taken captive in. Instead, they had been replaced with a pair of gray scrubs that almost matched the dull paint on the walls.

"It was a pleasant surprise to find you," Henley told me. "When we detected your healing powers, I wasn't sure if it was you or Michael. Although a part of me was hoping we'd find you both."

My head jerked up at the mention of Michael's name. I was surprised that he'd actually used it. Henley's half-smile reappeared. Something in my reaction interested him, and that scared me.

"You're protective of the people in your life, aren't you?" he asked as if we were old friends, catching up.

I didn't respond.

"Well, so am I," he continued, knowing my answer despite the fact that I hadn't provided one. "And that's why I've always wanted to bring Michael and Raina home. They might not be able to give me what you can, but there is still so much I could learn from their unique abilities. Ultimately, they belong here. They belong to *me*."

It would be impossible for Becca to locate Michael and his family now that the dream blocker was in place. Michael would've also activated the protocol to leave town after finding my note. Although I knew they were safe, I also knew it wouldn't take long for Henley to concoct another plan to try to find them.

I swallowed a lump in my throat, but it didn't go down easily. My throat felt dry and raw, like I hadn't had a sip of water in days.

"You belong to me now as well," he added, narrowing his eyes. "And since you belong to me and you are such a loyal, protective friend, I imagine you are going to be a good girl and do what you are told. Aren't you?"

It took every ounce of my self-control for me to nod. What I really wanted to do was leap off the table and squeeze my hands around Henley's throat.

"Good." He seemed pleased with himself. "If you do what you are told, I won't kill them *when* I find them, and you will have kept them safe. Everyone wins."

I noticed that Henley hadn't mentioned Becca's name, but I wasn't going to bring her up in case he hadn't figured out yet that I was there to save her. Maybe he didn't realize that I'd allowed him to capture me, so I could find her.

Henley turned to the guy in the corner. "Let's show our guest to her new home."

The guy walked over to me and grabbed me by my arm. He didn't grip ahold of me tightly, but I also didn't struggle or give him a reason to. I willingly stood up, accepting my fate. My legs wobbled beneath me, and he wrapped an arm around my waist to steady me, so I wouldn't fall.

With bare feet, I allowed this stranger to escort me out of the room and down a long, empty corridor. Henley walked ahead of us, proudly leading the way. I felt like I was on parade, being displayed as Henley's newest trophy, even though there was no one outside the three of us to witness it.

We passed several other rooms with closed doors. Each metal door looked identical to the next with nothing distinguishable about any of them. None of them gave any indication of who or what might be inside. Any of them could be the room where Becca was being held.

Henley stopped at the very last room at the end of the hallway and opened the door. He held it ajar as the other guy brought me inside. The door swung closed behind us and clicked as it automatically locked.

This room wasn't much different than the last, but it had an actual bed at least. It was plain with a white blanket, a single pillow, and no headboard. It didn't look very comfortable, but it was still better than sleeping on a metal table.

Just like I'd seen in the video Michael showed me of his childhood, there was a small, round metal table with two matching chairs to the far-left side of the room. On the wall beside it was a giant mirror that stretched from floor to ceiling. I knew the other side contained the observation room, where Henley could watch tests being performed and bark his commands from behind the glass.

Henley motioned for me to sit at the table, and his worker obediently sat me down in a chair. The coldness of the metal seat pierced through the thin fabric of my pants.

To the far right was a little room with only a curtain for a door. The curtain was pulled back, and from where I sat, I could tell it was a tiny bathroom with a toilet and a sink.

There was a soft click at the door, and then it opened. A nurse—the same one who'd been guarding Michael's room at the Charlotte facility—entered, carrying a metal tray of food and a glass of water. She didn't acknowledge me as she placed them on the table in front of me. Without a word, she turned and walked back to the door.

"Tonya, bring in her meds next," Henley ordered her.

Tonya nodded in response before placing her finger on a scanner by the door. The door unlocked for her to exit. I guessed Henley had been forced to make some upgrades in his security since my visit to the Charlotte facility. It was my turn to feel a little smug.

I looked down at the food, and my stomach turned. It appeared to be some kind of meatloaf, but the meat had an unusual gray tint to it.

Why is everything in this place gray?

Next to the mystery meat was a pile of soggy green beans.

The door opened again, and Tonya was back. This time, she was carrying a syringe. Without explanation, she walked over to me, forcibly lifted my sleeve, and plunged the needle into the side of my arm. I cringed. I'd always hated needles; plus, I had absolutely no idea what she'd just injected me with.

"The first thing I'm going to ask you to do is to eat all of your dinner," Henley said to me as Tonya exited the room. His tone was friendly, but I knew from experience that it was only friendly on the surface. It was just a mask to conceal the evil that really resided within him.

Henley watched me until I picked up the plastic spork and took a bite of the green beans. He smiled. "Good. When you're done, Tonya will give you something to help you sleep. You need to be up early tomorrow. We have a big day planned."

I stared at Henley until he left the room. As soon as he was gone, I let out a breath that I hadn't realized I was holding.

The gray meat sat in a blob on my tray. It jiggled as I poked at it with my spork.

The guy with blue eyes sat down in the chair across from me. "It's better to just get it down as quickly as possible. Dragging it out will feel like torture."

I stabbed off a small piece of the meatloaf and shoved it into my mouth. I tried not to think about the odd, sour flavor of it as I chewed and swallowed. It was terrible. I took a large gulp of water in an effort to wash the taste away.

We sat in silence as I forced myself to eat every disgusting bite. When I was finished, I expected him to grab the tray and leave, but he didn't. He just sat there, watching me.

"You're allowed to leave now, right?" I asked, motioning to my empty tray. I wanted to be alone.

He didn't move. "I'm trying to figure you out."

"What's to figure out?" I shrugged.

"Why you're here."

I looked away. "I'm here because I was captured."

He narrowed his eyes. "I don't think so."

I looked back at him and focused, attempting to read his mind. *What does he know?*

"It's not going to work," he said, interrupting my concentration.

"What?"

"Reading my mind." He sat back, a look of arrogance on his face. "First of all, that shot Tonya gave you suppresses all of your abilities, except your ability to heal. Henley knows how to isolate your healing powers, so he can study only that. Second, my mind is unreadable."

I pushed the tray further away from me on the table. Even though the food was gone, there was a strange smell lingering on it.

He reached out and took the tray. "Did you do it for Becca? Michael? Both?"

I shook my head. "Do what?" I didn't bother to hide the irritation in my voice.

"Surrender." He stared me dead in the eyes.

"I-I don't know what you're talking about," I stammered.

He smiled and stood up, tray in hand. "Sure you don't." He walked over to the door, scanned his finger, and pulled the handle to exit. "My name's Luke, by the way. We'll talk more tomorrow."

He held the door open for Tonya, as she was on her way inside. This time, she was holding a small plastic cup of water and two pink pills.

"Take these," she said, holding them out to me.

I obediently took them from her. "Are these sleeping pills?"

She raised an eyebrow but didn't answer me.

I popped the pills in my mouth, downed them with the water, and handed the empty cup back to her. She pivoted on her heels and marched out.

Luke looked back at me one last time before closing the door behind them.

At last, I was alone. I needed to strategize how to get out of here. The fact that Luke had already figured out that I'd allowed myself to be captured and suspected it was because of Becca was concerning. It meant Henley likely knew it too.

I got up from the table and paced around the room.

First step, I needed to figure out where they were keeping Becca. I would need to know her exact location in order to quickly get her out when the time was right.

Second step would be to figure out a weakness in their system to escape. The electricity was the weak point I'd used to get to Michael when we broke him out of the Charlotte facility. Although I was certain they'd fixed that defect by now, there had to be something else I could use here. Nothing was ever perfect. I would keep my eye out for a flaw in their security while I worked on finding Becca.

My legs began to feel wobbly again. Whatever the nurse had given me was starting to kick in. I managed to stumble to the bed before collapsing on top. It took every ounce of strength I had left to position myself correctly on the bed and pull myself under the thin, scratchy blanket.

I didn't know what time it was when I woke up. One moment, I had been asleep, and the next, I was dashing through the curtain to the makeshift bathroom. Dropping down on my knees, I lifted the toilet lid and released the contents of my dinner.

My stomach cramped until I was doubled over on the cold tiled floor. All I could do was lie there in a clammy sweat, praying that the nausea would go away.

Several minutes later, when I was confident that I was done being sick, I crawled back to the bed and climbed in. I felt better, but I wasn't sure that would last.

I barely slept the rest of the night, but I had no concept of how much time had passed. There were no clocks or windows in the gray room, so I could do nothing but wait for someone to come in to start my day—not that I was looking forward to whatever that would entail.

After what felt like an eternity, the door to my room finally opened. I immediately sat up, dreading whatever was going to come next but also anxious to leave the room.

Tonya entered, and I couldn't help but wonder if she'd even gone home the night before. She appeared to be wearing the same outfit as yesterday. The only difference was, her graying blonde hair was now pulled up into a tight bun instead of the ponytail she'd worn the night before.

She walked over to me, lifted my sleeve, and gave me another shot. Based on Luke's chattiness last night, this shot was likely another injection to suppress my abilities.

"Come with me," she said when she was done.

I obediently followed her out of my room and back down the long hallway. We passed the room where they had initially kept me and eventually came to a nurses' station.

On the other side of the nurses' station, there was a room with a patient chart on the door.

When I'd rescued Michael from the facility in Charlotte, there had been a similar chart on the door to the room where they were holding him. It was possible Becca was in there, but I needed to be certain before I tried anything.

Tonya led me through a set of doors and into a bathroom that reminded me of my high school locker room. The bathroom had multiple stalls inside, including a few that appeared to be showers. Placed on the bench outside of one of the shower stalls was a pair of fresh gray scrubs, underwear, and a white towel folded neatly on top.

"Take your shower and then put these on," she said, gesturing to the clothes. "You have five minutes."

I waited for a second, and then when I realized Tonya wasn't leaving and the clock was ticking, I decided to get undressed as quickly as I could and get into the shower. I turned on the water and gasped as the cold water gushed down on top of me.

Two dispensers were attached to the wall of the shower—one for soap and the other for shampoo. I dreaded the thought of trying to get a comb through my long, curly hair without the luxury of conditioner.

"One minute," Tonya called from the other side of the curtain just as the water had begun to warm up.

I finished washing the shampoo suds out of my hair and turned off the water. With the shower curtain wrapped around me, I reached out and plucked the towel off the bench. I closed the curtain back as I dried off.

Tonya reached through the curtain, my fresh clothes in her hands. "Henley is waiting. Hurry up."

I grabbed the clothes from her and promptly started getting dressed. It wasn't that I cared about what Henley thought per se, but I knew I had to be careful not to seem uncooperative. I needed him to eventually let his guard down to some degree and make a mistake. Without access to my abilities, the only way for me to get out of here with Becca was to find a flaw and outsmart him.

I also knew that Henley could be very unpredictable when he was angry. Of course, I was worried about what he would do to me, but I was even more worried about what he might do to Becca if I provoked him.

I knew that Henley had tried to leverage Raina against Michael when they were kids. He'd threatened to hurt her in an attempt to force Michael to do things with his powers that he wasn't capable of.

I'd also seen Henley try to use Seth and me to manipulate Michael when we were captured in Charlotte. Henley had warned he'd kill us unless Michael used his abilities to heal himself.

Punishment and control were Henley's go-to moves, and I couldn't give him a reason to use them on Becca.

When I finished dressing, Tonya led me out of the bathroom and back to the long hallway. Instead of going back to my room, she brought me to the room with the metal table. I hadn't comprehended it last night, but it was actually an exam room, like a twisted version of a doctor's office. I looked at the mirrored wall and realized it was also attached to an observation room.

Henley was already in the room, sitting in a chair, waiting on us. Luke took his place in the corner, and an older man in a white lab coat stood next to him. The man was holding a black medical bag, similar to the one Alexander had. I assumed he was some type of doctor.

"Good morning," Henley greeted me, almost cheerfully, as he gestured for me to take a seat on the metal table.

I didn't respond, but I obeyed his command and hopped up onto the table.

Henley smiled at me, but it didn't reach his eyes. He was playing games, trying to seem charming, but I saw through it. "I know you had a rough night. Are you feeling better?"

"Yes," I quietly replied, comprehending he must have been watching me as I'd gotten sick.

Henley motioned to the man in the white lab coat. "This is Dr. Leeman," he explained as the doctor walked over to me. "He's going to check you out to see how you are doing."

I couldn't understand why Henley was suddenly so concerned about my well-being.

Dr. Leeman robotically checked my blood pressure, pulse, and temperature. He then asked me a series of questions regarding what symptoms I had last night versus this morning.

"When would you say the stomach cramping and nausea stopped?" Dr. Leeman asked as he pressed on my stomach.

I didn't feel sick anymore, so I assumed whatever bug I'd had before must now be gone.

"Um, it's hard to say," I replied. "Maybe about twenty minutes after it started."

Dr. Leeman nodded thoughtfully. "Would you say that it progressively got better over a period of time or all at once?"

"All at once, I think." It was hard to remember with all of the sedatives they had given me.

"Extraordinary," Henley said with a pleased smile. "You said that it typically takes about twenty-four to seventy-two hours to fully recover from food poisoning. She recovered in less than half an hour."

I darted my eyes at Henley. I should've known. He'd given me food poisoning on purpose.

"That's correct," Dr. Leeman replied. "This was a remarkably fast recovery. The bacteria we put in her meal should have taken a minimum of twenty-four hours to clear her system. We need to run a few more tests to confirm it's completely gone, that her body truly healed her of it."

"Well then, do it," Henley ordered, a tinge of irritation in his voice. "She should have been hooked up to machines last night to thoroughly study the process." He shot an agitated glance at Tonya.

"My apologies, sir," Tonya replied, recoiling into the corner next to Luke.

My intuition told me that this wasn't the first time Tonya had messed up, and Henley's patience with her was wearing thin. I sensed that Tonya was forgetful, and that could come in handy.

Henley turned his attention back to me. The false friendliness had now returned to his face. "I'm sure you're wondering what's on the agenda for today."

I took a deep breath, and out of the corner of my eye, I noticed Luke looked down at the floor.

"Last night, we tested your ability to heal against a particular kind of bacteria, so we're going to give you a break today against illness and focus on repairing wounds."

Images of the scars on Michael's arms, back, and chest flashed into my mind, and I could feel my heart start to race. His scars were painful reminders of being slashed by Henley's doctors over and over as they'd insisted that he heal himself. This was going to be horrible, but I had to endure it. I'd known this would be part of the deal when I decided to surrender.

In my attempt to feel brave, I straightened my posture. Henley noticed and frowned. It hadn't been intentional, but I could tell that Henley had taken it as a sign of defiance. I slouched back down, but I was pretty sure the damage had already been done.

"Before we get started," Henley said, "I'd like you to tell me where you were living before I found you."

"I lived in Florida, where you found me," I lied.

"No, you moved away from Florida," he replied, clearly onto me. "I want to know where you moved to after Florida and whether or not Michael and Raina were with you."

I froze. I wasn't going to tell him anything about Michael.

"I haven't seen Michael since Charlotte," I lied again. "We went our separate ways."

Henley narrowed his eyes at me. "I doubt that. After all, you did almost die, trying to save him."

I looked away. Alexander and Michael had warned me about this. Henley would try to get me to tell him where Michael was.

Becca had told me that Henley viewed Michael as obsolete now because of my ability to self-heal, but I knew this was really about winning. Even if Henley didn't need or want Michael, he needed to succeed in catching him.

He leaned in a little closer to me. "We can do this the easy way or the difficult way."

My eyes slid back to him.

"I'm not going to lie to you; today is going to be tough." His tone was steady and uncomfortably calm. "But how cooperative you are will determine how tough it's going to be."

I straightened my back again, this time in deliberate defiance. I didn't care what he did to me. I would never tell him anything about Michael. "I have nothing to say."

He didn't move a muscle, but a vein bulged in his neck. "Then, just remember, this was *your* choice."

EIGHT

NATALIE

"There's no way I'm eating that," I told Luke as I pushed the metal tray as far away from me as possible. Although this was the only meal offered to me today, I wasn't going to allow them to make me sick again tonight.

What is Henley going to do if I refuse to eat? Torture me? That ship had already sailed.

Luke sat across from me at the table in my room and sighed. "It's not poisoned."

It was only the two of us in the room, but I was still surprised by his candor.

"Oh, so you knew they were going to poison me last night?" I raised my eyebrow at him.

He shook his head. "No, I didn't know about that." There was a hint of sadness to his voice that made me wonder if I could believe him.

"Then, how can you be sure this isn't?" I pointed at the tray.

With his eyes fixed on something across the room, he replied, "Because I looked at your chart, and the food poisoning test was marked complete. Congratulations, you passed." His tone was sarcastic, as if he didn't agree with what they were doing to me.

If he'd seen my chart, then he probably knew about the other tests they'd run on me today. I rubbed the tops of my forearms and then protectively folded my arms around my abdomen. Even though I had been able to heal the wounds Dr. Leeman had inflicted on me, the memory of the pain still lingered.

I had no idea how Michael had lived with being sliced open on a regular basis like that, especially without the ability to heal himself. I'd only gone through one day of it, and toward the end, I'd feared I would lose my sanity.

I shuddered, struggling to push the thought out of my head.

He nudged the tray back toward me. "I know it sucks, but you need to eat if you are going to survive."

He was right, but I couldn't understand why he cared if I lived or died. No one else at Henley did. That was how they all slept at night. They forgot that their test subjects were actual human beings.

Reluctantly, I stabbed a bite of broccoli with my spork and shoved it into my mouth. I had no reason to trust Luke, but I had to take a chance on eating dinner. I needed to keep my strength up if I was going to get out of here alive with Becca.

"I know why you're here, you know," he said with a smirk. "So, you can stop pretending."

Are we going to play this game again?

I swallowed the broccoli and looked as innocent as possible. "And why is that?"

He frowned. "You're here for Becca and to protect Michael."

The sound of Becca's name piqued my interest, but I tried to remain composed. This could be a trick to get me talking. "How would you know that?"

"Very little happens around here without me finding out. I know she's your sister."

"Was that in my chart or something?"

He smiled. "I knew before that. You're all anyone could talk about after the commotion you caused in Charlotte."

I didn't respond. I just took another bite of broccoli and attempted not to look smug as I waited to see if he'd offer up any more details about Becca.

"You're not going to escape with her," he said, his smile quickly disappearing. "I know that's your plan."

How does he know that? Does that mean Henley knows as well?

I looked over at the observation glass, but all I saw was my own exhausted, haunted reflection staring back at me.

"They aren't there," he said, understanding my concern.

I had no reason to believe him.

"Henley goes home at six every evening and doesn't come back until seven in the morning," he explained. "And Dr. Leeman only does observation during active testing periods, like last night when you were poisoned. They are the only ones allowed to hang out in that room. And don't worry; I checked just in case before I came in here. It's empty."

He could be telling me this in hopes that I would let my guard down and speak openly. Henley could be behind that glass, watching me, and I would never know.

He must have seen the hesitation on my face because he quickly added, "I wouldn't have told you about looking at your file if there was any chance they were in there."

There wasn't anything he could say that would convince me to trust him. He was a Henley employee after all.

"If you saw my chart, what other tests do they have planned for me?"

He hesitated for a second. "It's better if you don't know."

My heart jumped up into my throat. *Could it get worse than what I went through today?* I mean, today, Henley had intentionally punished me. I had chosen that over giving him information about Michael. *Would every day be like that—or* worse*?*

"I doubt that. If I knew what was coming, I could be better prepared for it." I wasn't one hundred percent sure I wanted to know what Henley had in store for me, but I was genuinely curious to find out what Luke had found in my file.

"If you know what's going to happen, then it's all you're going to think about," he said. "And what difference will it make? You can't change it. You can't stop it from happening."

The fear of the unknown began to make me feel uneasy, so I decided to change the subject. "Where does Henley go every day at six?" I took a sip of water.

If Luke was going to insist on chatting with me while I ate my dinner, I was going to try to get as much information out of him as possible.

"He goes home to his family," he replied matter-of-factly.

I almost spit out my water. "What? Like, to a wife and kids?"

"Believe it or not, he does. Well, just one kid, I think. I saw a picture of a little girl on his desk but only once. That was the only time I was allowed in his office."

I didn't know what to say or how to respond to that. All I could do was imagine Henley sitting around a nice dining room table with his family.

Is he listening to his daughter recap her day at school while pretending that he didn't spend his entire day torturing me? Does his wife have any idea what kind of monster she married?

The thought of Henley enjoying his time outside of these walls infuriated me.

"Pretty messed up, right?" he asked, raising an eyebrow.

"Just a little ..." I shook my head, trying to refocus the conversation to something more productive. "What is your role here at Henley, Luke?"

He hesitated again and then responded, "Right now, it's to see if I can find out anything about Michael and Raina's whereabouts."

I narrowed my eyes at him. "And how do you think you're going to do that? Nothing Henley did today worked."

Luke hadn't witnessed the whole thing, but he'd seen enough to know I wouldn't crack. He had been there for the first hour or so of Dr. Leeman's testing, but after I'd passed out from the pain and regained consciousness again, Luke had been gone. I assumed Henley had sent him away to work on something else.

He leaned in a little closer toward me. "Well, I've been trying to read your mind for the past twenty minutes, but it's not working."

I made no effort to hide the shock on my face. Luke wasn't a Henley employee after all. He was a prisoner, too, and just like Michael and Raina, he had powers of his own.

I'd developed an aptitude for reading minds after Michael healed me from the accident. Although Michael had said he couldn't read minds, the fact that he'd managed to unlock it in my brain probably meant that he really did have the ability, even if it was dormant somewhere within him.

When I'd rescued Michael from Charlotte, they'd had him strapped to a gurney. He certainly hadn't been roaming around Henley, unattended, like Luke was.

If Luke is a prisoner, how is he sitting here in front of me?

"I don't understand," I told him. "How are you walking around freely and stuff?"

"I've learned how to be valuable to them."

We sat in silence for a moment. My broccoli was now gone, and I debated on whether or not I wanted to try eating the meat. I wasn't completely sure, but I thought maybe it was ground turkey.

Luke's eyes shifted again to something across the room. This time, I followed his stare to see what kept distracting him.

He was looking at the blood-soaked scrubs I'd been wearing earlier. They were sticking out of the metal trash can, where I had placed them after changing into clean ones. No one had come in to retrieve them yet. Apparently, Henley didn't believe in proper disposal of hazardous waste.

Seeing the blood made me recall the feeling of Dr. Leeman's scalpel slicing into my flesh, and I instinctively looked down at my abdomen. I was prepared to see the worst, but there was no blood. My scrubs were still fresh and clean. The wounds from earlier were fully healed. Well, the physical ones were healed anyway.

"If you don't tell me where Michael and Raina are, they are going to take it out on both of us tomorrow," he told me, pulling me out of my thoughts. His voice was now low and desperate.

"I'm sorry." I actually felt sorry for him now that I knew he was a prisoner. "But I don't know where they are." And that was the truth.

Thankfully, they would be far from Texas by now. They were somewhere safe.

I had never been so grateful for Alexander's strict protocol.

"There has to be something you can tell me," he insisted. "Obviously, they have some sort of predictable plan in place, or they wouldn't have been able to elude Henley for so long. Even if you can tell me that, I think that will be enough to keep Henley satisfied—for now."

Sure, Henley would be satisfied because then he would have a leg up on finding them. I would never risk that.

"No," I said firmly. "Absolutely not. Do whatever it is that you plan to do to me. I'm not telling you anything."

Luke's eyes widened. "I-I'm not going to hurt you."

He seemed sincere, but I promptly reminded myself again not to let my guard down. Just because he had claimed to be a prisoner at Henley didn't mean I could trust him. It didn't even mean that he was who he'd said he was either. Henley was clever, and this could all still be a trick to get me to trust Luke. The fact that he was allowed to even sit here alone with me was highly suspicious.

Just like with Michael, my intuition didn't seem to work on Luke. It was hard for me to tell if he was being genuine. I needed to err on the side of caution.

"I can't help you," I repeated.

He stared at me for a second, his eyes pleading with me. "I don't understand why you are protecting him."

Because I love him, and I would rather die in this miserable place than betray him. I didn't say it aloud, but my expression must have said what my words hadn't.

Luke abruptly stood up, his metal chair tipping over and crashing on the floor behind him. He didn't even notice.

I tensed, unsure of whether or not he would hurt me. He'd said he wouldn't, but it could have all been a part of his plan to seem vulnerable, to get me to trust him so I would tell him what he wanted to know about Michael. Now that I'd refused, I wouldn't be surprised if his true colors surfaced.

I braced myself for him to lunge at me from across the table, but he didn't. Instead, he began pacing around the room.

He roughly raked his fingers through his hair, leaving it a tousled mess.

After a minute, he stopped pacing. He turned to me, his expression intense. "Why would you be loyal to someone like him?"

The question confused me. "To someone like Michael?"

He didn't reply, but he folded his arms across his chest and looked at me expectantly.

"He's a good person," I said, still not understanding the question.

Luke laughed and raked his hair again. "Sure he is. Mr. *Perfect*."

He returned, bracing his arms on top of the table. "Let me ask you this: if the situation were reversed and he were here instead of you, do you really think he would choose to be tortured over ratting you out?"

It was a ridiculous question. "Yes, he would. I know he would."

"All right, I'll ask you a different question." He eyed me, wanting to take in my reaction to whatever it was he was going to ask me. "Do you know who I am? Did he ever tell you about me?"

I shook my head. I had no idea who he was. Michael never really talked about his childhood or the people at Henley, except when it was necessary. They were obviously painful memories, so I never pried.

"If Michael is so wonderful and such a trustworthy person, then explain to me why he abandoned me here," he said, his eyebrows raised, forcing deep lines onto his forehead.

I shook my head, not wanting to hear whatever it was he was going to tell me.

"Tell me what kind of a person leaves someone behind to rot in a place like this?" he persisted.

I held my breath. Even without my intuition, I could tell what he was going to say before he said it.

Luke leaned in a little closer. His vibrant blue eyes pierced into mine. "What kind of person does that to their own *brother*?"

Nine

Natalie

If it wasn't for Tonya coming in at night to give me an extra dose of sedatives before bed, I'd have no concept of time at Henley. Because they were terrified that I would somehow regain my abilities in the middle of the night, Tonya always made sure to plunge that syringe into my arm and give me two pink pills to take every night before bedtime.

Instead of cutting me, Henley had spent the past five days testing another method to see how my body would react. He was starving me.

Not only was Henley curious to see how long I could survive, but I believed it was also his twisted way of chastening me.

Henley had made it clear that he was displeased by my lack of willingness to help him find Michael and Raina. He'd been punishing me for days because I refused to give him any information pertaining to Alexander's escape protocol.

The fact that Luke had failed on his mission to get this information from me meant that he was being disciplined as well. It had been five days since Luke told me he was Michael's brother, and I hadn't seen him since. A small part of me began to worry about him.

The first two days of starvation had been the worst. My stomach had growled angrily at me, but there was nothing I could do. I was trapped in this hell and had no choice but to try to ignore the hunger pangs as they occurred.

The last three days had become easier in some ways and more difficult in others. My stomach was no longer growling, as if it had accepted that it wasn't going to be fed. The growling had been replaced though by a nervous, shaky feeling. I was so tired that I struggled to even get out of bed. My energy was completely depleted.

The only time I left my room was when Tonya escorted me to the shower in the morning and then to the lab after for testing with Dr. Leeman. When testing was finished, Tonya would bring me back to my room, and I would remain there until the following day—when it would start all over. I wondered how long this phase of testing would last, not that I missed being cut open.

With nothing else to do to pass the time, I should've been able to come up with a brilliant plan to find Becca and escape. As hard as I tried and as much as I wanted to get out of there, I wasn't able to concentrate. My body felt fatigued, and my mind was hazy. I was too busy fighting to survive to focus on anything else.

I had no idea what time it was when the door to my room opened. I turned over in bed, half-expecting it to be Tonya. I was shocked, however, to find Luke standing in my room.

I quickly took notice of his face, which was covered in a collage of red splotches mixed with black-and-blue bruises. His right eye was almost swollen completely shut.

With unsteady legs, I forced myself up out of the bed. I didn't bother to ask him what'd happened. I already knew. This was his punishment for me not giving him any valuable information on Michael and Raina.

"Luke, I'm sorry," I said, and I meant it. Although I would never betray Michael, I was still sorry this had happened to Luke. No one deserved this.

He lifted up a hand to stop me and then motioned for me to sit down at the table.

I sat down, and he took the seat across from me.

"Is it safe to talk?" I asked, stealing a glance at the mirrored wall.

"Yes. I checked the observation room before I came in, and no one was in there. They are probably taking a nap, resting from all of the festivities." He half-smiled as he pointed to his face. "I'm sure this was exhausting for them."

I cringed, but he didn't even seem startled by how they were treating him. My guess was, this was typical in his world.

I reached my hand across the table, toward his face, but he instinctively recoiled from me.

"I can heal you," I explained. "It's the one ability they haven't suppressed, remember?"

He watched me curiously for a moment, as if he was considering it, but then he slowly shook his head. "No, that would just make things worse. They need to see me in pain for a few days to make sure I've learned my lesson for failing at my task."

I helplessly folded my hands back into my lap. Unfortunately, he was right about that.

"Why would you do that?" he asked.

I didn't understand his question. "Do what?"

"Heal me."

I blinked at him, unsure of how to answer. "Um … because you're a person … in pain." Who wouldn't want to help someone in that situation?

He narrowed his eyes. It was as if the idea had never occurred to him. "You would probably get in trouble for helping me. You'd risk that?"

I contemplated his question. Without a doubt, Henley would be angry with me for interfering with his punishment of Luke, but I didn't care. I wasn't going to let Henley take away my humanity.

"Yes."

He sat there, staring at me. "Why?"

"You're the closest thing I have to a friend right now, so …" We were far from friends, but he was the only person I'd met at Henley who hadn't attempted to hurt me. At this point, that almost made us friends.

He nodded thoughtfully but didn't say anything.

The door swung open, and Dr. Leeman entered with Tonya at his heels. Tonya was pushing a metal cart with syringes and bandages on top. They didn't seem surprised to find Luke in my room, so they must have told him to come.

Luke and I glanced at each other. We both knew what this meant, although I was astonished they were going to do it in here. For some reason, they usually brought me into the room with the metal table to do this type of testing.

Without being told to do so, Luke walked to the corner of the room. He stood, facing out, with his hands folded in front of him, but he looked down at the floor. He knew what was coming, and he didn't want to watch it again.

Dr. Leeman walked over to me and lifted my left arm. Tonya readily held the scalpel out for him. By now, they had this perfectly rehearsed.

Dr. Leeman took the scalpel and sliced it across the top of my forearm.

I never understood how Michael could get cut and not flinch. I still winced at the initial cut even though the scalpel was so sharp that I barely felt it go into my skin.

Normally, my body would heal itself just as the pain began to set in.

Today was different though. The throbbing pain began to intensify as blood started to drip from my arm. Dr. Leeman caught the droplets with gauze before they hit the floor.

"Heal yourself," Dr. Leeman demanded.

I sat there in shock. I didn't understand what was happening. "I-I can't."

Why am I not healing?

No one had ever believed Michael when he told them he couldn't heal himself.

What if they don't believe me? Will they just continue to slice me open until I bleed to death?

I started to feel light-headed.

Dr. Leeman eyed me, trying to decide whether or not I was telling the truth.

"I can't," I insisted again. My voice cracked from the panic I felt building inside.

Dr. Leeman looked away and back to Tonya. "Bandage her up and make a note in her file that she was unable to heal herself today."

Tonya nodded and handed me a larger piece of gauze. "Apply pressure," she told me.

As Dr. Leeman left the room, he stopped briefly to smile arrogantly at Luke.

The blood began to soak through the gauze in my hand.

"You need stitches," Tonya said, shooting me a dirty look as she handed me more gauze. "I'll be right back."

Sorry to inconvenience you, I shouted at her in my head as she left the room.

"What are you doing?" Luke asked me when she was gone. He took a step forward but stopped, making sure he stayed close to the corner. "Just heal yourself."

"I wasn't lying. I can't."

"Why not?"

I shrugged. "I don't know … maybe I don't have enough energy to. They haven't fed me in days."

Michael had once told me that our abilities were based on energy and we had our abilities because we could transform that energy differently than other people. I didn't know if my inability to heal was connected to the fatigue I felt due to lack of food, but it sounded feasible.

Luke just stared at me as Tonya came back into the room. He watched silently from the corner as she stitched me up.

When Tonya was finished, she began to gather her things together on the table, preparing to leave. Luke stepped out from the corner and approached her.

"Tonya," he scolded, his tone full of authority.

I raised my eyebrows at him. I was still learning the ropes around Henley, but I was pretty sure he wasn't allowed to address her like that.

I waited for Tonya to go off on him, but instead, she cowered. "I'm sorry, sir. I didn't see you standing there."

"How many days has it been since the subject has eaten?" he asked her.

"Five, sir." She refused to meet his eyes. "I thought that's what you wanted."

"Bring her ten meal replacement shakes, a yogurt, and a banana at once."

She nodded her head and scurried out of the room, closing the door behind her.

I gaped at Luke in shock. *What the heck?*

He looked pleased with himself as he assessed the surprise on my face. "You're not the only one with cool talents," he said. "I made her think I was Henley."

The door opened again, and Tonya reappeared, fumbling with a tray of all the food Luke had requested.

Luke's face returned to a serious expression. He was somehow still controlling her.

"Leave it and go," he commanded, sounding angry. His voice was his own, but his tone was very much like Henley.

She placed the food on top of the table and hurried out.

When she was gone, he gestured to the food. "Dive in."

I grabbed the banana, quickly peeled it, and took a bite. It tasted like heaven.

"Hide meal replacement shakes under your bed. It won't be much, but at least it will be something in case they decide to keep depriving you. Just make sure you only eat it at night when you know they aren't watching."

"Mmhmm," I replied, my mouth full of banana.

"They'll probably start feeding you again though," he continued. "I doubt Henley will want to pause his testing just for the sake of punishing you."

"Maybe." I lifted the lid off of the yogurt. "Although I'm not sure which is more important to him."

He sat down in the chair across from me. "I'm not going to lie to you. Henley enjoys all of this. But the most important thing to him is developing his magical cure."

I scooped a sporkful of yogurt into my mouth and swallowed. I could feel my energy returning and the pain in my arm subsiding.

"What is he trying to do exactly?" I asked. "I mean, I've heard he wants to create some kind of medicine that will cure anything, but why is he so fixated on that? It's not like he really wants to help people."

"I guess I forgot to ask him." He shrugged, a sarcastic smile touching his lips.

"Fair enough."

I wished I knew Henley's end game, his real reason for doing all of this. That might be the key to his weakness and my key to freedom.

Luke watched me as I finished my yogurt and hid the meal replacement shakes under my bed. I decided not to have one right now. After not eating for five days, I was worried if I had too much, I would just get sick.

I returned to the table and sat back down, feeling better than I had in almost a week.

"I don't understand why you'd put yourself through this," he said out of the blue.

His question caught me off guard.

"Why I would come to Henley?" I asked. "You already know I came here for Becca."

"But why? What's so special about Becca that you would want to do all of this for her?"

Again, I was at a loss on how to answer. "Well, she is my sister, and I love her."

I could tell from his expression that he had no idea what I was talking about. It dawned on me that he might not get notions like friendship and love. Those would definitely be hard concepts to grasp if you'd never known anything except being a prisoner at Henley.

On my first night at Henley, Luke had said he was trying to figure me out. He couldn't comprehend why I'd allowed myself to be captured. He wasn't trying to gather details on my plan to break Becca free. He really wanted to understand my motivation because he couldn't fathom making that sort of sacrifice for someone else.

"She's important to me. When you love someone, you want to protect them from hurt and harm even if it means making things harder for yourself. Love is being selfless for the sake of someone else." I wasn't sure if that was the perfect definition of love, but it was how I felt about the people I loved.

"You probably don't know this," he said, "but Raina is my sister."

I hadn't even considered it since Michael had told me that he and Raina weren't blood-related. "I didn't think Michael and Raina were really related."

"They're not," he clarified. "Michael and I share a donor mother, and Raina and I share a donor father."

I still couldn't believe that Michael had a living, breathing blood relative that he never told me about.

"The way you feel about Becca, I've never had that kind of relationship with Raina even though she is my sister," he said.

I couldn't help but smile a little. "Raina is such a delight. I can't imagine why not."

Luke laughed. "I guess she hasn't changed much since we were kids."

"Luke, can I ask you a question?" I unexpectedly felt brave and trusting enough to ask.

He looked at me expectantly but didn't respond.

"Is Becca here? Is she alive?" I asked the question even though I was terrified to know the answer.

Just because I was here did not guarantee that Henley had decided to spare her life. We'd already passed that three-day mark.

As much as I didn't want to think about how aggressively Henley was pursuing Michael, I also hoped he was keeping Becca alive, so she would help him. She could still be valuable to him if he thought she might lead him to Michael and Raina.

He nodded. "Yes, she's here, and yes, she is alive."

I felt flooded with relief. "Is she okay? Does she know I'm here?"

He shifted in his seat, suddenly uncomfortable with my questioning. "She's as good as she can be under the circumstances. I don't know if she knows you are here though."

I wanted to bombard Luke with a million questions, but I knew I needed to be careful. Just because it felt like he and I were becoming friends and just because he'd helped me today, it didn't mean I could completely trust him. He'd spent his entire life at Henley, and there was no way to know for sure where his loyalty lay. He could very easily go back to Henley and tell him I had been asking all of these questions.

If Henley knew how desperate I was to protect Becca, he would either kill her to punish me or use her against me to try to get information on Michael.

Luke stood up. "I should go. I'm going to find Tonya, so she can order me to come clean up your food trash."

He walked to the door.

"Thank you," I told him before he opened the door.

He turned and looked at me.

"For the food," I clarified.

He shrugged. "No big deal. If they find out, they'll just take it out on Tonya."

As Luke left and closed the door behind him, I realized that Henley trusted Luke to some degree. Otherwise, Luke would be drugged up and locked in a room, just like me. If Henley knew Luke was walking around, manipulating the thoughts of his employees, there was no way he'd allow Luke to roam around here as freely as he did.

Henley didn't have as much control over Luke as he thought he did.

This realization gave me a renewed sense of hope. Luke had somehow succeeded in gaining Henley's trust. Regardless of the painful testing and punishment inflicted on him, Luke must've never taken the easy way out by using his mind manipulation to stop it. He managed to keep a cool head and not abuse his special talent.

The result was, Luke had a weapon at his disposal that he could use, undetected, if he was careful.

That was what I intended to do. I would find my secret weapon and then use it at just the right time.

I smiled to myself. *I am going to find a way to get out of here.*

Ten

Natalie

Over the next several days, I came to realize that Luke had been right. Henley's desire to punish me did not outweigh his higher priority of understanding how my healing powers worked. I was back to eating three small meals a day, just enough to keep my energy at a level that would allow my body to heal itself.

The tests themselves had become more intense. Each wound got a little deeper and was more painful. Henley would constantly push the envelope to see how much I could take.

At some point, I lied to myself, *he'll have what he needs, and this will stop.*

As much as that thought comforted me in the moment, the truth was, I didn't know what would happen to me once the testing ended. Henley wouldn't need me anymore, and I was certain he wouldn't just release me.

"Hurry up," Tonya called through the shower curtain, interrupting my thoughts.

I gave my hair one last rinse and turned off the water. As I reached out of the shower to retrieve my towel, I caught a glimpse of the faint scar that remained on my arm. Although I'd gotten back my ability to heal and the wound on my arm had closed up at a remarkable rate, it'd still left a scar.

I dried off, got dressed, and followed Tonya out of the bathroom. It was quiet, except for the sound of Tonya's sneakers squeaking against the floor as she walked. She never attempted to make small talk, which was fine with me.

As we rounded the corner toward the hall that led past the nurses' station and to my room, Tonya stopped short. She reached her arm out to stop me as well. Not paying attention, I ran into her arm.

I looked up to see two Henley workers in blue scrubs, pushing a gurney toward us. I gasped when I saw that someone was lying on top of it. A white sheet was pulled over the entire body, and I realized that whoever was on the gurney was dead.

It can't be her.

Tonya pulled me toward the wall, so the men pushing the gurney could pass. As they walked by, I debated on pulling the sheet off the body to see who was beneath it. If I did it, Henley would surely punish me the second he found out. If it was Becca, I probably wouldn't care what the punishment was. But if it wasn't her, the action wouldn't get me any closer to escaping alive with her.

Instead, I decided to wait until I saw Luke later and ask him to confirm again that Becca was still alive.

There was also a possibility that the body could be Luke's. I hadn't seen him yet today, but I reminded myself that I usually didn't see him until after my morning shower.

"Let's go," Tonya instructed, nodding her head toward the direction of my room.

If she knew who was on the gurney, she didn't let on. I doubted that she even cared.

I silently followed her back to my room.

I let out an audible sigh of relief when I saw Luke standing in there, awaiting our arrival. He was alive. Tonya didn't hear me, but Luke did. He curiously watched me as I tried to stifle the overwhelming anxiety I was feeling.

I needed Tonya to leave, so I could get answers about Becca.

I walked over to the metal table and sat down. At this point, I didn't need instruction. I knew the routine. My usual breakfast—a container of yogurt and a banana—was waiting on me.

Seeing that I was going to eat my breakfast, Tonya turned around and left the room.

As soon as the door closed behind her, I jumped up and ran to Luke. Without thinking, I threw my arms around him, hugging him tightly.

"What's gotten into you?" he asked, stiff as a board and not hugging me back.

I released him. "I'm happy you're alive."

He furrowed his brow, confused.

"Is Becca still alive?" I asked.

He didn't answer.

"Is she?"

He seemed even more confused. "What are you talking about?"

I could feel tears of frustration and fear start to sting at my eyes. It was a roller coaster of emotions that I couldn't seem to escape.

"There was a dead body … in the hall." My breath became strained, and I felt the start of a panic attack coming on. I crouched over with my hands on my knees, trying to get it under control.

"Uh … sit down," he said, gently guiding me back to the metal chair.

I sat and focused on taking deep breaths. I needed to feel the air moving in and out of my lungs.

Once my breathing was under control again, I looked up at Luke.

"You okay?" he asked.

I nodded. "I'm fine now."

"Becca is still alive."

That was good news, but I needed confirmation. "Are you positive?"

"Yeah. They aren't going to let anything happen to her."

"How can you be sure?" I asked, recalling how she'd warned me that Henley didn't find her valuable anymore.

He shrugged. "Finding someone with her talents is difficult. Henley has never tried to create it because it does occur naturally—just very rarely."

I realized that he didn't know I had the same gift of intuition that she did. If he didn't know, maybe Henley didn't either. They must not realize that it was in my family's bloodline.

He furrowed his brow again.

"What?" I asked, my heart starting to race.

He looked at me as he opened his mouth and then closed it again. He lifted up a finger to indicate I needed to give him a minute. Then, he walked over to the door, opened it, and left.

I sat there, staring at the door, trying to figure out what was going on. *Where did he go?*

A minute later, the door reopened, and Luke returned.

"Sorry, I wanted to make sure no one was in there." He gestured toward the mirror and then sat down at the table across from me. "I know who died, so I know for sure it wasn't Becca."

"Who was it?"

"There have been others." His voice was low, as if he was worried someone might suddenly walk into the room and catch him telling me. I leaned in closer to hear him better. "I don't know how many exactly but at least five or six from what I've seen. They are people that Henley is testing his miracle cure on."

"But they are dead," I said, trying to keep my voice down. "He's not curing them; he's killing them."

"Because his cure isn't working."

"Who are they?" I asked, wondering if they were Henley's employees or other people held captive, like us.

"Runaways mostly. People who won't raise red flags when they turn up dead. If they are ever found, that is."

Even if they were runaways, they probably still had families who were clinging to hope that they would someday be found and come home. The idea pained me and reminded me of my own family's experience as we'd wondered what had happened to Becca after she went missing.

"I can't speak to all of the cases, but I did peek at one of the files," he admitted. "I think they are relatively healthy when they get here, but Henley infects them with a disease or something before he administers his cure to see if it will work. The problem is, I think the cure is actually killing them."

"What does he infect them with?"

"It might not be the same for everyone, but in the case I saw, he'd given him E. coli bacteria."

I sighed. "No one would even get suspicious if they did an autopsy. They would just think he had eaten undercooked meat. The only way someone might figure out something else had happened would be if they were able to detect the cure that Henley had given him."

"Henley's smart enough to think of that," he said. "He'd cover his tracks. The last thing he wants is for this to get out and ruin his chances of selling the cure once it's ready."

I looked around at the gray walls that surrounded the room, wondering if I was really the first occupant. Surely, Henley hadn't created this just for me. I would be willing to bet he'd held one of those runaways in this room before he killed them.

"I can't imagine the things you've seen in your lifetime," I told him. "Why haven't you ever left?"

I'd seen what Luke could do with other people's minds. If he wanted to get out of here, I was sure he would be able to find a way.

He looked at me, surprised by my comment. As I watched his reaction, I detected the sadness in his eyes despite his best attempt to cover it up.

"It hasn't been easy, but it's all I know."

I realized it wasn't the answer I'd been secretly hoping for. If Luke had told me that he wanted to leave and would do it if given the chance, I would've asked him to help me and Becca break free. But if he wasn't clear about how he felt about escaping Henley, I couldn't risk asking. It meant his loyalty could still be to Henley even if Luke didn't agree with what he was doing.

"Eat your banana," he said, breaking my train of thought. "Tonya will be back soon, and you're going to need your strength."

I shivered at the thought but obediently finished my breakfast.

I sat on the metal table, waiting for Dr. Leeman and Henley to enter the room. Luke hadn't said much as he and Tonya escorted me from my room to the exam room, but I didn't need his silence to tell me this wasn't going to be pleasant. I was now well aware that the metal table equaled physical pain. All I could do was wait to see what they had in store for me today.

By the time Henley and Dr. Leeman arrived, Tonya already had me hooked up to the various machines to record the changes to my vitals and brain activity. Henley appeared to be pleased as he noticed I had been well prepared ahead of his arrival.

"Very proactive," Henley said, smiling at Tonya. "You know I hate to waste time." He turned to me. "I have some good news for you. We're going to explore some new opportunities today."

I just stared back at him. I didn't like the sound of that. There was no way these "new opportunities" were going to be in my favor.

Anything sounded better than being cut with a scalpel, but I also didn't trust that Henley hadn't come up with something even worse.

"We're going to see how you do with using some of your other abilities." Henley turned to Tonya and Luke. "Let's get our subject nice and secure."

I didn't know what that meant until they approached me. Tonya pushed me down on the table and started fastening the thick straps to my left wrist and ankle. They were going to restrain me like I'd been on the day I woke up here.

Luke apologetically looked down at me as he tied up my right side.

"Safety first," Henley said to me with a wink.

Dr. Leeman held up a remote and hit a button that moved the table up at an angle, so I was more upright.

"So, here are the rules," Henley told me. "Tonya will give you medicine to counteract the sedatives, so you will have your powers back. You are to do as you are commanded and will only use your powers as instructed. If you do anything other than what Dr. Leeman authorizes you to do, I will bring Becca in here and take my frustration out on her. Understand?"

And there it was. We'd both known he had the Becca card in his back pocket. It had just been a matter of time before he played it. I needed to find a way out of here. Sooner or later, he would try to use Becca as leverage to get me to give up information on Michael. A part of me was surprised he hadn't tried that already.

"Nod to show you understand," he instructed.

With my jaw clenched, I confirmed with a nod.

"Good," he replied before leaving to watch from the safety of the observation room.

Tonya pushed a cart containing medical supplies toward me. I noticed a syringe on top. It still had the protective cap on it, and I assumed it was the medicine to give me my powers back.

The lights began to flicker. Dr. Leeman and Tonya glanced at each other before the lights went completely out.

We were now in total darkness.

It took a second, but the backup generator came on, providing a little bit of light in the room.

"Stay put," Henley said over the speaker, which must also be hooked up to the generator.

We waited in silence while Henley tried to figure out what was going on.

The straps dug into my wrists and ankles, and I did my best to try to adjust, but nothing helped.

A few minutes later, Henley's voice returned over the speaker. "Apparently, it's storming outside, and it's caused a power outage for the entire area. Go ahead and untie the subject and bring it back to its room."

Dr. Leeman attempted to lower the table, but it wouldn't move. Instead, Luke untied my right wrist and steadied me while Tonya undid my other wrist and ankles. Back on my feet, I was ready to go back to my room, relieved that testing had been halted for the day.

The backup generator lights transitioned to the regular lights as the power came back on. I started to worry that they would strap me back to the table and resume the testing, but luckily, the lights flickered and went out again.

Knowing the backup generator would come back on in a matter of seconds, I reached out and grabbed the syringe off the table. I tucked it into my waistband right before the generator lights came back on.

I discreetly looked at Tonya and then Dr. Leeman. Neither of them had noticed.

I obediently followed Tonya back to my room with Luke trailing closely behind.

I did my best to stifle the sense of victory I felt deep inside. This was the breakthrough I'd been waiting for. I had the syringe that could give me my abilities back. When they least expected it, I would use it to break myself and Becca free.

Tonya unlocked the door to my room and motioned for me to go inside. Once I was inside, I turned to see if either of them intended to stay, but the door closed and locked. I was alone.

I quickly removed the syringe from my waistband and pulled my bed out from the wall. Using some leftover gauze from the injury to my arm, I carefully secured the syringe to the top of the left leg of the bed. The gauze was wrapped tightly around it, and it would be hidden in the corner once I moved the bed back. It wasn't undetectable, but it wouldn't be obvious that it was there. Someone would really have to be looking for it in order to find it there.

After I slid the bed back into place, I lay down on top of it.

I was getting closer to making my move. Now, I just needed to validate that Becca was in that room by the nurses' station. Maybe I could get Luke to confirm it. If he knew Becca was here and that she was still alive, he had to know where they were holding her.

As I lay there, I began to fantasize about a life outside of Henley. Once Becca and I escaped, I would need to find Michael and apologize to him for everything. Now that they had the dream blocker, I wasn't sure how exactly I was going to do that though. The protocol had been designed to make sure they couldn't be found. Maybe I could find a way to contact Stan, Alexander's friend, who helped provide resources to Michael's family so they could evade Henley.

My thoughts were interrupted by the sound of my door flying open. I sat up in surprise, unsure of who had just abruptly entered. It was hard to tell in the dim light. I hoped Henley hadn't changed his mind and that Tonya hadn't returned to bring me back to the lab.

The person closed the door and took a few steps closer. I realized it was Luke.

"You startled me," I told him, feeling relieved.

He walked closer, and I noticed that his hands were clenched at his sides. "Where is it?"

Crap. He's onto me.

"What are you talking about?" I asked innocently.

Luke stormed over to the bed and gripped me by the sides of my arms. "I know you took it. Where is it?"

"I don't have anything."

Luke let me go, yanked my pillow off the bed, and shook it. When nothing fell out, he grabbed me by the arm and pulled me off the bed. He ripped back the blanket and raked his hand over the mattress but found nothing.

Frustrated, he slammed his fist into the mattress.

"You have to give it back," he said, turning back to me.

"You're going to have to be more specific." I was determined to keep playing dumb. There was no way I was telling *anyone* that I had the syringe. Not even Luke.

Luke ran his hand through his hair, yanking the top of it in aggravation. "He's going to kill you, Natalie, if he finds out you have it. He's going to see it as defiance, and trust me, he's not going to let you blow up his office again. He'll kill you first."

I didn't say anything in response. He wasn't telling me anything that I hadn't already known. I was willing to risk it for the chance of getting out of here with Becca.

"If you think he doesn't have enough information on your abilities to deem you expendable, then you're wrong," he continued. "He has a lot more tests he's going to run on you to see how far he can push your abilities, but he already has Dr. Leeman working on tweaking his precious cure based on all of the data they've collected on you. They can keep testing that with or without you."

All the more reason to stick to my plan and get out of here.

He stood inches from me, angrily glaring down at me. "I'm going to ask you one more time. Where is it?"

I looked him in the eyes and shrugged. "I don't have it."

He clenched his jaw, realizing I wasn't going to budge. "Fine. Have it your way. I read Tonya's mind, and she's pretty sure she put the syringe on the cart, but she is doubting herself. If she goes back and counts inventory, she'll know for sure. Henley might come and torture the crap out of you until you turn it over. Don't say I didn't warn you."

He walked out of my room without so much as looking back at me.

I was running out of time. Luke was right. It was only a matter of time before they confirmed the syringe was missing. I needed to escape—and soon.

I lay back down on my bed and stared up into the darkness.

Maybe I could hide the syringe in my waistband and take it with me to the shower in the morning. When I was behind the curtain, supposedly showering, I could inject myself. I wasn't sure how long it would take for the sedatives to wear off, but surely, I would have my powers restored before Tonya returned me to my room.

With my abilities back, it would be nothing for me to overpower Tonya. From there, I would just need to figure out exactly where they were holding Becca. The first place I would check was the room with the chart on the door. If that didn't work, I would just blow out every door in the building until I found her. Henley couldn't stop me if I had my powers back.

The door to my room opened, and Tonya stepped inside. She was here to inject me with my sedative and to give me my sleeping pills.

She turned on the light, so apparently, the power had returned.

As I took the two pink pills from Tonya, I realized that it was now or never. Instead of swallowing them, I hid them under my tongue.

The second Tonya was gone, I spit them out. Without the sleeping pills in my system, I hoped that I would wake up in the morning, feeling alert instead of sluggish and groggy. I needed to be able to think and react quickly if I was going to find Becca and break us out of here.

I didn't remember falling asleep, but I awoke to the sound of my door opening.

Is it morning already? I felt like I had just dozed off.

I was always awake before Tonya came in to get me, and that was with taking the sleeping pills before bed.

I rubbed my eyes. If it was morning, I had to wake up immediately. I needed to figure out a way to get Tonya out of my room for a few minutes, so I could retrieve the syringe and hide it in my waistband.

"Natalie?" a familiar voice whispered as the light in the room flipped on.

My heart leaped into my throat. *It can't be …*

I sat straight up, trying to blink the figure in front of me into focus.

"Michael?" I asked, my voice tight. *Please don't be a dream.*

He took another step closer, and it was really him. I leaped off the bed and threw myself into his arms.

I pulled back to look at him and placed my hands on each side of his face. It had been so long since I'd seen him.

"I can't believe you're really here," I said, tears of joy stinging at my eyes. "I'm so sorry for leaving you the way I did."

"We need to hurry," he replied.

"How did you find me? How did you even get in here?"

"It's a long story. I'll fill you in later."

Before he could step away, I wrapped my hands around the back of his head and pulled him into a kiss. He tensed for a second—obviously taken by surprise—but a moment later, he pulled my body firmly against his and kissed me back.

He reached up, cupping my jaw and deepening the kiss, wanting me as much as I desperately wanted him.

For a second, I forgot where we were. Breathless, I forced myself to part with him before we got too carried away. We needed to focus on escaping.

He stood there, staring at me.

"What's the plan?" I asked. "Are you alone?"

He shook his head, bringing himself back to reality. "Right … getting out of here is going to be trickier than getting in. Please tell me you have your abilities."

"I don't," I told him. "But I can get them back."

"How are you going to do that?"

"With this," I replied.

I pulled the bed from the wall and untangled the syringe from the gauze. I was about to pull the cap off of it when he placed his hand on top of mine to stop me.

"Not yet," he said, gently taking the syringe from me and placing it in his waistband. "Let me check and make sure the coast is clear first," he said.

He started to walk away, and I instinctively grabbed his arm. I didn't want him to leave me for a second. Wherever he was going, I was going with him. We'd already spent too much time apart.

As he turned to look at me, I realized something was off. I was touching Michael's arm, but it didn't feel like his. I looked down and saw perfectly even, smooth skin on his forearm.

"Where are your scars?" I asked, my voice shaking.

As he looked at me with apologetic eyes, I comprehended what was really going on.

"*No*," I gasped.

He didn't reply.

I let go of his arm and put my hands over my mouth. "How could you?" I asked beneath my hands.

I watched in horror as my vision of Michael faded into the reality that it was really Luke. He'd tricked me into handing over the syringe—the only option I had to get out of this horrible place.

Luke took a step toward me. Before he could say anything, I reached up and slapped him across the face.

"Give it back," I demanded.

"Keep your voice down," he snapped. "I'm doing this for you." A red handprint began to appear on his cheek.

"For me? That's crap. You're doing this for Henley."

"I'm not going to sit back and watch you get yourself killed."

"If you take this away from me, you *are* killing me." *Doesn't he understand that?*

Luke turned and walked away. I contemplated tackling him and trying to take the syringe back, but I knew it was no use. He was a lot bigger and stronger than me, and without my abilities, I would be no match for him. Besides, it would just cause a commotion that would likely send Tonya in to investigate.

Luke opened the door, looked back at me once, and then left.

It was silent, except for the echoing sound of the dead bolt sliding into place, sealing my fate.

Eleven

Natalie

"Michael?" I called out, but there was no response.

A song that I recognized from one of Aunt Gael's 1980s playlists blared from the speakers that hung in every corner of the room. A disco ball dangled from the ceiling, sending sparkles of bright light spinning throughout my high school's gymnasium. A thin layer of fog was lingering at my feet as I walked across the black-and-white checkered dance floor, continuing to look for Michael.

I glanced at the stage, set up for a DJ, but no one was there. I passed several empty tables, perfectly adorned with white tablecloths and glittery centerpieces that said Prom *on them.*

It was odd that I would dream about this, especially since I'd never even attended my own prom.

A table with a punch bowl was also prepared, but instead of having a bunch of delinquent students trying to figure out how to spike it, it remained untouched.

I felt someone's presence behind me.

I pivoted around in anticipation, hoping maybe it would be Michael.

When I'd fallen asleep, I'd tried to focus on remembering Michael's face in hopes that I would dream about him tonight. I needed to see him even if it wasn't real.

It wasn't Michael though. Instead, I was standing face-to-face with Becca.

She looked beautiful in a gown with a black lace top and a long skirt. The skirt was a mixture of black and white tulle, almost giving the illusion of vertical stripes. Half of her hair was pulled up, leaving her long mahogany hair partially covering her bare shoulders.

Since I'd arrived at Henley, Becca hadn't appeared in any of my dreams, and I hadn't seen her in person. I'd been going on faith that Luke had told me the truth about her still being alive. If this was really her visiting my dream and not a figment of my imagination, then I needed to know for sure.

"A little underdressed, don't you think?" she asked me.

I looked down at my own attire in horror as I realized I'd shown up in my gray scrubs from Henley.

"You never could quite get it together." She smirked. "I was so tired of always having to look out for you all the time."

I shook my head. She looked like my sister, but this didn't seem like her at all. I'd been hoping Becca had found a way to visit me, but this wasn't her. This was a depraved version of her that my imagination had concocted in my feverish state.

"You're sweating," she observed.

"One hundred point four," a woman's voice said through the loudspeaker over the music.

"Her fever is breaking," a man replied to her, his voice echoing throughout the gym. "That's good. She hasn't kept down food or fluid in over two days."

I recalled how my temperature had been one hundred point five degrees the last time Tonya checked it.

"Should I start an IV?" the woman asked.

"No. Henley gave specific instructions that we are to observe but not intervene."

Becca looked out onto the empty dance floor. "No one is coming for you," she said, turning back to me. "No one out there cares if you live or die."

Is that true?

Michael ... Seth ... my parents ... I hadn't wanted to push them away. I only wanted to keep them safe.

"We'll continue tomorrow," the man's voice said. "Either way, we're ready to move forward with Project Josie."

Becca looked down at the ground and shook her head. She seemed disappointed. "You're going to be responsible for her death, you know." She looked back up at me. "How are you going to live with yourself?"

She tilted her head to the side, without a doubt observing the confusion on my face.

"What are you talking about?" I asked. "Who is Josie?"

Becca smiled calmly. "You'll see." She turned and started to walk away.

"Who's Josie?" I shouted after her, but she slowly evaporated into thin air.

I didn't know what time it was when I finally woke up. I lifted my eyelids and saw Tonya walking out of the room. She'd placed a tray on the table.

I sat up, and from my bed, I could see a bowl of soup, a cup of tea, and two white tablets—medicine of some sort—on the tray. It was probably something for my fever.

I was positive this wasn't a gift from Henley or Tonya taking pity on me. I knew this was another attempt from Luke to get me to forgive him for what he'd done. I sat in bed, refusing to touch any of it.

My mind drifted back to my dream and Becca's comment. I racked my brain, trying to figure out who Josie could be. I'd never met anyone by that name, so how was I going to be responsible for her death?

I heard the familiar click of the door, and I tensed. Luke entered, and his face fell when he saw the table still full of the things he'd manipulated Tonya into bringing me.

I sat on the edge of my bed, staring at him with contempt.

"I know you're pissed," he said. "But you really should take the medicine and try to eat."

I shrugged. "My fever has already broken." I didn't need him or his pathetic attempt to mend things.

"You haven't kept down any food or water. You look …" His voice trailed off.

I knew what he was going to say, and he was right. I'd lost so much weight since coming to Henley from being poisoned, then starved, and now from this illness. I had tied the drawstring of my pants as tight as they would go, and I still had to be careful when I walked because they wanted to slide down my hips. I avoided looking at myself in the mirror as much as possible because I hated the fact that I didn't recognize myself.

Regardless, I didn't want anything he had to offer.

He sat down at the table and gestured toward his care package. "I didn't even know what to send," he said with a small laugh. "I had to pretend to be Henley, ask Tonya what you needed, and then tell her to bring it to you."

I didn't respond. I wasn't sure what kind of game he was trying to play with me, but I wasn't interested.

"Look," he said, "I'm not sorry for what I did."

"Great apology," I scoffed.

"You never would have made it out of here with Becca, and then Henley would have killed you."

"This," I said, motioning to myself and then the rest of the room, "is so much better."

Luke's eyes widened. "It *is* better than being dead. You can't give up."

As much as I hated to admit it, I was giving up. I had no way to get out of there without my abilities, and thanks to Luke, he had taken away the one shot I had at getting them back. I had been so stupid to believe that I could come in here and find a way to rescue Becca. I couldn't even save myself.

"You can go now," I told him.

He lingered, and I shot him another look of disdain.

"I need you to give me some information," he said.

I huffed at the ridiculousness of his request. "Of course you do."

He didn't care about me getting well. He was just trying to save his own skin.

Luke stood up and dragged the metal chair across the floor until it was in front of me. He sat down, less than a foot away, trying to force me to have a real conversation with him. I wished I had the energy to get up and walk away.

"I need you to tell me where Michael is," he said.

I leaned in a little closer and looked him in the eyes. "You can go to hell."

He frowned again. "I'm not going to tell Henley. I want to find Michael, so he can come and get you out of here—for real."

"You're lying. I'm not telling you anything." I looked away, done with the conversation. *Nice try, Luke.*

He sighed. "Look at me." When I didn't obey, he added, "*Please.*"

Reluctantly, I looked into his pleading eyes. Their resemblance to Michael's made my heart ache.

I swallowed a lump in my throat. I would give anything to see Michael one more time before I died. I wanted so badly to tell him how much I loved him and that I was sorry for leaving without saying good-bye.

"Do you know what Henley had Dr. Leeman inject you with?" he asked.

I shook my head.

"Avian influenza. Do you know what that is?"

"It's a flu that is passed from birds to humans." I recalled hearing about it on the news when I was little.

"I overheard Dr. Leeman telling Tonya that you could've died from it because you were so weak. Henley knew, and he didn't care."

"I'm getting better, so what does it matter?"

"Great. You passed Henley's test. Do you know what the reward is for passing? Another test. Haven't you figured that out by now?"

He wasn't telling me anything that I hadn't already known. Henley wasn't going to stop until I was dead.

"You don't get it," he continued. "They aren't planning to just inject you with another strain of the flu, Natalie. They are going to inject you with a bacteria called Yersinia pestis. Dr. Leeman said your symptoms will feel like the flu, and he told Henley that it's likely you will die without immediate treatment. He doesn't think your body can fight it on its own."

I didn't want to admit it, but deep down, I knew that I didn't have the strength to heal from another severe illness without treatment. Although my body was healing itself from Avian flu, overall, I still felt weaker and weaker every day from constant illness, injury, and lack of nourishment. One more illness, and I was confident I would be dead.

Then, it dawned on me that maybe Luke was bluffing. Maybe he was just making up this story about Henley plotting to make me sick again. Perhaps Luke was hoping I'd panic and give him information on Michael in an attempt to save myself.

"If this is true, then why hasn't anyone else here gotten sick? Isn't the flu contagious?" I questioned.

"I think Henley gave us some kind of vaccine. I didn't realize it at the time though because it's not like they tell me what they are injecting me with when they do it."

I couldn't tell if he was lying. After what he had done by pretending to be Michael, I didn't need my intuition to tell me he couldn't be trusted.

"If you're so worried about this next illness, bring me some antibiotics that will treat it," I told him.

He reached out to touch my arm, but I jerked away from him.

He quickly retreated, but his eyes were still pleading with me. "I can't guarantee that I can get them to you in time. I know I walk around here pretty freely, and I've managed to find a way to make things livable here, but I am still a prisoner, just like you."

"When are they going to infect me?" If his story was true, I wanted to at least know when it was scheduled to happen.

"The day after tomorrow." He looked down, now avoiding my eyes. "Dr. Leeman thinks the flu will be out of your system by tomorrow morning, based on your rate of recovery, and Henley wants the test done as soon as possible."

I nodded, more to myself than to him.

"If you can give me any info on where Michael is, I can try to get to him in time," he offered. He looked back up at me, hopeful I'd give in.

Even if Luke was genuinely trying to help me, not that I was fully convinced that was the case, I couldn't risk something going wrong and Henley finding Michael in the process.

Luke watched me in silence, waiting to see if I would respond, but I didn't. I just stared off into the corner of the room, accepting my fate. I would rather die than risk Michael's life.

He stood up and moved the tray to the chair where he'd been sitting, so I wouldn't have to get out of bed to reach it.

"Pretend it's not from me and try to eat," he said before turning and leaving. "You need to rebuild some strength."

As much as I didn't want to give Luke the satisfaction of eating the soup or drinking the tea he'd sent me, I picked up the cup of tea and took a sip. I had to set my pride aside and keep fighting—for Becca.

When I finished the tea, I attempted to eat the soup but started to feel nauseous. Instead of finishing it, I lay back down and closed my eyes despite the fact that I didn't want to go to sleep. This was likely one of my last days on earth, and as much as I didn't want to spend it at Henley, I felt like I shouldn't just sleep it away.

I heard the sound of my door unlocking, and I opened my eyes. Luke was back. I didn't know if I'd fallen asleep or if Luke had come right back.

"What do you want now?" I asked, my voice hoarse. I let out a deep, painful cough.

He approached my bed.

"Sit up," he said, pushing the chair out of the way and taking a seat on the side of my bed.

I tried to sit up but fell back onto the pillow. I felt even weaker than the first time he'd visited.

Luke grabbed me by the shoulders and helped me into a sitting position. I noticed a syringe sitting on the bed beside him.

"Jeez, you're burning up again," he said, placing his hand on my cheek.

I didn't have the energy to push him away.

He removed his hand and picked up the syringe. He pulled the cap off of it, exposing the long, thin needle.

"What are you doing?" I coughed again.

"I'm giving you your abilities back. You need to get out of here."

Luke lifted the sleeve of my shirt and plunged the needle into the side of my arm. It stung as he unleashed the contents of the syringe, but I stayed still, praying this would work.

When he was finished, he placed the cap back on the syringe and looked at me expectantly.

"How long does it take to work?" I asked, still feeling the same.

"How would I know?"

"If Henley finds out you did this, he will kill you." I knew I didn't have to tell Luke this, but I felt like it should be acknowledged. I couldn't believe he would risk himself, let alone do it himself instead of tricking Tonya into doing it.

"Let's not tell him then," he replied. "Try to stand up."

He stood up, and I twisted myself so that my feet were on the floor. Slowly, I eased myself up into a standing position. It didn't last long though, and my legs gave out underneath me. I started to fall forward, but he caught me. He sat me back down onto the bed and squatted in front of me, so we were eye-level.

"You've got to do this," he urged. "Do you feel any difference at all?"

I shook my head.

As much as I willed the medicine to work and give me my abilities back, I didn't think it was. My body was still drained and weak.

He glanced around the room, his eyes landing on the table and chairs. "See if you can move that chair."

Using my abilities took energy, which I did not have. Still, I looked at the chair and tried concentrating. I wanted it to move so badly, but nothing happened.

"Are you trying?"

"Yes. Shh." I continued to focus on the chair.

In the past, when my abilities had worked the best, I would have a burst of emotion to go along with it.

I closed my eyes and thought about my time here and my need to save Becca. Becca had been held here against her will for *years*. Who knew what she'd gone through in that time frame? It was unimaginable.

Even though I could feel myself getting upset, I didn't have the same emotional charge that I usually did. I opened my eyes and fixed my attention again on the chair, but it didn't move. I had nothing left to throw at it. Frustrated and exhausted, I lay back down.

Even if the medicine had worked to give me the ability to use my powers again, I lacked the mental strength to make them work.

I curled up on the bed, and Luke lifted the blanket to cover me.

"Please don't give up," he said quietly.

"It's hopeless."

"Nothing is ever hopeless. There's always a way. I promise you that I will figure something out."

I didn't look at him or respond. The truth was, I was going to die soon, and we both knew it.

TWELVE

MICHAEL

"Try Natalie's birthday," Raina suggested.

"I already tried that." I held Natalie's phone in my hand, staring at the keypad, willing her passcode to come to me. It was a four-digit number, and at this point, it felt like we'd attempted every possible combination.

Ever since Natalie had left, I had kept her cell phone charged and nearby. The one time I'd left it unattended to help Raina figure out why her hairdryer wouldn't turn on, there was a missed call on her phone.

What if that call was the clue we've been waiting for? Or what if it was Natalie, calling for help, hoping that we still had her phone? It was a longshot, but I was willing to consider anything at this point.

I looked helplessly at Seth and Jen. They were both deep in thought.

"Try her street address in St. Augustine," Jen suggested. "One, one, two, one."

I entered it, but it didn't work.

I was *this* close to hurling the phone across the room, but if I did, I knew I would never hear the message.

Seth snapped his fingers and stood up. "Becca's birthday. July 7. That has to be it. Try zero, seven, zero, seven."

I punched in the number, and it worked. We were in.

I clicked on the notification for the voice mail and hit play. Raina, Jen, and Seth gathered closer as I put it on speakerphone. Anxious to hear the latest voice mail, I quickly skipped past the messages Todd had previously left for Natalie.

"Next voice message, received today at nine twenty-three a.m.," the recorded message on her voice mail said.

"Hi, Miss Clark," a man's voice said. "This is Wayne Cartwright, and I'm calling with an update for you on one of those locations you asked me to check out. It turns out that G.G. Armand Designs is owned by C. Henley Labs Incorporated. The design company is just a front. I sent one of my guys up there yesterday, and he confirmed that Chad Henley went into the building at six fifty-eight a.m. and left at six p.m., so we believe he is still in the area. No sightings of the girl though. Give me a call back, so we can discuss how you want to proceed."

The voice mail ended, and I hung up the phone.

"Who's Wayne Cart-whatever?" Seth asked.

We shook our heads. None of us had a clue as to what was going on.

Jen grabbed her phone off the coffee table and started typing into it. A moment later, her eyes lit up. "Wayne Cartwright is a private investigator in San Antonio, Texas. Natalie must have hired him to look into Henley."

I stared at Jen in shock.

"I take it, you didn't know about that," she replied, eyeing my reaction.

I stumbled over to the couch and sat down.

Why would she have tried to find Henley? All we'd done for the past several months was try to avoid him.

"Who's the girl?" Jen asked. We all looked at her, confused. "In his voice mail, he said they spotted Henley but not 'the girl.' Who's the girl?"

Who the hell knows? I don't even know my own girlfriend right now.

Raina and Seth shrugged and then turned back to me.

"Yeah, like I know anything at this point," I replied sourly.

"This is good news!" Jen said. I looked back at her doubtfully. "It *is*!"

Jen sat next to me on the couch, putting her phone down and pulling Seth's laptop off the coffee table and into her lap.

"If Henley is going to such great lengths to set up a pretend company, it's because that's where he has Natalie," she explained while her fingers typed a million miles per minute on the keyboard. "I bet if we figure out where this company is, we will know where Natalie is."

Seconds later, she found a website for G.G. Armand Designs. The website looked legit. She was right; Henley had gone to great lengths to throw us off.

"But Natalie knew about the location," Raina chimed in. "That means, he was anticipating her surrendering."

"She didn't surrender there though," Jen reminded her. "She allowed herself to be captured, so she must not have been certain he was there."

"It still doesn't explain why Natalie wanted to go there at all in the first place," Raina said.

Seth nodded. "I'm telling you, he got to her somehow and threatened someone. Probably one of us."

A look of dread crept over Jen's face, and she grew pale. "The girl … you don't think Natalie thought I'd been taken by Henley, do you?"

Seth sat on the other side of her and put his arm around her shoulders. "I think Natalie would have contacted me if that were the case."

"Either way, it's not your fault. Natalie made this decision all on her own," I assured her, hearing the anger come through in my voice. I wasn't even sure if I was angrier with Natalie for being so reckless or with myself for not seeing it sooner and stopping her.

I should have been keeping a closer eye on things, and maybe I could have prevented this from happening. I was her boyfriend, and it was my job to protect her. I should have known if Henley had contacted her.

All of the signs had been there. Something had been on her mind, bothering her, and I hadn't pushed her to tell me. Instead, I'd decided to just let her talk to me when she was ready.

How could I have been such a fool?

"There's not a physical address anywhere on here," Jen said after clicking through every page of the website. "But give me a few minutes." She picked up her cell phone and stepped out of the room.

She knew a lot of people in the investigative field because of her work, and I had no doubt she would be able to locate it.

I stood up and aimlessly roamed around Seth's apartment. I needed to get my head together. I needed to focus on the fact that Jen was right. This *was* good news. If we knew where Natalie was, we could rescue her. This was the lead we'd been waiting for.

I pulled out my cell phone and sent a text to Alexander, asking that he and Lorena come over. They had temporarily rented a studio apartment in Seth's complex. Hoping it would just be short-term, Raina and I were crashing at Seth's.

About twenty minutes later, Alexander and Lorena arrived, and we filled them in on our discovery.

"I've got the address!" Jen announced proudly. "It's in Evanston, Illinois."

"I think we should call the police," I said.

In unison, everyone turned to look at me. They were in shock that I would actually suggest it. It was strictly against our protocol; even Seth and Jen knew that.

"Son, you know that's not possible," Alexander replied.

I looked at Lorena. Her eyes were full of sympathy for me, but I could tell she agreed with Alexander.

"He is hurting her. Right this second. Do you understand that?" I challenged.

The thought of Natalie going through the kind of torture that Raina and I had endured as kids was killing me inside.

Alexander took a step forward, his hands up, trying to get me to calm down. "I know you're upset. We all are. But it wouldn't be safe—for her or for us—if we got the police involved."

I knew he was right, but I didn't like it. Henley was well connected. If we contacted the police, word would get to Henley before the police ever got there. He'd have time to prepare, to move Natalie. Or worse, he could kill her and completely get rid of any evidence. Henley just had too many people in his back pocket. Without a doubt, he'd get away with it.

"Fine," I replied. "But I'm going to Evanston and getting her out of there."

I wanted to fly to Evanston, bust in there, and drag Henley out by his throat.

"He'll be expecting you," Alexander warned. "I know you love her, but you have to keep a level head about this. We have to formulate the right plan if this is going to work."

Again, the rational part of me knew that Alexander was right, but I couldn't shut off the images going through my head of Henley torturing Natalie. I knew better than anyone what he was capable of, and she was the last person I'd ever want subjected to that.

"I'm going to kill him," I said through gritted teeth. "I should have gone back a long time ago and ended him."

Lorena got up from the couch and walked over to me. She placed her hands on the sides of my face to get me to focus on her. "This is not your fault," she said.

I tried to pull away, but she wouldn't budge.

"It's *not*," she said again.

I nodded in response, and she released me. It might not be my fault, but I still felt guilty for not doing more to prevent it.

Why didn't Natalie just talk to me? We would've found another way to solve whatever was going on. No scenario would have landed on her willingly being captured by Henley.

Seth's cell phone rang. He glanced down at it and then quickly stepped out of the room to take the call.

I took a breath, admitting to myself that I was acting on emotion and not logic. It wouldn't do Natalie any good if we all ended up captured or dead. We needed to think this through and be careful.

"Let's talk through some options," I said to Alexander, feeling a little calmer.

He nodded. "I say, we go there and stake out the place for a few days. Let's see the patterns of who is coming and going and how often."

"What if Natalie doesn't have a few days?" I asked. I wasn't trying to assume the worst, but she had been there for weeks now. "The voice mail said that Henley had been seen leaving around six. What if we nabbed him when he came out? Used him as leverage to force our way in?"

A minute later, Seth came back into the room, pale as a ghost.

"Uh, guys," he said to us, although he was still on the phone, "it's a strange coincidence, but you need to hear this."

I stood next to him as he lowered the phone from his ear and put it on speaker.

"Dad, are you there?" he asked, shooting me a wary glance.

As soon as I realized he was talking to his dad, I contemplated pulling the phone away from Seth and hanging it up. His dad had been secretly working with Henley and done absolutely nothing when

Henley shot Natalie in Charlotte. She had been lying on the floor, *dying*, and that spineless excuse for a man had just stood by and watched.

I didn't trust him, and I certainly didn't want him to know we were planning to rescue Natalie.

Seth must have seen the look on my face because he shook his head at me, telling me to stop. *He doesn't work for Henley anymore*, he mouthed.

"I'm here," William Weber said.

"Tell them what you just told me."

"Well," William replied, "I just received a phone call from Luke."

An alarm went off in my head. I looked at Raina, who had the same concern written all over her face.

I yanked the phone out of Seth's hand, as if I were grabbing ahold of William himself. "What did *he* want?"

"He asked me to get in touch with you. He said that Henley has Natalie, but Luke has a plan for you to come rescue her."

"Why would he call you?" I asked, not bothering to hide the accusation in my voice.

"Probably because I'm the only person on the outside that he knows who has a mutual connection to you," he replied. "I took a chance, calling Seth, hoping he'd be able to contact you."

Alexander walked over to us and placed a hand on my shoulder. "What's his plan?" he asked William.

William cleared his throat. "He said that Henley leaves at six p.m. every night. He wants you to come at nine. He'll make everyone on duty believe that you are Henley and that you have a new medical team coming to take Natalie to a more secure facility for testing."

I looked at Raina again. She stared back at me with scared, wide eyes.

"When does he want us to do this?" I asked.

"Tonight."

"I don't know about this," Raina whispered to me.

We were on the plane, on our way to Evanston.

"Me neither, but what choice do we have?"

"Yeah, but trusting Luke of all people?"

Her fear was valid. There was nothing trustworthy about our brother. He'd proven that to us over and over again. It did feel like we might be walking right into a trap. The fact that this was being coordinated through William Weber didn't help to ease my apprehension.

We'd spent about an hour debating on what to do at Seth's apartment while Jen and Lorena checked on flights. Then, we'd debated it again on the drive to the airport and while we were waiting to board the plane. The plan didn't sit well with any of us, but we also didn't have any better ideas. Without some help on the inside, we knew we wouldn't get very far. This might be our only chance to rescue Natalie and escape, undetected.

After going around and around in circles, we'd decided to chance it. We had to get Natalie back. I couldn't stand the thought of her being there for one more night, and on top of that, the longer Henley had her, the closer he'd get to replicating her powers. The last thing Henley needed was more power.

Although they were on the plane with us, Lorena and Jen wouldn't be joining us on the rescue mission. Once we landed, they were going to head to a house that Stan had set up for us in Barrington, Illinois, a town about an hour outside of Evanston.

Alexander and I had tried to talk Seth out of coming with us to the Henley facility. We explained to him that it might be a repeat of last time, that he might be captured again. If that happened, he might not be as lucky. He had been adamant though about coming with us, and there was nothing I could say to change his mind.

I glanced at him and Jen in the row across from me and Raina. Seth sure was a loyal friend. Natalie had always told me that we could trust him, and he had proven her right.

Growing up, I'd never thought I would have real friends outside of Raina, my adoptive parents, and their friend Stan. I didn't think it would be possible for me to be honest about who I was, much less be accepted for it. Natalie, Seth, and Jen had changed that misconception for me, and I would be forever grateful.

Once we landed at O'Hare International Airport and debarked the plane, we took a shuttle to an off-site airport parking lot, where Stan already had two SUVs waiting on us. We loaded all of our luggage into the SUV that Lorena and Jen would be driving to Barrington.

Alexander, Seth, Raina, and I planned to use the other SUV to travel to Evanston.

Lorena kissed Alexander good-bye and then turned to me. "Please be careful," she said.

Although she had never met Luke, she'd heard the stories, and she understood the risk we were taking by trusting him.

"I will," I assured her. "At the first sign that something is off, we'll get out of there and regroup on a new plan."

I knew it would be hard to leave, knowing Natalie was still inside, but we had to be smart about it. We couldn't help her if we were in captivity ourselves.

Lorena gave me a hug and then turned to say her good-byes to Raina.

I walked over to Alexander as he shut the trunk on Lorena and Jen's SUV.

"It should take us about thirty minutes to get to Henley," I told him. "Do we need to make any stops along the way?" Without saying it, I was asking him whether or not we had weapons.

Alexander nodded toward our SUV parked a few spaces away, understanding my question. "No. Stan already took care of it. They are inside."

Although we shouldn't require our guns if everything went as planned, I still felt better, knowing we would have them on us. Henley was armed, and we didn't want a repeat of last time.

"It's time to go," I announced.

We only had an hour until Luke was expecting us, and we needed to get on the road, just in case we got caught in traffic. If by some miracle this wasn't a trap, we couldn't be late. We had to be on-site and ready to execute our part of the escape plan. If this was for real, our window of opportunity wouldn't last forever, and there was no way I was going to miss it.

THIRTEEN

MICHAEL

From the outside, you'd never suspect that G.G. Armand Designs was a front for a Henley facility. The architecture was exactly what you'd expect from a trendy, up-and-coming design firm. The building was modern with large, tinted windows that stretched all around, from ground to roof. It gave this illusion of total transparency despite the secret horrors taking place inside of it. I was positive that the majority of windows were actually fake.

Despite the fact that it was after hours and the building was technically closed, we found the front door unlocked, as promised.

The lobby was empty, and all of the lights were turned off. As we quietly passed by the receptionist's desk, I noticed an unwashed coffee mug that had been left behind. The desk was so ordinary, and I realized that a normal person probably occupied it. This person probably had no idea that they actually worked for Henley and not an architectural design company.

Around the corner from the reception area was a door that required a fingerprint verification in order to enter.

"Here goes nothing," Seth said as he knocked, following the directions we'd been given.

This is it. Moment of truth.

I quickly scanned the lobby, double-checking for signs of an ambush. The lobby was fairly dark. The only light coming in was from the giant windows from the streetlights outside. Still, I didn't see anything suspicious.

We waited in agonizing silence for what felt like an eternity. Finally, we heard the door click and crack open.

A tall, lanky security guard, only a few years older than me, poked his head out.

"Good evening, sir," the security guard said, looking directly at Alexander. The guard took a step back, opening the door wide for us to pass.

We hesitated but only briefly before walking through to the other side. So far, so good, but there was still the possibility that this was part of a plan to lock us inside. I couldn't help but tense, waiting for Henley to appear out of the shadows.

The guard turned back to Alexander once the door clicked shut behind us. "Sir, I'm sorry to hear about your hand." He looked down at Alexander's right hand, as if seeing something wrong with it.

"Yes, thank you," Alexander replied, playing along.

This must have been the delusion that Luke had put on the security guard. Luke had made the guard believe Alexander was Henley and that he couldn't scan his finger because he'd hurt himself. If Luke wasn't such a self-serving, manipulative jerk, I'd actually be impressed by his creativity.

"This is my team," Alexander said, gesturing to us. "We've come to retrieve the subject."

"Very good, sir," the guard replied. "Just the one?"

Raina and I exchanged a quick glance.

Who else does he have here?

"That's correct. Just the one that is able to self-heal," Alexander replied calmly.

Alexander was doing his best to sound detached like Henley and not break the guise.

"Of course," the guard replied. "Let me know if you need any assistance. Have a good evening, sir." He turned and walked over to a room that said *Security Office* on it, went inside, and shut the door behind himself.

"Creepy," Seth muttered under his breath.

I glanced around. There was only one way to go, which was a long, wide hallway that was completely vacant. It reminded me of a horror movie that I'd taken Raina to see. The movie itself hadn't been scary, but the resemblance of the Henley facility we'd been raised in had sent

Raina into a full-blown panic attack. She couldn't make it to the end of the movie.

I looked over at her. "You okay?" I whispered.

She nervously looked back at me and nodded. "Let's just hurry up and get this over with."

Either Henley didn't staff up much at night, or Luke had made sure to warp everyone's minds so that they were conveniently occupied at the moment. I was willing to bet it was the latter, which meant we needed to move quickly. His ability to manipulate minds was never an exact science, and the people under his manipulation could come out of it at any time. Even the slightest deviation from the plan could trigger them to realize something wasn't right, and then they'd see the truth for what it was.

We trailed behind Alexander down the hallway, giving the illusion that Alexander was Henley and we were just his mere lackeys. In the event we passed anyone else in the hall, this should appear normal to them. No one ever dared to walk alongside Henley and pretend to be his equal.

We passed by several offices with their doors closed until the hallway came to an end. To the right was a maintenance closet. To the left were several more offices as well as a nurses' station and various rooms with closed doors. Most likely, Natalie would be down there.

"This looks kind of familiar," Seth whispered to me.

The area to our left looked very similar to the layout at the Charlotte facility.

We headed left, but before we reached the nurses' station, a nurse popped out from behind the desk. It was as if she'd been waiting on us. I looked down and took a step behind Seth. I knew this woman. She was the same nurse who'd been assigned to me in Charlotte. Even if she was under Luke's spell, I didn't want her to somehow recognize me and blow our cover.

"Sir," I said to Alexander, still looking at the ground. Out of my peripheral, I saw him stop and turn to me. "Would you prefer that I wait for you by the lobby?"

I was sure Alexander had no idea what I was talking about, but luckily, he played along.

"Yes, I told you to wait there," he replied, sounding irritated, like Henley would be at a disobeyed command.

I quickly turned and hurried down the hall in the opposite direction. As much as I wanted to turn around to see what was going to happen next, I resisted the urge. I needed to stay out of the nurse's eyesight if this was going to work.

I waited in the empty hallway instead of going back into the lobby. The hallway was completely silent, and everyone was still under Luke's ruse.

Even as kids, Luke had always had this unique talent of reading and manipulating minds, and apparently, he had continued to develop it after we left. I'd never seen him do anything of this magnitude before.

The crazy part was, Luke could probably mind-manipulate everyone into just letting him walk right out of here if he wanted to. In fact, he really didn't even need us here to break Natalie free. There was nothing stopping him from waltzing out the door with her. The problem was, Luke actually *preferred* to be here.

As I stared into the darkness, hoping Alexander would emerge with Natalie and also listening for signs that they needed my help, my mind wandered back to the first time Raina and I had attempted to escape Henley when we were six years old.

It had been raining all day, and it hadn't slowed down at all despite the fact that it was well into the night. I didn't know what time it was, but I knew I was supposed to be in bed. It had felt like hours since the nurse had come in and turned out the light.

I didn't mind the dark. Raina, on the other hand, hated it. I wished that I could just open my door, go to her room, and reassure her that everything was going to be okay.

A loud rumbling noise made me jump. Alexander had told me it was something called thunder and nothing to be afraid of, but I wasn't so sure. If I was still feeling uneasy about it, I knew Raina had to be freaking out.

I got up out of bed and quietly crept to the door of my room. I reached out and placed my hand on the doorknob. To my surprise, it turned. It never turned.

For a second, I froze. What if I get caught? *I didn't even want to imagine what my punishment would be if that happened.*

With a pounding heart, I slowly pulled the door open and peeked out. The nurse wasn't at her station, and the coast seemed to be clear.

Is Raina's door unlocked too?

I didn't know where the courage had come from, but I found myself leaving my room and heading down the hall to Raina's.

I tried her door, and it opened.

She sat up in bed when I entered. I carefully closed the door behind me.

"What are you doing in here?" she whispered, and I could tell she was afraid.

"I wanted to check on you," I said.

"I'm scared," she admitted.

As if right on cue, the thunder roared again, and she jumped.

"Alexander says it's nothing. He says it's normal," I reminded her.

We liked and trusted Alexander. He was the only one at Henley we could say that about. He was different. He was actually nice to us.

I hated that I couldn't even check on my sister without worrying about breaking the rules and being in trouble for it. The last time I'd broken a rule, Henley had put me in a dark room for what felt like days. I had been grateful it was me though and not Raina. Still, I didn't want to go there again.

"I wonder if the front door is unlocked," I said, not even realizing the magnitude of the idea as I said it.

Raina gasped. "We can't do that!"

I shrugged. "Why not?"

"It's against the rules."

I sat down on the edge of Raina's bed. "What if we never had to be afraid of Henley again?" I asked her.

Raina stared at me, as if she had never pondered the question. "I don't …"

"What if we left? According to Alexander, there is a whole world out there that is nothing like this one. We could live there."

Raina shook her head.

"Alexander says there are carousels there. Real *ones," I said.*

Raina's eyes lit up. Alexander had given her a small musical carousel for her birthday, and it was her most treasured possession. Actually, it was her only possession, and she kept it hidden under her bed. She knew that Henley would take it away if he knew she had it.

I reached out my hand to her. "I'll protect you. Always. I promise."

Raina hesitated and then took my hand.

She let me lead her out of her room, and luckily, the nurse was still gone.

Raina tugged on my hand. "What about our brother? We can't leave him."

Raina was still having a hard time adjusting to calling Luke by his name, which was understandable because we could only use it when we were alone or with Alexander. Henley didn't want us to have names, but Alexander offered to help us choose names if we promised to only use them in secret.

I nodded in agreement. We weren't as close with Luke as we were with each other, but he was still our brother.

We quietly made our way to Luke's room and opened the door. He was sound asleep in his bed. Apparently, the storm didn't bother him at all.

Raina shook him by the shoulder, and he turned over.

He opened his eyes, and they narrowed when he realized we were in his room. "What are you doing?" he asked a little too loudly.

"Shh," I whispered. "We're leaving. Come on."

Luke looked scared, which was strange because he never seemed scared. "We can't do that," he whispered back. "Henley would find us and kill us."

"Henley might kill us if we stay," I insisted.

He had to know that was true.

Luke turned to Raina. "You aren't seriously doing this, are you?"

Raina looked at me. "Yes. I'm going with Michael, and I want you to come too."

"No way," Luke said. "This is too risky. Just do what Henley says, and you'll be fine."

It was easy for Luke to say. He got to spend the majority of his days reading the minds of Henley's staff, so they could test his accuracy. He wasn't getting cut open every day like I was.

"We're going," I told him. "Are you in, or are you out?"

My patience was wearing thin, and as much as I didn't want to leave him behind, every second we wasted debating about it decreased our chances of escaping.

Luke looked at Raina again, who nodded at him in encouragement. He closed his eyes for a second and then nodded. "Fine. Let's go."

I took a step closer to the door with Raina and Luke behind me.

"We should probably sneak to the kitchen and steal some food to take with us," Luke whispered before I could open the door.

Raina stopped. "Why?"

"Because, otherwise, we'll starve out there," he told her.

She looked at me. "Is that true?"

"No," I said. "We'll figure it out. We'll be fine."

"How?" he asked. "Do you know how to get food out there?"

I narrowed my eyes at him. Of course I didn't, but I would find a way.

"Someone will feed us," she rationalized.

"Maybe. Maybe not," he said, giving a nonchalant shrug. "People in the real world are meaner than in here."

Raina's eyes got wide. She hadn't considered that. She looked at me, but I didn't have the answers. I had never been in the outside world, but Alexander lived there, and he wasn't a bad person. I was willing to chance it.

"But if you want to go, we'll go," Luke said, taking a deliberate step forward.

Raina remained where she was. "I don't want to go."

"Stop scaring her," I snapped at Luke. "You're such a jerk."

He smiled. "I didn't do anything. She made the decision not to go, not me."

He could pretend to be innocent, but he had known exactly the effect his words would have on her. He knew how to manipulate her, and unfortunately, because he knew I wouldn't leave without her, he had successfully manipulated me as well.

We didn't end up escaping that night. Instead, I quietly walked Raina back to her room, tucked her back into bed, and returned to my own prison cell to anticipate the hell that awaited me the following day.

I snapped out of my memory as I heard footsteps echoing from down the hall. I braced myself. It could be them, with Natalie, and if so, I needed to be prepared to leave. Or it could be Henley's men; in which case, I needed to be ready to fight.

I rested my hand on my gun, which was holstered on my hip and concealed by my jacket. It was loaded, and thanks to many lessons from Alexander over the years, I knew how to use it. Raina did, too, and she was a better shot than I was. I hadn't heard gunshots, so I didn't think anything had gone wrong. But just in case, I kept my hand on the gun anyway.

The footsteps grew closer, and once they rounded the corner, I released my gun as I realized it was Alexander, Seth, Raina, and Luke. I could tell Seth was carrying Natalie in his arms. In the dim lighting of the hallway, I couldn't tell if she was hurt or not.

I rushed down the hall to meet them halfway. All I could think about was ripping Natalie from Seth and holding her in my arms. I was almost to Seth but stopped short as I got a better look at her. It was for sure Natalie, but she didn't appear to be herself at all. She looked like the skeleton of my girlfriend.

How could she have changed so much in only a matter of weeks?

Seth glanced at me, his eyes full of concern, as he shifted her from his arms to mine. I could feel her bones protruding from beneath her clothes. Her cheekbones were sunken in. She was awake but seemed incoherent. I had to choke back the emotion I felt just from laying eyes on her.

"We need to get her out of here and get her stable," Alexander said.

Natalie moaned.

I was worried that if I held her too tight, she might break.

"I've got you," I told her, my voice catching in my throat. "You're safe now." I laid my hand on her cheek, trying to heal her.

She pushed my hand away. "No. You're … not … real."

I took her hand and placed it on my cheek instead. "It's me, Natalie. I promise."

"Bec," she said, barely above a whisper.

"What?" I asked her, shaking my head. I leaned in closer. "What's wrong?"

"She's not really awake," Luke said. "The nurse gave her sleeping pills about an hour ago."

"Becca," Natalie said.

This time, I heard her. So did Seth.

Seth took a step closer to us. He put his hand on Natalie's arm. "Did you say Becca?"

Natalie closed her eyes, as if mustering up the strength to speak. "Here."

Natalie moaned again, and I looked at Seth.

Is Natalie telling us that Becca is here too?

Seth's expression twisted into a blend of torment and confusion. He turned and looked back down the hallway in the direction from where they'd come.

I looked at Luke. "What is she talking about?"

Luke glanced between me and Raina. "You need to get Natalie out of here."

Seth got in Luke's face and shoved him backward. "Answer the question. Is Becca here?"

Luke hit the wall behind him. He closed his eyes, defeated. "Yes, she's here."

Seth rubbed his hands over his face, as if trying to see if it was all a dream.

If Natalie hadn't said something, would Luke have let us leave Becca behind? Unbelievable.

"I can't leave her," Seth said. "I have to go back for her."

"That's not a good idea. You need to take Natalie and get out of here," Luke insisted. "I can't keep everyone under control here forever. It's going to wear off soon."

If I wasn't holding Natalie, I would have lunged at Luke. Seth's hands were free though, and he charged at Luke, pushing him against the wall once again.

"Where is she?" Seth demanded.

I had no doubt Seth was ready to beat it out of him.

"If I take you to her, will you get Natalie out of here?" Luke asked.

"I'll go with them," Raina said, looking between me and Alexander. None of us trusted Luke, and we couldn't let Seth go alone, especially since he was unarmed. "Get Natalie to the car. We'll be right there."

Normally, Alexander and I would argue with Raina, but we knew we had to act fast. Natalie's condition was dire, and we needed to get her outside, so Alexander could try to help her. We had to trust that Raina would be able to take care of herself and Seth. Without hesitation, Alexander moved past me and held the door to the lobby open for me and Natalie to pass through.

I hurried past Alexander, through the lobby, and out the front door with Natalie in my arms. Alexander climbed into the backseat of the SUV. He held out his arms for me to hand Natalie to him, but I didn't want to let her go.

"You need to get in the driver's seat in case we need to get out of here quickly," he told me.

As much as I didn't want to hand her over, I knew I had to. There was no telling what was going on inside the building right now, and we might need a fast getaway.

I carefully handed Natalie to Alexander and helped him pull her back into the third-row seat. When she was secure, I rushed around the car, into the driver's seat, and angled myself, so I could not only see what Alexander was doing in the back, but to also keep an eye on the main entrance to the building.

I heard Alexander unzip his medical bag. He'd brought it, knowing there was a strong possibility that someone would end up needing medical attention. He pulled out his stethoscope.

"Try to take a deep breath for me," he told Natalie, although I wasn't sure she could hear him.

I watched helplessly in painful silence as he continued to examine her.

"I need you to text Stan," Alexander told me. I opened the glove box and fumbled for a phone. "Text: 9-1-1-I-V."

I typed it out as fast as I could and hit Send. "What does that mean?"

Alexander shone a light into Natalie's eyes, checking her pupils. "She needs an IV. Hopefully, Stan can have one delivered to the house before we get there."

"Why isn't she better?" I asked. "Why didn't she heal when I touched her?"

"I don't think what she has can be healed by you," he replied. "This isn't an injury. She's severely dehydrated and obviously malnourished. I detected fluid in her lungs, so I suspect she has pneumonia."

Natalie whimpered in pain.

"It's okay," Alexander assured her. "We're going to take good care of you and get you better."

Alexander and I jumped in our seats at the sound of a loud popping noise. We froze, waiting to see what would happen next. It was silent for a second, and then we heard two more popping sounds. Those were definitely gunshots.

"Get ready," Alexander warned.

I cranked the car and shifted it into drive. A moment later, the main door to G.G. Armand Designs burst open, and Luke emerged, carrying an unconscious girl in his arms, who I assumed was Becca.

Seth came out next, holding his shoulder. He was moving unusually slow. Then, I noticed a trail of red running down his arm. He was bleeding.

I held my breath until I saw Raina run out behind them. She had her gun drawn.

A spark flew up next to Seth. Someone was shooting at them. Raina turned around and fired twice back into the doorway. She must have hit whoever it was because she immediately turned and ran toward the SUV.

Luke reached the SUV first. He shoved Becca inside on the floor between the two bucket seats and climbed over her to take his seat. Seth was about to get in the back with them.

"Get in the front!" I yelled to him. I couldn't heal him if he was back there.

Seth heard me and climbed into the passenger seat next to me. He was clammy and pale, and judging from the condition of his shirt, he'd lost quite a bit of blood. As soon as we got out of harm's way, I would need to pull over somewhere and heal him. I wasn't a doctor, but it didn't seem like he would be able to make it all the way to Barrington with that wound. He looked like he might go into shock or something.

Raina hurled herself into the backseat. "Go!" she yelled.

Before Raina could even shut her door, I hit the gas pedal and peeled out of the parking lot.

Fourteen

Natalie

I opened the tall iron gate and stepped inside. The light from the moon cast a distinct glow on something sticking out of the ground across the field. It was as if it were drawing me in, wanting to be discovered. My bare feet sank into the soft dirt as I walked toward it.

Trees surrounded me from every direction as I stood in a clearing about the size of a football field. It was empty with the exception of me and the illuminated item on the other side.

I was halfway across the field when I realized what the object was. I froze.

It was a headstone on a grave.

Is that my grave? Am I dead?

I wanted to turn around and leave, but where would I go? I didn't know if this was a dream or reality, but I needed to find out.

With one foot in front of the other, I closed the gap between myself and the grave. It took me a minute to get up the courage to look at the headstone.

It was blank.

As much as I'd thought I would be relieved that my name wasn't on it, in a way, it was actually worse. The fact that there was no name on it left too much room for me to worry that it belonged to someone else—someone I cared about. That was more terrifying to me than my own death.

What if this is Becca's grave? What if I'd failed and Henley killed her?

Or it could be a stranger's grave, *I reminded myself.*

I'd previously dreamed of Becca telling me that I would be responsible for someone else's death, perhaps someone named Josie. I still hadn't decided if that was a feverish nightmare or my intuition trying to tell me something, but if it was my intuition, maybe this was Josie's grave.

I heard a flutter behind me and instinctively turned around.

A raven flew across the yard and straight toward my face. It squawked angrily as it struck my cheeks and forehead. I threw my hands up, trying to protect myself, but it continued to peck and claw, ripping apart my hands. I screamed and stumbled backward, still trying to fight it off.

I lost my balance and fell backward into the grave. Although the grave had appeared filled in before, it was now a hollow plot, welcoming me into it. I screamed again right before I crashed into the ground.

I lay in the dirt, a good six feet below the surface. Above me, there was nothing but stars in the sky. The raven was gone, and everything seemed peaceful in the world above.

I could feel my heart pounding, and I was surprised I hadn't woken up by now. Usually, when I had a nightmare this terrifying, it was enough to send me back into the conscious world.

Maybe I am dead …

"Natalie?" I heard a familiar voice ask as a shadow appeared at the top of the plot. "Can you hear me?"

"Michael?" I asked. "Yes, I'm here."

Oh, how I wished he were really here.

"Please wake up," he replied.

"Michael, help me!" I yelled as loud as I could.

"I think she heard me," I heard Michael say to someone, although I didn't see anyone else up there.

The next thing I knew, I began to float to the top of the grave, back toward ground level.

When Michael came into view, he reached out his arms, and I lightly drifted into the safety of them.

He smiled down at me. "We got you back. You're safe now."

Even with my eyes closed, I could tell it was daylight and that sun was hitting my face. My mind slowly registered that I couldn't be at Henley. There was no sunlight at Henley.

Vague images of being rescued began to come back to me.

I was asleep in bed and heard someone come into my room. At first, I thought it was Dr. Leeman or Tonya, so I pretended that I was still asleep, hoping they would go away and leave me alone. If they were coming to start the next test, I knew I wouldn't survive it. I wasn't ready to die yet.

Instead of getting injected with another disease or a sedative to suppress my abilities, someone picked me up out of the bed and carried me across the room. I was scared to open my eyes. If it was Henley or Dr. Leeman, it probably meant they were taking me to the room with the metal table. I whimpered at the thought.

That was when the arms carrying me squeezed a little tighter, and I heard Seth's voice. "Hang in there. We're getting you out of this place."

I dared to open my eyes and confirmed it was Seth. I was convinced that I must only be dreaming, but I closed my eyes and rested my head on Seth's chest anyway.

Seth came to a stop and handed me to someone else. The second I felt his strong, protective arms, I knew it was Michael. As much as I wanted to be excited about seeing him, I knew it was either likely still a dream or maybe Luke was playing more mind tricks on me.

When Michael put his hand on my cheek, it took every ounce of strength I had to push him away. If it was Luke, I didn't want him touching me.

It wasn't until Michael took my hand and put it to his face that I started to believe maybe—just maybe—it was really him. Just in case, I decided to tell him about Becca. If they were there to rescue me, they needed to get her out too.

I couldn't remember anything after that.

"Her eyes just fluttered," I heard Michael say. It was followed by footsteps that grew closer to where I lay.

I wanted to reply, but the words weren't coming to me yet. I managed to make a noise, but it sounded like a groan.

"Natalie, are you in pain?" Alexander asked.

I shook my head. Nothing hurt, but I felt stiff. I must have been asleep for quite some time.

"Try to open your eyes," Alexander told me.

It was a struggle, but I forced them open. It took a minute, but then everything slowly came into focus.

Alexander was sitting on the side of my bed. "It's good to have you back."

I looked around the room. Michael was standing by the window, his arms folded across his chest, biting his thumbnail. They were the only two in the room with me.

"Becca?" I croaked as I attempted to sit up. "Where is she?"

Alexander helped me, propping up the pillows so I could rest against them. "Don't worry. We were able to get her out."

Alexander reached for the stethoscope hanging around his neck and slid the earpieces in his ears. He pressed the diaphragm to my chest and listened, and then he leaned me forward slightly and placed it on my back. "Take a deep breath."

Michael watched silently as Alexander examined me, but he didn't come any closer.

After listening to a series of breaths, Alexander removed the stethoscope and hung it back around his neck. He grabbed my wrist and took my pulse. "You've improved drastically in the past few days. That's good."

"How long was I asleep?" I asked, afraid to know the answer.

"A week," Michael replied.

I looked at Alexander. A week was a *long* time. Even when Michael had healed me from my accident, I hadn't slept an entire week.

"You needed to rest, so your body could heal," Alexander said, giving me a comforting pat on the arm.

I looked around the room. Wherever we were, it was unfamiliar. The room was fairly small with only the twin-size bed I was lying on, a dark blue upholstered armchair, and an oak dresser. The walls were painted a pewter-blue color, and the window Michael stood by had navy-and-cobalt paisley curtains. We were definitely in a house of some sort and not a hospital.

"I know you just woke up, but is it okay for us to talk about what happened?" Alexander asked.

I could sense the urgency in his voice, and I understood why. He wanted to assess the threat level of Henley finding us, wherever we were. That was Alexander, always trying to figure out how to keep everyone safe.

I nodded.

"I need you to answer this first question honestly," Alexander said. "Did you give Henley or Luke any information about our protocol?"

"No."

"Are you one hundred percent positive?" Alexander asked. "I know Henley would have taken extreme measures to try to get you to talk. I wouldn't blame you if you did."

I adamantly shook my head. "Henley tried, but I never told him anything. I'm confident I didn't."

"I know that wasn't easy. Thank you for protecting my family." Alexander smiled kindly at me. "What made you decide to go to

Henley? Was it because of Becca?" Alexander's tone was calm with no trace of accusation.

"Yes, partly," I replied. I looked over at Michael. "I was also trying to protect you. Henley wasn't planning to capture you if he found us. He was planning to take me and kill you."

Michael didn't reply. He just stood there, staring at me, giving me no indication of what he was thinking.

"How did you know that was his plan?" Alexander asked, his voice gentle. "Did he somehow contact you to threaten you, to threaten us?"

"No. Becca told me," I said. Alexander and Michael exchanged a look, but I continued, "She told me his plan and warned me that he was going to kill her in three days if she failed to locate us and turn us in. I attempted to find her on my own, to get to her first, but I was hitting dead ends. So, that's when I decided to—"

"Take matters into your own hands," Michael interrupted. He unfolded his arms and then refolded them again.

"Try to save my sister by allowing Henley to capture me on his own," I clarified.

Surely, he could understand that. He would have done the same for Raina. I knew he would have.

"I'm confused," Alexander said. "How did Becca contact you?"

"She visited my dream a couple of days before I left. I hoped that if I could just get behind Henley's walls, I could find a way to escape with her, to save her, but I never saw her there. I'm so glad you found her." I sighed with relief.

Alexander flashed Michael a worried look.

Oh no.

"What?" I asked, feeling the relief quickly fade away. After everything Henley had done to me, I couldn't imagine what he must have done to Becca. "Is she hurt?"

Michael turned away and looked out the window. Alexander smiled, but I could see the worry in his eyes.

Is she dead? Please don't let her be dead.

"Tell me," I demanded.

"She's not hurt," Alexander assured me.

"Well, is she here? Can I see her?"

If they rescued her and she isn't hurt, where is she? Why haven't they told her I am awake? I was certain she'd want to see me as much as I wanted to see her.

"I think you should talk to Seth," Michael told me, glancing over his shoulder.

Seth? Why? What is going on?

Alexander stood up. "I think that's a good idea. I'll go get him."

"Wait," I said, recalling another piece of important information that I needed to make sure Alexander knew about. As much as I wanted him to go get Seth so I could find out what was going on with Becca, they needed to know that there was the potential of looming danger. "There's one more thing you need to know."

Alexander sat back down, and Michael turned away from the window to face me.

"Henley is killing people. Mostly runaways. He's making them sick or something and then testing his cure on them." I hesitated briefly before adding, "Luke thinks it's the cure that's actually killing them."

Alexander frowned. "I knew that would only be a matter of time. Henley had talked about wanting to test it back when I was still working for him, but I kept telling him it wasn't ready yet. I'd warned him it could be dangerous."

Alexander went to stand up again, but I reached out for him to stay.

"Have you ever heard of something called Project Josie?" I asked.

Alexander pondered it for a moment and then shook his head. "No, I haven't. What is that?"

"I don't know," I replied. "I was hoping you did. I dreamed about it, and I think it's because someone around me was talking about it at Henley. But I had a fever at the time, so it's possible it didn't really happen at all." I hated this feeling of not knowing what was real and what wasn't.

"Do you remember exactly what they said?" Alexander asked. "Every detail you can recall is important."

The memory was fuzzy, but I tried to remember. "I think they were talking about how sick I was, but they weren't going to intervene because they had what they needed for Project Josie." As I said it, I realized none of it made any sense.

I glanced at Michael, but he didn't notice. He was staring at the floor.

Alexander took a deep breath. "Anything else?"

"Not that I can recall," I replied. "But I was dreaming of Becca, and she told me I was going to be responsible for *her* death. I'm assuming she meant whoever this Josie person is. I don't even know if she's real though. It could have just been a dream."

"Could she be one of the runaways?" Michael asked.

"Maybe … but how would I be responsible for her death? I've never met her."

"Do you think Luke knows who she is?" Alexander asked.

I shrugged. "I don't know." I'd never mentioned it to Luke because I had been mad at him for tricking me.

"I doubt he'll give us a straight answer, but I'll ask him what he knows," Michael told Alexander as he walked toward the door to the room.

"Luke is *here*?" I asked, not attempting to hide the shock in my voice.

Michael stopped and turned back. He opened his mouth to say something and then hesitated before replying, "I'll send Seth in to talk to you about Becca." Then, he turned and walked out of the room.

I stared helplessly at the empty doorway. I wanted to go after him, but I had no idea what I would even say. He was obviously upset with me, and he had every right to feel that way. I needed to figure out a way to make things right with him.

Alexander stood up. "He just needs a little time. This has been hard on him."

Michael's reaction had been obvious to him too.

I felt tears stinging my eyes, and I willed myself to keep it together. I managed a smile and nodded at Alexander.

"Try to take it easy for the next day or so. I'll be back to check on you in a couple of hours."

"Thank you for everything, Alexander."

Alexander smiled before leaving.

Less than a minute later, Seth appeared in the doorway, out of breath. He must have run when Michael told him I was awake. He smiled widely as he sat next to me on the bed.

"I thought you'd never wake up. I mean, how much beauty rest does one girl need?"

Despite his joking, I could sense his concern. I knew him too well.

"It's good to see you too."

Seth shook his head and took my hand in his. "Let's get this out of the way," he said. "You know what you did was really dumb, right?"

I leaned my head back against the headboard. Out of everyone, Seth should understand why I had done it. "What was I supposed to do? He'd had Becca this whole time, but I'm sure Becca told you that."

He furrowed his brow. "My dad was actually the one who admitted that. I called him after we returned. I can't believe it was him all along."

I never would have thought Mr. Weber would fess up to Seth about what he had done. As messy as it was, I was glad it was at least all out in the open now.

"All this time, I thought it was some psychopath who'd broken into your house and taken her. But my *own father*?"

I could hear the anger and hurt in Seth's voice.

When Becca had disappeared, it had completely devastated Seth. It was hard to believe that his father had been able to sit by and watch his son suffer such loss and heartbreak and never say anything about his part in it.

"When did you realize that Becca was there?" Seth asked.

"Three months before I was captured. I figured it out in Charlotte after you left."

"And you didn't think to tell me? I would've helped you." Seth squeezed my hand.

"That's exactly why I didn't tell you. I didn't want you to come with me. I was scared if it went bad again, Henley would kill you. He wanted to last time."

Seth released my hand. "He almost did again. Well, one of his goons almost did anyway. I got shot when we went back for Becca."

"What?" I asked in disbelief.

"Yeah, in the shoulder. It was pretty nasty, but Michael healed me, so it's all good now. Plus, Jen's been giving me extra attention, so that's nice."

The gravity of the situation weighed heavily on me despite Seth's attempt to make light of it. The only reason I had gone to Henley alone was to keep those I loved safe.

What if Seth had died, trying to rescue me? I wouldn't have been able to live with myself.

"What have they told you about Becca?" he asked, changing the subject.

I shook my head. "Nothing. They won't tell me anything. I asked to see her, and they sent you in. What's going on? Is she okay?"

Getting Becca back was the only good thing to come out of all of this.

Seth took a breath but said nothing.

"What?" I asked.

Is she really dead, and they just don't know how to tell me?

"She …" Seth hesitated, trying to find the words. "She's … well … she's changed."

"What does that mean? Changed how?"

Seth stared down at the comforter on my bed.

"Tell me," I insisted. The suspense was going to kill me.

Seth looked back up at me, and I could see it in his eyes. Something was *seriously* wrong.

"She was there for a long time, Nat. It's understandable that she's not herself."

Well, of course she was going to be traumatized. Who wouldn't be after being there all that time? But she would be okay. She was safe with us now.

Alexander had said that she was resting, but I knew my sister. Unless something was majorly wrong with her, she would have come to see me by now. I needed to see what was going on for myself.

I peeled the covers back, but Seth grabbed them and pulled them back over me.

"What are you doing?"

"I'm going to see her!" I resisted against him, trying to get the covers off so I could get out of bed.

Seth reached out and grasped me by the sides of my arms to stop me. "You need to rest, and so does she." His voice was firm and insistent, but I didn't want to hear it.

"Why does everyone keep saying that? I'm fine!"

"You're not fine," he said, still holding me tightly.

"I haven't seen her in five years. I'm going to see my sister." I struggled weakly against him.

"You almost died. *Again.* You know that, right?" His tone was now somewhere between sad and just plain agitated.

I stopped fighting him. I knew I had been weak and sick, but surely, it hadn't been that close of a call. They hadn't started the next test yet.

Seth must have seen the confusion on my face because he let go of my arms. "Like, if we had shown up a day later—heck, maybe an hour—you would probably be gone."

I sat there, speechless. That couldn't be right. Yes, I had been really sick, but I wouldn't have died until they injected me with the next illness.

Seth looked me square in the eye. "You were in such bad shape that Michael couldn't even heal you. You had pneumonia, and between all of the crap in your body and how malnourished and dehydrated you were, it's a miracle you are still here. The only reason you are is because Alexander was there to treat you. For real, it was touch and go for a bit."

Although I couldn't see my reflection in the mirror above the dresser from where I sat, I recalled the last time I'd caught a glimpse of myself at Henley. I remembered how frail and weak I'd looked and not at all like myself. If I still looked like that, or worse, it was no wonder they were all worried.

"Alexander told us to say our good-byes to you, just in case." Seth looked away.

I reached out and took Seth's hand. "I'm so sorry that I put you through that." The words felt insignificant for the pain I'd caused him. I couldn't even imagine how hard that would be if the situation were reversed.

"I'm just glad you are back and getting better."

"At least someone is," I mumbled, more to myself than to Seth.

"What are you talking about?"

"Michael can barely even look at me," I admitted even though the words stung as I said it.

"He's hurt, Nat, and worried. What did you expect?"

I shrugged. I knew it was what I should have expected, and it was what I deserved, but it was still painful.

"He loves you, and trust me, he is happy to see you. Even if he isn't showing it," Seth continued. "He'll come around."

"How can you be sure?"

He leaned in a little closer. "Because I was with him after you left. He was determined to find you and was willing to do anything to save you."

I nodded but couldn't help but worry about what would happen if Michael never forgave me. Now that I was back, I couldn't imagine my life without him in it.

"He might be angry with you, but he didn't leave this room for almost an entire week," he continued. "Eventually, I had to tell him to go shower. He was kind of gross."

I looked at Seth for a minute and decided he was telling me the truth. He wasn't just saying it to make me feel better.

"It'll be okay," he reiterated.

I nodded again even though I knew there was no guarantee that things with Michael would go back to normal.

"I'm mad at you too, just to be clear." He playfully nudged my leg. "But I'm used to your shenanigans by now."

"Oh my gosh! You are awake!" Jen cried from the doorway of the bedroom. She clapped her hands together before running to my bedside and giving me a tight hug.

Lorena and Luke filed into the room behind her. Lorena stood at the foot of my bed while Luke lingered uncomfortably in the doorway.

"How are you feeling?" Lorena asked.

I smiled in an attempt to reassure them that I was fine. I didn't want them to worry about me any more than they already had. "Pretty good. A little stiff but okay."

Jen plopped down on the side of my bed, opposite of Seth.

"I bought you some clothes," she said. "They are in your dresser."

"Thank you," I replied.

"I hope you like them. I tried to find things that were your style."

"I'm sure I will," I replied and then coughed.

"Time for you to rest," Seth said, standing up.

"We'll see you soon," Jen told me.

Lorena and Jen left, but Luke remained where he was. Seth stopped at the door and seemed to be waiting to make sure he left as well.

"I'll only be a minute," he assured Seth.

Seth eyed him, as if deciding whether or not he'd allow it. Finally, he nodded and then turned back to me. "Just holler if you need anything." He threw a final warning glance at Luke before leaving the room.

Luke walked over to the armchair and sat down. He let out a sigh. I wasn't sure if it was out of relief or frustration.

"I'm surprised you're here," I said to him.

"Me too." He looked around the room, taking it in. I realized this must all be so foreign to him. "I wasn't planning on leaving, but when everything went south, I really didn't have much of a choice."

"Are you glad now though? To be out?"

He swayed his head back and forth. "Yes, and no. Yes, it's nice to have my freedom, but the unfamiliarity of everything takes a little getting used to."

"Is this your first time ever outside of Henley?"

He ran his hand over the upholstery on the arm of the chair. "No. They would take me out sometimes—when they wanted my help in trying to find Michael and Raina."

He looked down, seeming ashamed to admit that he'd attempted to hunt down his own siblings. I'd seen enough at Henley though to know he hadn't been given much of a choice.

"For what it's worth, I'm glad you are here," I told him, and I meant it.

Sure, Luke and I'd had our differences, but I believed that he wanted to be a good person. The fact that he'd chosen to save my life proved that.

He looked up at me, clearly surprised by my comment and then immediately uncomfortable by it. "Well, next, you're going to spout off some nonsense about us being friends or something."

I shrugged. "Maybe we are after all."

I saw the hint of a smile tug at the corner of his lips before he stood up. "I'd better go and let you rest. I'm pretty sure it's been longer than a minute."

"Hey, Luke?" I asked.

He turned and looked at me.

"Is Becca okay? No one is really telling me anything."

He frowned. "Just try to rest. Becca isn't going anywhere."

He turned and left the room without any further explanation.

I sat in silence for a few minutes, processing it all. I was happy to be reunited with Michael and my friends, but it was also difficult to enjoy the moment, not knowing what was really going on with Becca. I felt like everyone was holding back. For some reason, they were afraid to just be honest with me.

As much as I recognized that I needed to rest and heal, I also knew I would never be able to sleep again until I saw Becca. I needed to see for myself that she was here and healthy.

Without a doubt, Becca was dealing with the trauma of being at Henley. Now more than ever, she needed to know that I was here for her. I wanted to reassure her that I would help her get through this.

I decided that I would just go to her room, give her a big hug, tell her how much I loved her, and then leave. After I did that, I would be able to rest and focus on getting better myself. Maybe I could ask Seth to move my bed into her room, so she and I could get better together.

I slipped out of the covers, glad that there was no one to stop me this time. I placed both feet on the floor and leaned on the bed until I was confident my legs were sturdy enough to allow me to walk.

Wearing a pair of pajamas and nothing on my feet, I snuck out of the bedroom and into the hallway.

My room was at the end of the hallway. Directly across from it was another bedroom with the door open. The bed was neatly made, but a suitcase lay open on the floor.

In the middle of the hallway was a staircase. Apparently, we were on the second story of the house.

Next to my bedroom was another bedroom with the door open. No one was in the room, but a black jacket was sprawled out on top of the unmade bed. That must be Raina's room.

I could hear people talking downstairs, but everything was quiet upstairs.

There were two other bedrooms on our floor. The door was open to one but closed to the other. I quietly crept down the hall.

When I reached the bedroom with the door open, I took a peek inside. No one was in there.

I turned my attention to the door that was closed and contemplated what to do next. There was a good chance that Becca was inside, resting, but it was also possible that someone else was inside, and then I would be busted. I decided to risk it anyway.

What's the worst that can happen? They'll yell at me and tell me to go back to bed?

I walked to the closed door and attempted to turn the doorknob, but it was locked. I jerked my hand back, expecting whoever was inside to open the door, but that was when I realized that the door was locked from the outside. It was as if someone had put the doorknob on backward.

That's odd. Why would someone be locked inside?

I pressed my ear to the door but heard nothing, except silence, coming from the other side.

There was no guarantee that Becca was inside, but I needed to know for sure. I quietly knocked on the door, hoping no one downstairs would hear it.

There was no response.

I rested my hand on the lock, ready to turn it. A knot formed in my stomach, giving me a clear warning signal. I wasn't sure what I was going to find in the room, but I needed to know for myself. If Becca was in there, I had to see her. It had been too long.

With my breath held, I unlocked the door and slowly pushed it open.

The room was quiet and dark despite the fact that it was daylight. The curtains were tightly drawn, and beneath them, I could see that the windows had been boarded up. That was strange. The windows hadn't been boarded up in my bedroom or any of the other rooms I'd passed.

My eyes adjusted as the light spilled in from the hallway.

I noticed a bed with a black metal frame, but it wasn't until I was a few steps closer that I realized someone was lying in the bed. I couldn't tell who it was, but they hadn't moved when I entered the room.

"Becca?" I whispered.

There was no response.

I took a step closer and then another.

The knot in my stomach intensified, but I did my best to ignore it. In spite of knowing something was off, I continued to move forward. I needed to know if it was her.

I reached the side of the bed, and although the person was sleeping with their back to me, I could see long, dark hair spilling out onto the white pillowcase. It was Becca.

With a shaking hand, I reached out and gently touched her shoulder. I felt her tense beneath my fingertips.

Becca rolled over, and her eyes widened at the sight of me. I desperately tried to keep my emotions in check as I stared back at her.

Becca slowly sat up, never taking her eyes off of me. "Natalie?" she asked in disbelief.

I nodded, unable to speak. I was in awe that she was right there in front of me. This wasn't a dream.

"Is it really you?" She tilted her head.

"It's me, Bec," I told her, my voice quivering.

I thought she was reaching out to hug me. I assumed she had missed me as much as I'd missed her.

It wasn't until my back slammed against the wall behind me that I realized that she had lunged off of the bed to attack me. Her hands firmly clasped around my throat. I pushed against her, but I was still too weak to fight her off.

What is she doing?

I tried to talk, to rationalize with her, but I couldn't breathe, let alone speak. I attempted to read her mind, desperate to understand what was happening, but all I heard was silence.

I helplessly tugged at her arms as everything around me started to fade to black.

FIFTEEN

MICHAEL

"That's not how you cut into an avocado," Raina said as she nudged me out of the way, so she could take over the cutting board.

I gladly handed the knife over to her. I'd had no idea what I was doing.

I looked around the kitchen to see if there was something else I could do to be useful, to stay busy.

Lorena was making a sweet mango salsa for me and Raina, Jen was making a spicy salsa for everyone else, and Seth was just stirring chopped lettuce in a bowl, claiming it was a salad. Maybe I could go help Alexander on the grill. I hesitated though, wondering if Luke might be out there.

The ceiling to the kitchen rattled ever so slightly. Raina looked up from the avocado but then dismissed it and began cutting again. I stayed still, listening carefully for any additional noise.

Becca's room was directly above the kitchen, and when we'd left her earlier, she had been lightly sedated and resting. We'd locked her in her room to keep her from leaving and hurting anyone, particularly Natalie. It was possible that maybe she'd gotten up and started roaming around the room.

I should go check on her and make sure the room is secure. Just in case.

The ceiling rattled again, this time with more force, and it was followed by a thud. Raina locked eyes with me. She'd heard it too.

I ran out of the kitchen with Raina at my heels.

"What's wrong?" I heard Seth call behind us, but we didn't stop to answer him.

When I reached the top of the stairs, I instinctively looked at Natalie's room. Her door was open, but there was no sign of her. I raced into Becca's room.

Becca had Natalie trapped against the wall. Her fingers were around Natalie's neck, literally squeezing the life out of her. Even in the dark room, I could see the contrast of the whites of Becca's knuckles against the bruises already forming on Natalie's neck.

I slammed into Becca with so much force that I was worried we might go through the bedroom wall as we hit it.

Although the impact with Becca was significant, she didn't immediately let go of Natalie. She dragged Natalie with her as long as she could until she could no longer hold on to her. The moment she let go, Natalie fell to the ground, gasping for air.

I held Becca against the wall and pinned her arms to her sides. Her green eyes were wild, like an animal, and they were still set on Natalie. If I wasn't restraining her, she'd surely lunge at her again. It was what we had all been afraid of since rescuing them both.

Raina stood behind me, and I could feel her peering over my shoulder. She was ready in case I needed help.

I didn't have trouble holding Becca still though. My adrenaline had fully kicked in the moment I realized Natalie was in danger.

Seth appeared in the doorway and flicked on the light.

"Go get Alexander!" he yelled to someone in the hallway, probably Jen.

Seth ran to Natalie's side as she gagged and battled to catch her breath.

"Michael, she needs you," he said.

Raina reached around me and grabbed ahold of Becca. "Go. I've got her."

I hesitated even though I didn't need to. Raina had the same ability that I did and could easily tap into her adrenaline. She could handle Becca.

"Go," Raina insisted.

I let go and rushed to Natalie's side. Out of the corner of my eye, I saw Becca attempt to fight against Raina, but it was useless. Raina held her own, and Becca couldn't get loose. Seth jumped up and was ready to assist Raina, if needed. It was crazy how we'd all somehow learned to work as a team, anticipating what each person might need.

I crouched down by Natalie's side. Her hand was clasped around her neck as she struggled to breathe.

"Let me see," I told her, lightly tugging at her arm.

She lowered her hand, exposing deep purple bruises where Becca's fingers had clamped down on her throat. I could see where each finger had latched on.

I reached my hand out, touching the soft skin on Natalie's neck. The color slowly returned to her face, and her breathing became even again. She settled her terrified eyes on me.

"Thank you," she said, her voice small and hoarse.

I didn't know if I wanted to scream at her or take her in my arms and never let her go. The urge was equal for either option.

Instead, I just stood up and pulled her to her feet. "Let's get you back into bed."

Alexander ran into the room, ready to help. He came to assist Natalie.

"Are you all right?" he asked her. "What happened?"

I could tell that Natalie was struggling to find the words, not so much from the physical pain, but from the emotional pain of almost being murdered by her own sister.

"Becca attacked her, but she'll be okay. I healed her," I responded on her behalf.

Natalie didn't protest as I led her out of Becca's room and back down the hall to her own room. Without a word, she climbed into bed, pulling the covers up to her waist. She sat there in a daze, understandably in shock about what had just occurred.

Becca had woken up about eight hours after we rescued them from Henley. Seth was the first to go in and see her, and he quickly detected something was off about her behavior. Thinking she was traumatized, he tried to comfort her by talking to her about Natalie. With just the mention of Natalie's name, Becca completely lost it. She went into a rage, tearing the sheets off her bed, overturning her mattress, throwing a lamp against the wall. She incoherently babbled about Natalie and how she must be stopped as she destroyed whatever she could get her hands on.

At the time, I was in Natalie's room, hoping that in her unconscious state, she could sense that I was there with her. I heard the commotion from Becca's room and didn't know what to think. When I entered the room, I saw Seth desperately trying to calm Becca down, but it was no use. She was threatening Natalie and trying to escape past Seth to go find her. I restrained Becca while Seth got Alexander, so he could give her something to calm down.

We debated on tying Becca up because we were worried that she might try to make good on her threats, but it felt inhumane, and we decided against it. Instead, we had agreed to lightly sedate her and lock her bedroom door.

Now, the option of tying her up might be a necessity. If Becca found a way out of her room, I had no doubt she would go after Natalie again.

Anxious to get back to Becca's room and figure out a better way to restrain her, I edged toward the door.

"What's wrong with her?" Natalie asked softly before I could go.

I knew how much Becca meant to her, and I couldn't imagine what she must be feeling right now.

We had intended to tell her about Becca when we believed Natalie's condition was more stable. Natalie had been through a lot of physical trauma at Henley, and based on my own experiences there, I knew she'd been through a lot mentally as well. Seth, Alexander, and I were concerned that maybe Natalie wouldn't be able to handle the truth about Becca right away. We'd wanted to assess her mental state first, but after what had just occurred, I had no choice but to level with her now.

I stopped and turned around. Natalie looked so lost and scared.

As much as I wanted to go to her, take her in my arms, and tell her everything would be okay, I didn't know if she would want me to. I still had no idea where we stood with each other and if she'd really meant what she wrote in her note. Instead, I walked over to the armchair by her bed and sat down.

"She's been brainwashed by Henley," I told her.

I wished there were a better way to say it, to soften the blow a little, but there wasn't. She already knew the gravity of the situation. Now, it was a matter of giving her the details.

Natalie let out a breath, and I remained silent to allow the revelation to sink in.

She ran her hand through her long hair. It fell gently over her shoulders.

"She hates me," she said, more to herself than to me.

"She thinks she does," I clarified.

From what Natalie and Seth had both told me about Becca, I didn't believe the real Becca hated Natalie. Unfortunately, this programmed and tormented version of her did.

Tears welled in her eyes. "Why?"

"I don't know." It was the truth.

Becca had made it clear to us that she hated Natalie, that she wanted Natalie dead, but we had not been able to get her to tell us why exactly.

"It doesn't make sense."

"I think Becca set you up," I said carefully.

Natalie lifted her eyes to mine. "What are you talking about?"

She knew what I meant, but it was reasonable for her to be in denial of it. She wouldn't want to believe that all of the pain and torture she'd recently experienced had been deliberately set up by her own sister. But Alexander and I were fairly certain that was exactly what had happened.

"Think about it. Becca showed up in your dream to warn you that unless you did something, she and I were both going to die. She knows you, Natalie, and anyone who knows you knows that's going to trigger a response in you to take matters into your own hands."

She didn't say anything, and I couldn't tell if she was following me or not.

"I think she created a sense of urgency for you to take action and then led you to the idea of surrendering yourself to Henley," I stated, confident I was right. "She manipulated you on Henley's behalf."

"No," she said. "Becca wouldn't do that to me."

"Let me ask you this: did you ever see Becca while you were at Henley?"

Natalie thought for a minute and then slowly shook her head.

"I used to see Raina and Luke daily when we were there even if it was just in passing," I told her. "Henley liked to test our abilities together, so I actually saw them more than you'd think. How did Becca seem in your dream? Did she seem like herself?"

Natalie frowned. "No, she didn't, but I guess I just dismissed it. She was actually a little cruel toward me. She asked me if I would be selfish enough to let you die." She briefly closed her eyes. "Henley did this to her. He used her to trap me."

"She made you believe that conceding to Henley was the only way to keep everyone else safe."

She looked defeated. "You're … right."

"Can I ask you something?"

She nodded.

"When did you figure out that Becca was the raven?" Something told me that the dream she'd mentioned earlier today wasn't the first one Becca had visited.

She lowered her eyes. "In Charlotte. The night we rescued you."

So, Natalie had been keeping that secret from me for *months* before she disappeared.

I sighed but didn't respond.

Raina stepped into the doorway of Natalie's room. She didn't acknowledge Natalie but set her eyes on me. "Can I talk to you?"

I looked back at Natalie.

"I'm okay," she told me.

Of course she would say that, but I had no idea if that was the truth.

I stood up and followed Raina to the hall, closing the door to Natalie's room behind me.

"This isn't a good time," I said.

Seth and Alexander joined us in the hall, relocking the door to Becca's room behind them.

"We need to figure out what to do with Becca," Raina told me. "We have her tied to the bed right now, and she is pissed. I'm waiting for her head to start rotating or something."

"She's *not* possessed," I reminded her.

Raina raised her eyebrows. "Are you sure about that? She's acting like it. She tried to bite me."

I didn't know what to do with Becca. Tying her to the bed didn't seem right, but at the same time, we couldn't risk her escaping and killing Natalie either.

"I think keeping her tied up for now is the right thing to do," Alexander said. "At least until we can figure out how to get through to her."

"How do we do that?" Seth asked.

Alexander shook his head. "I'm not sure. I need to do some research on it. I'm not a psychiatrist. I've never treated anyone who's been brainwashed before."

"It's like she's not even the same person," Seth said.

"Right now, she's not," Alexander agreed. "For the moment, she is whoever Henley wanted her to be."

Raina looked at me. "We have other things we need to decide as well."

I knew she was referring to Luke.

I glanced back at Natalie's closed door. "Not here. Let's talk outside."

We walked downstairs, through the kitchen, and out onto the back patio. Lorena and Jen were still in the kitchen, anxiously waiting for us to return. Seth stopped off to give them an update while Alexander, Raina, and I went outside. There was no sign of Luke, so he was likely in his room, which was on the first floor, just off the living room.

The screened-in porch was set up almost like a second living room with a cream-colored couch, two armchairs, and a matching ottoman sitting in the center. Alexander sat in one of the armchairs while Raina and I sat on the couch.

"How did Natalie take the news?" Alexander asked me.

"As good as can be expected."

Alexander smoothed his palms out on his knees. He was stressed out but was trying his best not to show it. "We have Becca secured for now, but we need to talk about Luke."

Raina sank back onto the couch. Neither of us had ever expected to see Luke again, let alone have him stay in the same house as our family.

When Alexander had made the decision to break Raina and me out of Henley, he'd actually wanted to take Luke as well, but Luke had refused to go. In fact, Luke attempted to mind-manipulate Alexander into believing that Henley had caught him. Luckily, Raina and I realized what was happening and managed to snap Alexander out of it.

It hadn't been an easy choice, but we had chosen to leave Luke there. Coming with us would have been the best thing for him, but we couldn't convince him. I was of the opinion that, deep down, Luke had been too scared to go. He knew how to survive at Henley and manipulate his way around to make it livable. He would've had to figure that out all over again in the outside world, and I believed the possibility of failure had deterred him.

As guilty as I'd felt over the years for leaving him behind, I always knew we'd made the right choice. Raina and I didn't have any loopholes of survival at Henley. If we hadn't left, we'd both be dead by now.

Luke had been furious when we left, and he'd promised to do everything in his power to help Henley find us. I'd had no doubt that he'd make good on that promise, and he was one of the primary reasons that Henley had been able to locate us so many times.

"He needs to go," Raina said firmly, pulling me from my thoughts.

"Are you sure that's what you want?" Alexander asked.

He was trying to be neutral, for our sake, although I knew he'd jump at the chance to kick Luke out. Alexander didn't trust him either.

Raina sighed. "I don't know …"

Alexander gave her a quick nod. It was the answer he had expected. He looked at me.

"We can't just turn him loose," I said. "He knows where we are, and he could easily go back to Henley and tell him everything. With Becca tied up and Natalie healing, I don't think we can change locations quickly right now. It was hard enough, getting them both here in one piece."

"It might be wise to have him here, so we can keep an eye on him," Alexander agreed. "Especially since we don't have any information on this Project Josie that Natalie told us about."

"What's Project Josie?" Raina asked.

"We don't know," Alexander replied. "It might be nothing, but I highly doubt it."

"Luke said he didn't know what it was when I asked him, but who knows?" I added. "I don't think he'd tell us even if he did."

The truth was, Luke liked having an advantage over everyone else. If he knew what Project Josie was and that we were desperate for information on it, he would hold out on us as long as humanly possible. He was like that with anything that was valuable; he'd hoard it until it served him best.

"Why is he even here?" Raina asked. "Why did he contact us in the first place? This could all still be a trap."

I couldn't argue with that. I felt the same way about the situation. Luke had never shown a genuine interest in anyone, except himself. The fact that he'd contacted us to help rescue Natalie was out of character for him.

"Well, if Luke really was trying to help Natalie, he must know that he can't go back to Henley," Alexander said. "He would be killed. He wouldn't be able to return unless he had something to offer Henley in exchange for his life."

"Like us," I said.

We had come full circle. We didn't trust Luke, but we had no choice but to let him stay. At least if he was here, we could keep tabs on him.

Raina stood up. "I'm going to help Mom with dinner." She pursed her lips and walked back into the house.

Raina had always been more conflicted about Luke. Although Raina was my sister, she wasn't my blood relative. We'd been created with different donor mothers and donor fathers. Luke, on the other hand, was a blood relative. He was also the only blood relative that Raina and I had ever met. This fact gave Luke a strange power over Raina that had always concerned me. Luke was quick to sniff out any weakness and find a way to use it to his advantage. He'd mastered that with Raina, even at a young age.

I'd always believed that your family was who you made it. For me, it was Raina, Lorena, and Alexander. Within the past year, that family had extended to Natalie. And strangely, it now felt like Seth and Jen had become a part of it as well.

I hadn't considered Luke to be family after we left Henley. If I was being honest, I'd struggled with it, even when I was there. Luke was manipulative and selfish and, at times, cruel. On more than one occasion, his failed attempts to manipulate Henley's staff had backfired, and he'd blamed me. I'd taken several beatings and punishments on his behalf during my childhood, and he'd never expressed any remorse for it.

"How are you doing with all of this?" Alexander asked me. "That was a close call with Natalie."

"Which one? I'm losing count," I replied sourly.

Alexander waited patiently for me to continue.

"I don't know," I admitted. "On one hand, I'm grateful that Natalie's here and she's alive. But on the other hand, I'm frustrated that she put herself into the situation to begin with. *Again.*"

"Have you talked to her about it?"

"Not yet. I was going to talk to her about it tonight, but now, I don't know."

Alexander nodded thoughtfully. "This Becca situation is a real problem."

"I know."

"We have to be extremely careful not to offer up any details about our whereabouts to Becca. If I had to guess, she will probably attempt to contact Henley through dream visitation." Alexander looked tired. The stress was taking a toll on him.

I nodded in agreement. We were going to have our hands full, trying to keep an eye on both Luke and Becca. Either one of them could pose a threat of exposing us to Henley.

"I should probably go check on Natalie," I said, standing up.

"Good idea. I'm sure this is devastating to her."

I walked into the house but stopped short when I noticed Luke in the kitchen, talking to Raina and Seth. They jumped when I entered the room and stared at me, like I had caught them doing something illegal.

"What?" I asked. At this point, I didn't even know what to expect.

Raina looked at Luke and then back at me. "Luke just brought up a valid point."

"This oughta be good." I made no attempt to hide the cynicism in my voice.

"It's about Project Josie," she replied.

I looked pointedly at Luke. "I thought you said you didn't know what it was?"

"I don't," he insisted. "But I think I might know who does." He nodded his chin upward, toward the ceiling.

I sighed. It made sense, and I should have thought of it myself. We needed to talk to the other enemy under our roof.

We needed to talk to Becca.

Sixteen

Natalie

Michael looked up from a laptop that had been set up on top of a card table in the middle of Raina's bedroom.

"What is she doing in here?" he asked Seth, but he was referring to me.

"If Seth is going in there to talk to Becca, I want to hear what she has to say," I replied before Seth could.

It wasn't Seth's fault. He'd tried to talk me out of it, as I was sure Michael had instructed him to, but I had been insistent on attending. I knew they were both trying to protect me, but Becca was my sister, and I needed to understand why she wanted me dead.

I glanced around the room, which had been converted into what looked like a makeshift command center. Raina's bed had been pushed up against the wall to make room for the table. Seven chairs, painted in an antique-white finish, were crammed around it. I assumed they were from the dining table downstairs.

Michael walked over to me. "Are you sure you want to see this?" he quietly asked. "We have no idea what she is going to say. It might not be pleasant."

"I need to understand what's going on with her, whatever it is," I explained. "Plus, I want to help. Maybe she'll say something that will jar one of my memories from Henley that can help us connect it all together."

Aside from understanding what had happened to Becca while at Henley, we needed to figure out if Project Josie was a real threat or not. The sooner we did that, the better.

Michael didn't argue with me. Instead, he just gestured for me to sit at the table. He picked up the laptop and moved it to the dresser, next to a larger computer monitor. I took my seat as he began to connect the laptop to the monitor.

Alexander and Raina hurried into the room.

"We're almost ready to go," Raina said, joining Michael at the dresser.

As Raina punched something into the keyboard of the laptop, Alexander held up a flesh-colored earpiece to Seth.

"You'll be able to hear us with this," he told Seth.

Seth put in the earpiece while Alexander turned on a microphone that sat in the middle of the table. A red light came on, indicating that it was on mute.

Michael joined me at the table, taking the seat next to me. "After Becca attacked you, Alexander gave her a stronger sedative to calm her down and help her sleep," he explained. "While she was asleep, we set up surveillance in her room, so we can see and hear what's going on in there. She's awake now, but we think it's better if she doesn't know the camera or microphone are in her room. Alexander wants to observe her natural reaction, not one put on because she knows she's being watched."

"Here we go," Raina announced as the monitor turned on, reflecting the inside of Becca's room in a clear black-and-white picture.

I flinched as I realized Becca was restrained to the bed. She was awake and just sitting there, propped up with pillows. Her hands were tied to the bedposts.

"Is that really necessary?"

Michael turned to me, his expression doleful. "She tried to kill you, so, yes, it's necessary."

Jen and Lorena walked into the room and joined us at the table. Jen sat next to me while Lorena chose to sit on the other side of Michael.

Luke arrived less than a minute later. He shot me a quick smile before taking his seat, which happened to be the farthest one away from Michael.

"All right," Seth said, clapping his hands together, "let's get this show on the road."

"Okay, it's just like we discussed," Alexander said to him. "You need to be personable with her. Try to connect with her before you bring up Project Josie. She needs to remember that she trusts you before she opens up about anything."

Seth gave a nervous nod before walking out of the room.

Alexander and Raina sat down at the table and angled their chairs, so they could see the monitor. We were all silent, staring at the screen in anticipation. I noticed Alexander had a pen in his hand and a notebook in his lap, ready to take notes.

A moment later, Becca's head turned toward the direction of the door. We couldn't see or hear Seth yet but knew he must be there, unlocking her door.

She clenched her jaw as he entered the room.

There was an armchair in the corner of the room, and Seth dragged it closer to the bed. Becca didn't say anything, but she carefully watched his every move.

"It's good to see you, Bec," Seth said with a sincere smile as he sat down.

She glared at him.

He was silent for a moment, likely contemplating what he wanted to say next.

"Over the past five years, I think I've gone over every single memory of us, just replaying them in my head like a movie that's supposed to have a fairy-tale ending," he finally said. "It's funny how I only thought about the good memories, and then this morning, it dawned on me that it's actually the tougher moments that bond people together. It's the scary, difficult things that you overcome that give you the confidence to believe you can make it through anything as long as you stick together."

He paused to see if there was any reaction from her, but there wasn't. She just sat there, stoically watching him.

"Do you remember that summer when our parents took us to Folly Beach?" he asked.

She didn't respond.

"We were fourteen, and our parents allowed us to hang out on the beach by ourselves for the first time ever. We'd begged and begged them to let us go, and I promised that I would look after you. I'd sworn to keep you safe, and they finally agreed. You and I spent the day attempting to surf. Of course, you were so much better at it than I was. You were always better at everything." He let out a small laugh. "After falling off my board for the hundredth time, I was calling it a day. I took my board back to shore and planned to sulk the rest of the afternoon."

Becca's expression remained firm, unchanged, despite the fact that she knew this story well. She'd told this story so many times herself that I knew there was no way she'd forgotten it.

"But then you screamed and started thrashing around in the water," he continued. "You'd been stung by a jellyfish, but I thought you were being attacked by a shark or something. Without even thinking about it, I ran into the water and swam out to you. I didn't even care that I might get eaten by the shark in the process. All I wanted was to get you and bring you safely back to shore."

He leaned in closer to her. "That's all I want now too," he said. "I know you have to be scared. Heck, I am too. You're panicking on the inside and thrashing in the water, and all I want to do is reach in and save you. I'll do it, if you let me."

I swallowed a lump in my throat.

We were silent in the room, anxiously awaiting Becca's reaction to Seth's heartfelt attempt to reach her.

I squeezed my hands in my lap. *Please let this work. I need my sister back.*

She stared at him for what seemed like an eternity.

"It's interesting …" she finally said.

"What is?" he asked, his expression filled with hope.

"For the life of me, I can't figure out what I ever saw in you." She continued to stare curiously at him, as if she were really contemplating it.

He sat back in the chair, without a doubt stung by her comment. He cleared his throat. "This isn't who you are."

"You're right," she replied. "I've changed."

"What happened to you?" Seth barely choked out the words.

She smiled at him. "I'm finally free of you. I no longer have to be the girl that you follow around like some pathetic, lovesick puppy."

Seth flinched.

Before he could respond, Becca continued, "I have a real purpose now. I'm going to destroy her."

Alexander unmuted the microphone. "Ask her if she's talking about Natalie."

I was positive she was talking about me, but I held my breath anyway, waiting for her to confirm it.

"Natalie?" Seth asked.

Becca tensed at the sound of my name.

Seth shook his head in disbelief. "But she is your sister, and I know you love her."

Alexander ran his hand over his forehead, trying to figure out how to guide Seth to get the conversation under control.

"Love her?" Becca let out a laugh as her eyes darkened. "No, Seth. *I. Hate. Her.*"

It felt like someone had just stabbed me in the heart.

Michael looked at me, but I couldn't bring myself to make eye contact. I knew if I moved my eyes from the spot on the screen that I was staring at, I would burst into tears.

"Ask her why," Alexander said into the microphone.

"Why do you hate her?" Seth pressed. "I don't understand. She's never done anything to you."

I didn't want to continue listening to the conversation, but I also knew it was necessary if we were going to figure out a way to get through to her.

Seth's comment sent Becca into a rage. She began to thrash in the bed, trying to free herself. He stood up and took a step back, unsure of how to intervene.

"I hate her!" she yelled. "She's evil!"

Seth continued to back up toward the door despite the fact that Becca's restraints remained perfectly intact. I sensed he wanted to leave her room more for his own sanity than out of fear for his physical safety.

She continued to tug against the restraints. "You need to destroy her before she kills us all."

"Go ahead and leave," Alexander told Seth.

"You need to kill her, Seth. She won't stop until you kill her!" she screamed as Seth opened the door and walked out.

Once Seth was gone, Becca relaxed and sank back into the bed, exhausted from her outburst.

I felt all eyes on me as we waited for Seth to come back into the room, but I couldn't bring myself to look at anyone. Jen reached under the table and took my hand in hers, trying to offer me silent comfort.

A moment later, the door opened, and Seth walked in.

"All right, Doc, time for plan B," Seth told Alexander.

He was trying to seem unfazed about what had happened, but I knew Seth better than that. He was just as disturbed by his interaction with Becca as I was. This wasn't her at all. She seemed like a completely different person than the one we had known and loved.

I stood up and walked closer to the monitor, staring at my sister as she lay, tied up on the bed. Her eyes were now closed, but I was certain she wasn't sleeping.

What is going through her head right now?

"Does anyone have any idea why she hates me?" I asked. "She called me evil and said I needed to be stopped. She thinks I pose some kind of a threat to her, but why?"

I turned back around to face everyone in the room. I was met with blank expressions. One by one, they each shook their heads in response. Everyone, that was, except for Luke.

He looked down at the floor.

"Luke, do you know something?" I asked.

He jerked his head up, almost surprised that I had called on him. "No."

I didn't believe him. My intuition told me that there was more to it.

"What was it like for Becca at Henley?" I asked him.

He sat up straighter in his chair as he realized everyone's attention was on him. "Pretty similar to yours, I guess, but less tests and more training to try to strengthen her ability to track Michael and Raina."

I could feel my heart begin to race as I asked the next question, "Did Henley torture her?"

He frowned. "Yes. That's a given if you're a prisoner at Henley. You know that."

I nodded as I held back the flood of emotions building inside of me. Of course I knew it.

"Things shifted though when Henley found out about you," Luke added. "After he realized your potential and made the connection that you were related, he took a different approach with her. He started treating her really well. He began to make her feel special and important to him. That's why I thought maybe she'd be able to tell us about Project Josie."

Michael leaned forward, folding his hands on top of the table. "Did Henley use Becca to trap Natalie into surrendering to him?"

Luke looked at Michael and then back to me. "Yes."

"Why didn't you tell me about her before, when we were at Henley?" I asked Luke. "I specifically asked you if Becca knew I was there, and you said you didn't know. You never told me she'd been brainwashed into hating me."

Luke glanced around, like he was embarrassed to answer my question. Finally, he responded, "It would have hurt you, and I thought you might give up. I didn't want you to die."

As much as I didn't want to admit it, even to myself, that would've been true. I might have given up. The only thing that had kept me going at Henley was the fact that Becca was depending on me in order to escape. I'd believed that I was her only hope of surviving.

I turned my attention back to the monitor. Becca hadn't moved.

All I'd wanted for the past five years was to be under the same roof with her again. Now, we were, but I'd never felt like she was further away.

"I need some air," I said as I briskly walked out of the room.

I didn't stop until I was down the stairs and outside on the front porch.

It was the first time that I'd been downstairs or outside at all since waking up after the rescue. The sun felt strange yet wonderful as it touched my skin.

It was quiet and peaceful outside. The only noise was a bird happily chirping up in a nearby tree.

A few minutes later, I heard the front door to the house open and close again.

"I'm okay," I said, not turning around to see who it was. I looked down at the stone steps that led up to the front porch and sat down on the top step.

"I know," Jen replied, sitting down beside me. "Getting some air sounded like a good idea anyway though."

"I just don't understand," I said. "Becca was there for years, and she helped us. What could have happened to her for her to change her opinion of me so drastically that she wants me dead now?"

She watched me with sympathetic eyes. "I have no idea."

I shifted my body, so I was facing her. "Luke knows something that he's not telling me. I think he knows what happened to Becca at Henley."

She hesitated for a second, as if debating on whether or not she should say what was on her mind. "I know everyone else doesn't like Luke, but … I don't know … how bad can he be if he helped get you out of there?" She eyed me for a second before continuing, "Maybe he just doesn't want to hurt you. Whatever happened to Becca must have been really bad, and maybe he's just trying to protect you from it."

"Maybe."

I did believe that on some strange level and in his own way, Luke cared about me. The situation didn't feel right though, and I couldn't ignore my instinct.

"You might get some answers in a few minutes though," she said. "They are getting ready to send Luke in to talk to her."

The news surprised me, and she noticed.

"Alexander wants to see if she's more comfortable talking to Luke. His theory is, if Becca sees you and Seth as the enemy, maybe she'll see Luke as an ally," she explained.

"Yeah, I guess." As much as it pained me to think that she'd trust anyone over Seth and me, it did make perfect sense.

She stared off into the distance, and I felt a shift in her mood. There was now a sadness about her.

"What's wrong?" I asked.

Jen looked at me and seemed a little embarrassed that I'd picked up on it. She quickly looked back down and shook her head.

I gently nudged her with my arm. "Come on. Tell me."

It wasn't like her to be sad about anything. Jen was the most optimistic person I'd ever met.

She frowned and shook her head again. "No, I can't. It's so selfish."

"I won't judge, I promise."

She nervously wrung her hands. "I'm happy that you have Becca back. *I truly am*," she said, and I could tell she was being sincere. "But I don't know what this means for me and Seth. He's not acting any differently toward me or anything, but I know he loved her. What if he decides he wants to be with her again when she gets better?"

I scooted closer to her and put my arm around her shoulders. She leaned her head against mine.

"I mean, I would understand, but it would hurt so much," she continued. "I'm sorry. I shouldn't talk to you about this. I'm such a terrible person."

"You're not a terrible person," I assured her. "It's true that Seth did love Becca, but that was a long time ago. And I know he loves you very much. I don't think Becca's return changes how he feels about you at all."

"How do you know though?"

"Because I know things. I'm psychic, remember?" I said lightheartedly, trying to be the one to cheer her up for once.

She attempted to smile, but I could tell she wasn't convinced.

"And because he gave you *that*." I pointed to the diamond ring on her finger. "That ring belonged to Seth's grandmother. They were very close, and I remember when she gave it to him right before she died. I know Seth better than anyone, and for him to give you that, he had to be ten thousand times sure he wanted to spend the rest of his life with you."

She looked at me hopefully. "I don't want to lose him."

I gave her a squeeze. "You won't."

She straightened her back and quickly wiped away a single tear that had escaped. "You're right. What Seth and I have is special."

"I agree. You two are perfect for each other."

"And this *is* a beautiful ring," she said with a sniffle, but the sparkle began to return to her eyes.

"It really is."

She stood up and smoothed out the blush-pink sweater she was wearing. "We should probably head back in if we're going to see what happens when Luke tries to talk to Becca."

Not wanting to miss anything, I stood up and followed her back inside.

When we reached the top of the stairs, Luke was in the hallway. I assumed he was on his way to Becca's room to talk to her. He stopped when he noticed us.

"For the record, I think this is a bad idea," he told me.

"Why do you say that?" I asked.

"Becca and I were never close at Henley. She isn't going to tell me anything."

I didn't know whether or not that was true, but either way, I needed him to try talking to her. He might be our last hope.

"I think we're out of options," I said. "No one knows what Henley is up to, and we could all be in danger, including you."

"Are you sure you didn't just imagine the whole Project Josie thing?" he asked. "You did have a really high fever."

I wished I could reassure him, but I couldn't. "I don't know, but I don't trust Henley for a second. Do you?"

He shook his head, and without another word, he walked to Becca's room. He waited with his hand on the doorknob until Jen and I were back in Raina's room before going inside.

Michael looked at me expectantly when I entered the room.

"You good?" he whispered to me as I took my seat beside him.

"As good as I can be."

He nodded once and then turned his attention back to the monitor.

Luke stood confidently by the door inside Becca's bedroom.

Surprisingly, Becca laughed. "Seriously? What could you possibly want?"

Luke, not one to beat around the bush, got right to it. "What do you know about Project Josie?"

The smile faded from her lips. She seemed taken off guard by the question but quickly composed herself. "I don't know what you're talking about." She casually shrugged, but I could tell she was lying.

"That's a load of crap," Luke challenged, also seeing through her. "You know exactly what it is."

"Then, why don't you just take it out of my head, Luke? Oh, wait, *you can't*." She grinned sardonically at him.

I looked at Michael.

As if anticipating what I was going to ask, he leaned over and whispered, "Luke is unable to read her mind. He said he's never been able to read hers or yours at all. You both must have some kind of natural immunity to it, like we do."

It would be so much easier if Luke or I could just read Becca's mind. If we could read her mind, we could get to the bottom of Project Josie and maybe even the reason she believed she hated me so much.

"Whatever Henley is cooking up, it isn't in your best interest. Trust me on that," Luke told her.

"Trust you? That's a good one." Becca laughed again. "News flash: no one trusts you, Luke—not even your precious Natalie. You're so gullible. One kiss from her, and you're wrapped around her little finger, willing to betray us to save her."

How did Becca know about that?

Out of the corner of my eye, I saw Michael stiffen in his seat.

Luke didn't respond, and Becca saw it as an opportunity to put the nail in his coffin.

"Too bad you had to trick her into believing you were someone else," she said with a smirk. "No one has ever wanted you, Luke. Never in your entire, miserable life. Why would she be any different?"

Becca was a lot more dangerous than I had anticipated. This went beyond a perception that she believed she hated me. If Becca knew about Luke tricking me, it must have been because she'd been spying on us. It was becoming more and more evident that we had drastically underestimated Becca's role at Henley after he brainwashed her.

I glimpsed at Michael, wanting to gauge his reaction to all of this. As I would have predicted, he wasn't taking it well. His eyes were glued to the monitor, and his jaw was set tight. As soon as this was over, I needed to explain to him what had happened. The last thing I wanted was for him to think I would cheat on him with Luke.

Luke's confident demeanor was completely gone, and he didn't know how to respond to Becca. Instead of trying, he just walked out of her room, slamming the door behind him.

Becca smiled arrogantly. She knew that she'd gotten to him, and she had enjoyed doing it. It was a side of her I didn't think I would ever get used to seeing. The Becca I knew pre-Henley had always been careful with people's feelings. She'd always been an encourager, not a person who would use someone's insecurities to tear them down.

The second Luke opened the door to our observation room, Michael was on his feet and charging at him. Michael grabbed him and pushed him back out of the room, throwing him up against the wall in the hallway.

"Get off of me," Luke said, trying to push him away, but Michael's adrenaline was high, and there was no way Luke was going to escape him.

"You tried to take advantage of Natalie," Michael accused through gritted teeth.

I jumped up and ran into the hallway. The veins in Michael's arms and neck bulged, and I needed to break this up before he hurt Luke.

Luke sneered, "Don't be pissed just because I was there for her when you weren't."

"Stop! Please!" I begged, tugging at Michael's arm. "It's all a big mistake. It's not what you think."

"You're defending him?" Michael asked, tightening his grip on Luke's shirt.

"No," I replied adamantly. "What he did was wrong, but I don't think he was trying to take advantage."

Michael threw a hurt glance my way. He released Luke but not without giving him one last shove into the wall. Without another word, Michael turned and stormed downstairs.

Luke started to say something, but I cut him off, "Don't. *Just don't.*" I darted down the stairs after Michael.

I was still ticked at Luke for how he'd tricked me at Henley, but at the same time, I did believe he'd been trying to help me. Regardless, making sure Michael was okay was my top priority.

I found Michael downstairs, pacing around the kitchen. He stopped when he saw me.

"I'm sorry," I said.

"For what?" Michael asked with an exaggerated shrug. "For keeping the truth about Becca from me? For not telling me that you hired a private investigator? For deciding to break up with me so you could go surrender yourself to Henley? Or for kissing Luke? You're going to have to be a little more specific about what you're sorry for."

"For all of it," I admitted. My voice was stable, but I was so nervous that I thought my heart would pop out of my chest. I hated that I'd hurt him so badly, and I was terrified that he detested me now. "For the record, I didn't mean to kiss Luke. He was pretending to be you."

Michael shot a hateful look upward, as if Luke would be able to see it from upstairs.

"Before you go back up there and rip his head off," I continued, "you should know that he was trying to stop me from doing something stupid. Something that probably would've gotten me killed."

"Well then, maybe I should go to Luke for some pointers." Michael wasn't yelling at me, but I could tell it was taking him effort not to. "Because I have severely failed at protecting you from you."

I stood there, not sure how to respond to him. He needed to get this off his chest, but I was afraid that I would say something to make things worse between us.

He closed his eyes, took a deep breath, and then looked at me again. "You broke up with me. Even if you did kiss Luke, it's none of my business." He sounded defeated, and I could see the anguish in his eyes.

"I didn't want to break up with you. I did it because I thought that was the only way to keep you safe."

"Do you know what hurts the most out of all of this?" Michael's brows creased together. "It's the fact that you didn't trust me enough to tell me the truth. Even before Becca showed up in your dream, you didn't tell me that she was at Henley. You didn't trust that I would help you rescue her."

I wanted to throw my arms around Michael and reassure him that I did trust him. But just as the thought crossed my mind, he folded his arms across his chest.

"I do trust you," I explained. "I was just trying to protect you."

Michael looked down at the floor and shook his head. "I think that's just what you tell yourself."

I opened my mouth, unsure of what else to say, but I desperately wanted to find a way to fix this conflict between us.

Before I could formulate the words, I heard footsteps behind me. Michael looked up at whoever it was, and I turned around to find Raina standing in the doorway.

She shifted uneasily on her feet, glancing between us. I wasn't sure how much she'd heard, but I was positive that she hated me now more than ever.

"They need you both upstairs," she said.

Without another word, Michael walked past me and into the living room. I heard the sound of his feet as he stormed back up the stairs.

Reluctantly, I started to follow but then stopped when I felt Raina's judgmental eyes on me.

"I really was just trying to protect him," I insisted, although I wasn't sure if I was trying to convince her or reassure myself.

"Maybe, but what you did was really messed up," she replied. "You don't give him enough credit. He's been doing this a lot longer than you. He would've figured out a way to help you without getting caught."

I sighed. "I know. It's just … I was worried about stressing him out more because of his nightmares."

Raina tilted her head, confused. "What do you know about his nightmares?"

"He was dreaming about Henley …" I replied slowly, certain she was already aware. "He was having nightmares about going back. I couldn't bring myself to ask him to return, to put himself in danger for me."

Raina huffed at my response. "You don't know anything."

I didn't understand why she was pretending it wasn't true. "You know he was having nightmares. I mean, that's why you volunteered to test the dream blocker instead of making him do it." There was no way she could deny that.

Raina took a step closer and fixed her hazel eyes on me. "Yeah, I did volunteer, so Michael wouldn't have to do it, but his dreams weren't about him being at Henley. His dreams were about *you* being there."

I stood there, completely dumbfounded. *Can that actually be true?*

Raina looked me up and down. "So, congratulations. You made his worst nightmare come true." And with that, she pivoted on her heels and trotted upstairs.

Seventeen

Natalie

I avoided eye contact with everyone as I took my seat next to Jen. Instead of reclaiming his seat on the other side of me, Michael chose to stand away from the table. He leaned against the wall with his arms folded across his chest.

Raina entered the room, closing the door behind her. As she took her seat, I quickly surveyed the room, relieved to confirm that Luke wasn't there. I hadn't seen him come downstairs, so they must have sent him to another room upstairs to let things cool down between him and Michael.

Alexander leaned forward, folding his hands on top of the table. "Breaking through to Becca isn't working." He looked briefly at me. "I'm not saying we'll never get through to her, but we don't have the luxury of time right now. We need to know if Project Josie is a threat, so we can be prepared for it."

"I could try," I offered.

Alexander regarded me apologetically. "I don't think that's a good idea. Honestly, I think if she sees you, she might regress even further. We need to know what's really driving her hatred and address that before we consider sending you in there."

As much as I didn't want to admit it, if I were to walk into Becca's room right now, it would likely send her into another rage.

"Her conscious mind believes that you are the enemy," Alexander added.

That gave me an idea. "What about her unconscious mind?" I asked. "I could try to connect with her while she's sleeping."

"I didn't think you could connect with her when she was sedated?" Lorena questioned. "We've been having to sedate her pretty heavily to get her to go to sleep."

The dream connection would only work if Becca was actually asleep, and based on how she'd reacted during today's interviews with a mild sedative in her system, there was no way she was going to relax enough to sleep without something heavier. But still, I believed we could find a way to work around it.

"Yeah, but what if I can get in while her sedation is starting to wear off?" I asked, watching Alexander's reaction and hoping maybe my idea would work.

Alexander dipped his head side to side as he considered what I'd proposed. "It's a possibility, but we would need to time it just right. Even then, there's no guarantee that it will work or that we'll get the outcome we want. Regardless though, I think it's worth a try."

"What do we need to do?" I asked.

Alexander contemplated it for a moment and then replied, "If we go ahead and increase Becca's sedative now and put her to sleep, it should start wearing off around nine p.m. If we can get you into your REM sleep cycle around the same time, you should be able to connect with her before it completely wears off and she wakes up."

"How long do you think I'll have before she wakes up?"

"Thirty, maybe forty minutes," he replied. "We'll give you a mild sedative around seven thirty to help you fall asleep. It typically takes about ninety minutes to enter into REM sleep, where dreaming occurs."

It sounded complicated and chancy, but I was willing to give it a shot. I glanced over at Michael, who was deep in thought.

"Is everyone okay with me doing this?" I asked the group in general, but I was mainly checking to make sure Michael was comfortable with the plan.

Everyone nodded from around the table, including Michael.

"Now," Alexander said to me, "it's absolutely critical that you do not disclose anything about our location to Becca. We have no way of knowing whether or not she is using her dream-visitation abilities to contact Henley. We cannot give her any information that Henley could use to locate us."

"I'll be careful," I assured him. Then, I felt the urge to address something else that we hadn't spoken about. "There's one more thing."

They all looked at me expectantly.

"I don't want Luke to know about this."

"Why do you say that?" Michael asked, concerned, although I knew he wouldn't object to my request.

"I have this feeling … like he's not being completely honest about what's going on with Becca. I don't want him manipulating anything behind the scenes."

"Well, if Luke's talking, he's lying," Raina said, agreeing with me for once.

Everyone nodded, and it was settled.

A few minutes later, we dismissed, so Alexander could give Becca her sedative to start the process. I lingered in the hallway as everyone else headed downstairs.

Seth paused at the top of the staircase. "You coming?"

"Maybe later," I replied. "I need some time to collect my thoughts. I want to go into this with a clear head."

"If you need to talk it out, let me know," Seth said before continuing down the stairs.

I walked back down the hall to my room, closing the door behind me. I turned around and jumped as I realized Luke was in there, waiting on me.

"Why are you so jittery?" he asked.

I crossed my arms across my chest. "Why are you in my room?" I was annoyed by the fact that I was being denied my moment of peace.

He was ignorant to my aggravation as he sat down on the armchair, obviously not planning to go anywhere anytime soon. "How did it go with Michael? He seemed pretty pissed."

Jeez, Luke, you think?

"That's none of your business." I had no intention of discussing my relationship with Michael with him.

"He's always been a little bit dramatic," he said, staring off into space and smiling to himself, likely recalling some memory from their past together.

"Can I help you with something?"

If all Luke wanted to do was bash Michael, he could go.

Luke's gaze returned to me, and his expression became serious. "I wanted to check on you to make sure you were okay."

His sincerity surprised me.

"I'm great." My response was curt. I hoped he would just accept it and move on. I honestly didn't want to talk about it, especially with him.

He stood back up and walked over to me. His eyes carefully inspected me, and I suddenly felt exposed.

"Oh yeah?" he asked. "Then, why are you digging your fingers into your arms?"

I looked down and loosened my grip. Even though my arms had been crossed, I'd been drilling my fingernails into my forearms. I tried to rub away the red indentions they'd left behind.

I'd been trying to hold it all in, but now, I could feel the tears begin to well in my eyes. This was exactly why I'd wanted to be alone. Sooner or later, the stress of both Becca and Michael hating me was going to boil over, and I didn't want any witnesses.

As the first few tears slid down my cheeks, Luke took a step back, unsure of what to do. He stood there awkwardly for a moment and then stepped forward again. He hesitantly wrapped his arms around me.

My first instinct should have been to push him away, but instead, I allowed myself to sob freely into his chest. The pain I felt was overwhelming, and now that I'd given in to my heartache, it felt nice to be comforted.

"Shh," he whispered, stroking my hair.

I felt him lower his head so that his lips lightly rested on the top of my head. The gesture was soothing and intimate, and when the reality of what was happening hit, I pulled away from him.

What if Michael walked in? I wouldn't want him to get the wrong idea.

"Natalie," he whispered hoarsely as he moved to close the gap between us again.

I stepped further back, wiping the remaining tears from my face. "Thank you for checking on me, Luke. I really do appreciate it, but I think it's probably best if you go."

Luke had done so much to help me, and I truly owed my life to him, but it felt like we were teetering into dangerous territory. I was upset about my fight with Michael earlier, and I recognized that I was feeling vulnerable. I still loved Michael, and I knew that I would deeply regret it if I allowed anything to happen between Luke and me.

Luke frowned and eyed me for a moment. "Is that really what you want?"

"Yes," I replied firmly.

I didn't want to hurt Luke, but I also didn't want to lead him on. My heart belonged to Michael even if he didn't love me anymore.

Luke waited a second, but when he finally decided that I'd meant what I said, he walked past me and to the bedroom door. He glanced back before leaving and said, "If you change your mind, you know where to find me."

After Luke left, I curled up in bed and didn't move for what felt like hours.

I finally stirred when I heard a light knock on my bedroom door.

"Come in," I called, sitting up.

Lorena poked her head in. "You should try to eat something," she said, opening the door wider to reveal a plate consisting of a grilled cheese sandwich and a sliced apple. "You're still in the process of getting your strength back."

Seth had tried to get me to come downstairs for dinner about an hour ago, but I wasn't ready to face everyone yet. To be honest, I hadn't been hungry anyway. I just wanted to get this dream visitation over with, so we could hopefully figure out how to proceed with getting through to Becca.

I smiled gratefully at Lorena as she handed me the plate. "Thank you."

"I know this has been hard on you," she told me. "I promise things will get better."

"I hope so."

I appreciated Lorena's encouragement, but it was hard to imagine. In order for things to get better, I needed Michael to forgive me and for Becca to remember who she really was. Both seemed impossible at the moment.

Lorena sat on the side of my bed. As if she knew the struggle that was going on in my head, she said, "My son is incredibly stubborn. When he gets mad, it takes him a minute to get over it, but he always does."

"I really hurt him," I admitted after swallowing a bite of the sandwich. "I thought I was making the right decision at the time, but I wish I could go back now and change everything."

"You're not perfect, and neither is he, but you genuinely love each other, and that's what matters. Everything else is just background noise." She said it so confidently that it was no wonder she and Alexander had such a good relationship.

They'd been on the run from Henley for the majority of their marriage, and I knew that couldn't have been easy, especially with two kids, but I never sensed anything, except complete adoration for each other.

We sat in silence while I finished the rest of the sandwich and ate my apple.

When I was done, she took my plate and patted me on the leg. "It'll work out. You'll see."

Lorena stood up and walked to the door. Before she could reach for it, there was a knock. She opened it to find Alexander standing on the other side. I glanced at the clock on the nightstand. It was seven twenty-five p.m.

Alexander handed me a glass of water and a pill. "I figured you would prefer this instead of getting a shot."

"Yes," I agreed with a shudder. I never wanted to see another needle again in my life.

I put the pill in my mouth and took a big gulp of water to wash it down.

"It's a mild sedative," he reminded me as I handed the glass back to him. "Just enough to help you fall asleep."

"Fingers crossed," I said nervously. "Any advice on how to interact with her, if I'm able to make contact?"

Alexander sighed. "I'm not sure you should. If possible, try to just observe what's going on and not disturb her. If she discovers you have dream capabilities of your own, it could put her on the defensive."

I hadn't considered that. Since I had never successfully initiated the dream visits with her, she might not know that I possessed the same ability. I hadn't found out that it was a family trait or that I had the ability to do it until long after she disappeared.

"Won't she be able to sense me if I'm there?" I asked.

"It's feasible," Alexander said. "But it's also possible that she's so troubled right now that she might not detect you."

"It'll be fine," Lorena reassured me. "We're just downstairs if you need anything."

"Thank you," I told them as they left the room.

I lay back down, grateful for the sedative and hopeful that it would help me relax enough to sleep. Sure, I was emotionally exhausted, but I wasn't convinced that I'd be able to calm my mind enough to actually fall asleep.

Thankfully, after about ten minutes of lying in bed, I could feel the sedative start to kick in. I snuggled further under the covers and closed my eyes.

Becca was seated in a chair in the center of the room. She sat perfectly straight with her arms positioned on the armrests. There was nothing in the room with her, except the metal chair she was sitting on and me. I stood quietly behind her, hoping she wouldn't notice that I was there.

Three of the walls that surrounded us were a familiar shade of gray that made my stomach turn. The fourth wall was a mirror. Without a doubt, she was dreaming of being at one of Henley's facilities.

Although Becca was facing the mirrored wall and I was standing behind her, the only reflection in the mirror was hers.

I waited quietly to see what would happen. As much as I hated the idea of her dreaming about Henley, I remained out of her view.

Just when I began to think Becca would just sit there in silence for the duration of her dream, I heard a screeching noise that made my ears hurt, even in my sleep. Metal shackles emerged from the metal armrests and legs of the chair. They grew in size and locked into place around Becca's wrists and ankles. She twisted and tried to get them to release, but it was no use. The chair didn't move at all. It was as if it were bolted to the floor.

Becca started to panic, and I wanted so badly to go to her and remind her it wasn't real. But I remembered Alexander's advice and forced myself not to engage with her. If I intervened, I could make it all worse, and we might never know the truth about Project Josie or what had really happened to make her hate me so much.

The door to the room opened. It was Tonya but not quite as I remembered her. In Becca's dream, Tonya appeared taller, stronger, and more intimidating than in real life.

Tonya was dragging a metal cart with her. On top of it were multiple syringes, scalpels, knives, and even a drill. My heart began to pound at the sight of it. I could almost feel the scalpel moving across my skin even though it was still sitting on top of the cart.

Becca squirmed again, clearly expecting a pain that we both knew all too well.

Tonya seemed unfazed as she looked toward the mirror. "Where would you like me to start?" she asked. "She hasn't been cooperating with us today."

There was a pause, and tears began to stream down Becca's cheeks. She closed her eyes, as if silently praying for it all to go away. When she opened them and looked at the mirror, the reflection faded, exposing the observation room on the other side. I wasn't surprised to see Chad Henley standing in there, ready to give orders to Tonya.

Henley looked at Becca, and he seemed ... empathetic. The expression seemed so unfamiliar, coming from him.

"I'm sorry, Becca, but this is for your own good. She broke in here once, trying to kill you. If she does it again before we catch her, you need to be able to heal yourself. You have to practice."

Becca nodded as tears rolled down her cheeks. She believed him, but I couldn't understand why. I'd never given her a reason to believe I'd ever harm her, much less try to kill her.

Tonya pulled the largest of the knives from the table. Becca screamed, and thankfully, before Tonya could reach her, Becca transitioned to another dream.

I could feel my heart pounding in my chest, and I knew that if I wasn't sedated, I would surely have accidentally woken myself up by now.

Becca and I were now walking down the long hallway at Henley. I'd walked this hallway so many times that I would recognize it anywhere. I trailed quietly behind Becca as we headed in the direction of the bathroom where the showers were, but instead of going inside, we passed it.

We walked to another door, and despite the fact that I knew it would be locked in real life, Becca was able to easily push it open in her dream. I didn't know what was on the other side, but I followed her inside.

The room was large and cold. I peered from over Becca's shoulder and found myself observing at least a dozen dead bodies lying on top of gurneys. They were covered with white sheets, much like the one they'd pushed past me in the hallway. Henley stood in the middle of the room, between them all.

"Do you see it now?" he asked Becca. "Do you understand what she's capable of doing?"

Becca shook her head. "Natalie wouldn't do this."

"You saw what she had done to my office and how she'd hurt my security guards. Is that something you would've thought Natalie was capable of?"

"No …"

"She needs to be stopped before she kills us all," Henley told her. "You need to stop her before this is you or the rest of your family."

He motioned to the bodies, and they began to stir beneath the sheets. One by one, they slowly sat up on the gurneys, the sheets sliding down their faces and torsos to reveal the person beneath. Each of them looked like Becca, only with blank, zombie-like eyes.

Becca screamed and ran past me, out of the room.

I followed her into the hallway, but we were no longer at Henley.

I was now standing in a dark room. Even though I had been in this room a million times in real life, it took me a moment to register it. We were in Becca's bedroom at our parents' house.

Photos of me and Seth hung on a corkboard above her desk. Her favorite childhood teddy bear, Sonny, sat attentively on the cushion of her bay window. Everything was exactly as she'd left it.

It was silent as I looked around the room for Becca. She was lying in her bed, asleep, and as the moon cast a soft glow on her sleeping face, I realized she was dreaming of the night she'd been taken.

I cringed at the thought of her waking up to see Mr. Weber's face. As betrayed as I felt by him, I couldn't imagine what it must have been like for her. He'd been like a second father to us. It must have been terrifying to wake up in the middle of the night and realize that someone you'd trusted and loved was forcing you to leave your home against your will. Because Mr. Weber had knocked me out, I had no idea what he had done to get Becca out of the house.

Did he sedate her and carry her out? Or did he drag her out as she desperately tried to fight him?

I didn't want to watch what would happen next, but I knew that I had to be strong and press on. It was the only way to piece it all together.

Becca didn't move as footsteps approached her door. A moment later, the door opened, and two figures appeared. As they stepped closer, I realized one was Mr. Weber … and the other was me.

The me in her dream went to the side of her bed and shook her by the arm. She startled awake.

"Becca, you need to get up. We need to go," the imposter of me said.

Becca's eyes opened wide, and she sat up once she realized Mr. Weber was in the room as well.

"What's going on?" she asked.

"Seth's been in an accident. He's in the hospital. We need to go to him," Mr. Weber told her.

"What?" she cried, jumping out of bed and running to her dresser.

"No, there isn't time. We need to go now," the fake me said, grabbing her by the hand and pulling her out of the room.

I glanced into the hallway. There was no indication of where the real me was lying, unconscious.

None of this made any sense.

The room started to fade away because Becca was no longer dreaming of it.

I had a choice to make. I could either continue to follow her or allow myself to retreat back into my own dream world. As much as I wanted this confusing world to disappear and to go somewhere safer, I was prepared to force myself to push forward. One of these dream sequences could lead us to information on Project Josie.

I took a step and then stopped.

I had only been at Henley for a few weeks, and by the time I'd left, I'd begun to have a hard time telling what was real and what was false. Becca had been there for years and likely experienced the same, if not more, manipulation and torture than I had.

These obviously weren't real memories of Becca's, but she thought them to be true. She believed them enough to hate me for them. She was terrified of me and thought I was evil. This wasn't the truth, but it was a truth she'd been manipulated into accepting. And there was only one person I knew of who was capable of making her believe this was her reality.

Luke.

I was so stunned by the revelation that Luke had been involved in turning Becca against me that I was forced out of Becca's dream and back into my own. As hard as I tried to wake myself up, I was still too sedated. Instead, I lingered in my own imaginary world, floating from one to the next. It was as if I were stuck in a never-ending waiting room, anticipating the moment my subconscious would allow me to break free.

When the sedation finally wore off, I woke up with a start. My anger was fresh and ready for Luke.

I climbed out of bed, catching a glimpse of myself in the mirror above the dresser. I wore a navy T-shirt and navy-and-red plaid pajama pants. My hair was a little wild, but I didn't even bother to smooth it out as I stormed out of my bedroom and down the stairs.

I had no idea what time it was, but the sun was up. If Luke was still in bed, I had no doubt that I would drag him out by the hair on his head.

No one was in the living room as I walked through on my way to Luke's bedroom. A giggle came from the kitchen, and I realized it was Jen. Seth said something, but I didn't comprehend what it was. I was only fixated on my instinct that told me Luke was in there with them.

I entered the kitchen and stopped about six feet away from the dining table. Seth and Jen were giggling to each other while they ate bowls of cereal. Luke sat quietly at the other end, scooping up a spoonful of yogurt. They each looked up at me as I stood there, glaring down at Luke.

Out of the corner of my eye, I could see Seth smile and start to say something, but he must have seen the look on my face because he abruptly stopped. Without a word, Seth stood up and reached for Jen's hand. He quickly ushered her out of the room. My eyes didn't move from Luke.

At first, Luke stared back at me with curiosity. Then, I watched with deep satisfaction as his face grew pale with the realization that I was finally onto him.

He slowly stood up, his arms out, as if it would somehow calm me down. "It's not what you think."

I didn't want to hear it. The rage inside me was burning heavily, and it needed to come out. I could feel that my strength had returned. It might not be back in full force yet, but I was positive it was enough to get my point across.

I imagined giving Luke a shove, and he immediately flew backward, hitting the wall behind him with a thud. A small clock that hung on the wall fell and shattered into pieces on the floor.

Luke bounced off the wall and landed facedown on the hard tiled floor. He pushed himself up and looked up at me. There was fear in his eyes.

Good.

"I know you're mad," he said, standing back up. "But I can explain."

I laughed, not a genuine laugh, but one of a person on the brink of losing their mind. "Of course you can!" I taunted him. "Go ahead, Luke. I can't wait to hear it."

"You know I didn't have a choice. Henley made me do it."

I used my mind to shove him back up against the wall, holding him there. "Give me one reason why I should believe you."

"Because you know what Henley is like," he challenged, raising his voice despite the fact that he was pinned and couldn't move. "You know how sadistic he is. He wanted you, and he couldn't find you, so he used Becca to get to you. And he used me to turn her against you. He made me change her memories, including the one of the night she had been taken."

I eyed him for a second and then released him. I hadn't expected him to admit his wrongdoing so easily. I had fully anticipated this to turn into a long back-and-forth of me accusing him and him denying it. I'd even prepared myself for him to try to use his mind tricks on me to escape the situation.

He regained his balance and took a careful step toward me, but he stopped when he noticed my body tense up. I still wasn't above lashing out at him again with my powers, and he knew it.

"I didn't know you then," he explained. "I was doing what I had to do at the time in order to survive."

My instinct told me that he was telling me the truth, but my guard was still up. Even if it was the truth, it still didn't make it right.

"Why did you lie to me then? I asked you if you knew why Becca hated me, and you denied knowing about it."

Luke's brows creased together, his eyes pleading with me. "I didn't want you to despise me … I didn't want to lose you."

"Were you lying about Project Josie too?"

He adamantly shook his head. "No. I swear I have no idea what that is."

I closed my eyes, trying to stifle my anger. My intuition told me to believe Luke, but I was still furious with him. My temper could be dangerous when I was this worked up, and as much as I'd wanted to physically hurt Luke when I came downstairs, I knew deep down that I would regret it later if I did. Not to mention the fact that every time I used my powers, I put us all at risk of being discovered by Henley.

"You need to leave," I told him, my eyes still closed. I didn't hear him move, but I heard someone else run into the kitchen behind me. "For your safety, I can't be under the same roof as you right now."

Luke didn't respond.

"You heard her. Now, get the hell out," Michael said, and I felt him move to my side. His voice wasn't raised, but it was firm, and I knew his adrenaline was itching for a reason to be unleashed on Luke.

I felt a soft wind brush my arm as Luke hurried past me. I didn't open my eyes until I heard the front door to the house open and close and I was sure he was gone.

Michael moved, so he was now standing in front of me. He carefully watched me, his eyes still red from sleep but full of concern.

"What happened?" he asked.

I took a deep breath and slowly let it out, trying to calm myself down. It was something I'd learned to do when I used to have panic attacks. It seemed to work for helping me control my hostility as well.

As the fury wore off, it was replaced by a mixture of emotions. I felt betrayed but also scared, regretful, and vulnerable. I wanted nothing more than to throw myself into Michael's arms. The fact that I couldn't made the emotional roller coaster feel even more intense. I buried my face in my hands.

Michael waited patiently as I took a moment to get myself together. I heard someone else come into the kitchen but sensed when Michael gestured for them to leave because it quickly fell silent again.

Finally, I removed my hands from my face. "Can we talk outside?" I motioned to the door leading out to the back patio.

Michael nodded and walked over to the door. He held it open for me as I walked outside.

I sat down in one of the chairs, and Michael moved another chair so that he was sitting directly in front of me. He took my shaking hands in his, waiting for me to talk.

"It was Luke," I explained. "He made Becca think I was behind her kidnapping. He admitted that once Becca turned on me, they used her to lure me there." My throat felt tight as the words came out. "Henley tortured her to see if she had the same healing power I did but made her believe it was to keep her safe from me. He told her that I was trying to kill her. She's convinced I murdered all of those runaways. That's why she thinks I'm dangerous … why she hates me."

Michael squeezed my hands. "I'm sorry."

I looked up at him. "You're sorry? I'm the one who hurt you. I'm so naive. They played me, and I fell right into it."

If I looked back, honestly, all of the signs had been there. Becca hadn't been her usual self in my dreams—not since Charlotte. She'd pretended to have my best interest at heart, but she'd also said things that were out of character for her, things that were borderline cruel. I had just wanted her back so badly that I hadn't allowed myself to dwell on the fact that something seemed off.

I could kick myself for not figuring out the truth about Luke sooner. Not only had I witnessed and been victim of his manipulation techniques firsthand, but now, I knew he'd been lying about Becca. It was no wonder he had been so elusive at Henley every time I brought her up. He'd been playing games with me the entire time.

"Don't beat yourself up," Michael said. "Luke is a master at manipulation. Trust me, I've been fooled by him more times than I can count."

It definitely made sense now why Michael disliked Luke. I could just imagine what Luke had done to him and Raina at Henley.

"It was awful," I said quietly. "Her dream. It was everything I had feared from the moment I knew she was at Henley."

He looked down, sadness weighing heavily in his eyes as he stared at the scar on my arm. I realized that when he'd rescued me from Henley, his nightmares had been confirmed as well. It was clear that I'd been tortured while I was there, just as he'd feared.

I reached out and touched his face. "I had no idea about your dreams. I didn't know they were about me," I said. He looked up at me, and I removed my hand, realizing he might not want me to touch him like that. "I never meant to hurt you."

Michael swallowed hard. "I don't think you'd hurt me on purpose, but I always feel like I'm one second away from losing you forever."

I wanted to assure him that I wasn't going anywhere, but I knew that those would just be words. I'd broken his trust in me, and now, all I could do was own up to it. He had every right to hate me for what I'd put him through.

I would give anything to go back and make this right.

"What I did was wrong," I admitted. "I should have told you what was going on the second I realized that Henley had Becca. Keeping it from you was a mistake, and I completely understand why you hate me now. I don't blame you."

Michael flinched at my apology, and I worried that I'd said something to hurt him even more. "Hate you? Is that what you think?"

How can he not?

Michael cupped the sides of my face with his hands, letting his fingers trail into my hair. "I was terrified of losing you and angry that you'd lied, but I don't *hate you*. I could never hate you."

"I love you … so much," I whispered like a breath that I had to take. I wasn't sure if it was what he wanted to hear, but I needed to say it. I needed him to know that my feelings for him hadn't changed.

He leaned forward and kissed me. I'd forgotten how his soft lips made mine tingle when they touched.

He pulled back slightly to look at me. At first, I thought that maybe he regretted doing it, but as he stared into my eyes, I saw the longing that matched my own. He pulled me toward him until I was in his lap. With his fingers tightly laced in my hair, he kissed me again.

EIGHTEEN

MICHAEL

As I glanced in the rearview mirror to make sure we weren't being followed, I caught a glimpse of Becca sleeping in the backseat.

"Maybe we should've given her another dose of the sedative before we left," I thought aloud, looking at the clock.

It was almost ten a.m., and although Alexander had given her a dose in the middle of the night, she could wake up at any time now.

Natalie looked nervously back at Becca. "I think she'll be okay if we get there soon." She didn't sound convinced.

According to Alexander, the new safe house was approximately thirty minutes away from our old one. We would have liked for it to be farther away, but based on our situation with Becca, our mobility was limited. We were actually pretty lucky to get this new place as quickly as we had. It wasn't easy to find a fully furnished house that was available immediately and could accommodate all of us.

Natalie had kicked Luke out of the house around a quarter to nine, and within an hour of that, we'd gotten everyone up, packed, and on the road to the next place.

"I hope I did the right thing, throwing Luke out," Natalie said. "I mean, I know it needed to happen, but maybe I should have talked to you and Alexander first to weigh in on the consequences before I did it."

"If you hadn't kicked him out, I would have," I assured her. "You did the right thing."

I would rather move ten times than have to live with Luke. At least Natalie had had the self-control to stop herself from hurting him. If I had known that he had been in on the plan to get Natalie to surrender herself to Henley before she threw him out, I couldn't guarantee I would've had the same level of restraint. My fist still felt like it had been denied the pleasure of making contact with his face for kissing her.

"Yeah, but there's a good chance that I sent him right back to Henley."

I reached over and squeezed her hand. "It's for the best. Trust me."

She threw another wary look back at Becca. "I'm glad that she's calm, but I hate that she's probably dreaming right now. It's like she's trapped in this imaginary hell that she believes is real."

My heart ached for Natalie and how devastating this situation with Becca was for her. I wanted so badly to make it all better, but this was out of my control. The only thing I could do was be there for her and try to understand what she was going through.

"I don't think Henley realizes that I got my ability to heal from you after the accident," she said suddenly. "He hasn't figured out that I got my abilities after you transferred your energy to me when you healed me."

"What makes you say that?"

"Becca's dream," she replied. "I think Henley was torturing her and trying to get her to self-heal. If that's true, then it's probably because he believes I was born with my ability and thinks it could be hereditary."

That would be the logical assumption for Henley to make. After all, they both have the same natural abilities of strong intuition and dream visitation, and apparently, those traits did run in Natalie's family.

Natalie could be onto something. In all of the testing that Henley had conducted on me as a kid, my abilities never transferred to anyone else. Natalie was the first and only person that had happened to.

I felt a twinge of guilt, as I always did when I thought about her accident. That was the night I'd messed up Natalie's life forever in exchange for saving her. I never regretted saving her life, but I definitely second-guessed the way I'd gone about it. I always wondered what would have happened if I'd handled things differently.

Of course, I would never have let her die, but what if I'd just warned her instead? Sure, she probably would have thought I was crazy. But maybe I could've planted enough doubt in her mind to keep her off the road that night. Or perhaps, I should have followed her to the restaurant where she'd met Seth and slashed her tires. It would have been inconvenient for her, but again, she wouldn't have been able to drive home. Either Seth would have brought her home or she would have been delayed, trying to get new tires. Any of those scenarios were better than her living a life on the run, in constant danger, with powers she'd never wanted. She deserved so much better than this.

Becca shifted in the backseat. Natalie fumbled through her purse and pulled out a syringe containing the sedative that Alexander had given her in case Becca started to wake up. We'd been hoping we wouldn't have to use it.

Alexander turned down a residential street, and I followed behind him.

"I think this is it," I said.

I hoped Becca would stay groggy long enough for us to get her inside without Natalie having to inject her. Aside from not wanting to put Natalie through that, the last thing we needed was a conscious Becca seeing Natalie poking her with a needle. That would probably cause Becca to regress even further.

At the end of the street was a large three-story house. It was situated away from the other houses in the neighborhood, which was good. We didn't need to deal with nosy neighbors in close proximity.

Alexander pulled over to let me pass him and go into the driveway first. He pulled in behind me, followed by Seth. I stopped just short of the closed garage that was attached to the house.

We waited patiently while Alexander got out of his car and went to the front door. He found where the key had been hidden, unlocked the house, and went inside. A moment later, the garage door opened, and I pulled inside. Alexander closed it behind us as Natalie shoved the syringe back into her purse.

Natalie and I hurried out of the car. I carefully pulled Becca out of the backseat and carried her into the house. She was definitely in the process of waking up but wasn't completely coherent yet. Not enough to try to fight me anyway.

"Stan said there is a bedroom on the third floor. I think that would be a good place to put Becca," Alexander said as we walked past him.

I easily found the stairs on the first floor and carried Becca all the way up to the third. Natalie and Alexander were close behind me.

At the top of the stairs, there was a door that led into a large bedroom. The room looked like it had once been an attic that the owners had converted into an additional bedroom.

As we passed through the doorway, I noticed a dead bolt had already been installed to the outside of the door. I had no idea how Stan did what he did so quickly, but the man had it down to a science. It didn't matter what we needed or where; he always managed to make it happen. I could just imagine the story he'd told the installer of this dead bolt to get them to do it without being suspicious. If someone asked me to mount a dead bolt that way, I would automatically assume they were a psychopath.

Becca stirred again as I laid her on the bed, but her eyes were still closed.

I turned to Natalie. "Maybe you should go help them unload the car."

We needed to hurry up and get Becca tied back up before she was fully awake. I didn't want Natalie to see us tie up her sister. Not to mention, if Becca realized Natalie was in the room, it could send her into a rage.

Natalie quickly covered Becca with a blanket and then left.

Alexander handed me a scarf to use to tie up Becca's left hand while he worked on the right. The first time we'd tied her up in the previous house, we'd used rope, but we'd later switched to the scarves after we saw burn marks on her wrists. We wanted her secure, not in pain. Still, I was always a little concerned that the scarves weren't as durable as the rope.

I checked my knot three times before I was satisfied that it would hold.

Alexander decided to hold off on giving Becca another sedative. It was a delicate balance of trying to keep her calm but not drugging her up too much. We needed her to gain mental clarity about how Henley had brainwashed her, and she wasn't going to get there, being doped up all the time.

"We'll check on her in a little while to see how she's doing," Alexander told me as we left her room. He secured the dead bolt, so she couldn't escape.

"How long do you think we'll have to keep her locked up like this?" I asked, positive Natalie was out of earshot.

This whole situation was messed up, and we all knew it. None of us wanted to be holding Becca prisoner.

The look on Alexander's face said it before he did. "There's no way to know. At least we know what triggered her hatred toward Natalie. Now, we need to figure out how to change her warped perception of reality back to true reality."

I nodded in acknowledgment and then followed Alexander back downstairs.

Within the hour, we finished unloading our cars and got situated in our rooms.

Alexander and Lorena had the master suite on the first floor, and Raina took the bedroom next to theirs. I offered to take the couch in the office, but Seth insisted that he didn't mind. That left the three bedrooms on the second floor for me, Natalie, and Jen. Seth would probably end up in Jen's room more than his own anyway.

I was moving folded T-shirts from my suitcase to the dresser in my room when Natalie appeared in the doorway.

"Can I talk to you for a sec?" she asked timidly.

"Of course." I closed the drawer and gave her my full attention.

She sat down on the bed and looked nervously down at her hands, avoiding eye contact. Although she was starting to look healthier and more like herself, she still seemed somewhat fragile, especially when she was upset.

I sat down beside her, ready to relieve whatever was troubling her.

She looked up from her hands, her beautiful green eyes full of worry.

"What's going on?" I asked.

"Becca asked to see me, and I think maybe I should try talking to her."

My first reaction was *hell no*, but I didn't verbalize it. That wouldn't help her feel any better. I needed to stay calm and hear her out. "Why are you considering that?"

She was making the effort to include me in this decision, whereas before, she would have just done it and put herself in danger. If I pounced on her for asking, she would lose trust in me. I wanted her to confidently know that I was someone she could always count on to have her back, no matter what.

"We still have no idea what Project Josie is. Every day that passes by gives Henley an advantage."

"Do you think Becca will tell you?" I couldn't imagine Becca just handing that information over, especially to Natalie.

Natalie shifted, so she was facing me. "Not really, but I want to try. I need to at least explain to her that what she believes happened isn't real. It kills me that she thinks I am this evil person out to get her. If she's asking to see me, that must be a good sign, right?"

I didn't know how to answer her question. I'd witnessed Becca trying to choke the life out of Natalie. It was hard to imagine that she'd somehow come around on her own to rekindle their relationship. But at the same time, who was I to stop Natalie from trying to get through to her? Becca was tied up and secure. I could check the knots one final time before letting Natalie anywhere near her.

"If you want to talk to her, I'll help you prepare," I said.

I watched as relief flooded Natalie's expression. Her worry hadn't been so much about seeing Becca as it had been about my reaction to her request. Yes, I wanted her to talk to me before she ran off and did things, but I also didn't want her to feel like she had to walk on eggshells around me.

"Thank you," she said quietly.

She shifted to stand up, but I reached for her, stopping her.

"I love you, and nothing you could ever do will change how I feel about you. You know that, right?" I asked.

She nodded but not convincingly.

"I mean it," I told her, pulling her close and hugging her against my chest. "Even though I was hurt and angry with you for leaving, I never once stopped loving you."

I wanted to protect Natalie from all of the dangers that threatened us on a daily basis, but I also didn't want her to lose the spark that I had fallen so deeply in love with.

Natalie had a lot of fears, but she always managed to push through them. Doing things while afraid was so much braver than not having any fears at all. I'd always admired her for that. I didn't want to change that about her. I just wanted her to get better at thinking through her plans before acting so impulsively on them.

"I promise I will never do that to you again," she whispered.

I really wanted to believe her.

"Let's get you set up to talk to Becca," I said, giving her another squeeze.

Less than two hours later, we were almost finished with putting all of the surveillance equipment in place.

We'd contemplated whether or not we should once again hide the fact that we had cameras on Becca. Ultimately, we decided it probably didn't make much of a difference at this point. She'd already figured out that we were keeping a close eye on her, and to be honest, it gave me a little bit of comfort, knowing she was aware of it. I wanted her to be cognizant of the fact that she wasn't really alone with Natalie even if Natalie was the only person in the room with her.

Becca watched silently as Alexander and I set up the camera and microphone in her room.

As I left her room, I turned to her. "Natalie will be in shortly to see you."

I mainly wanted to check her reaction before we sent Natalie in. I anticipated a spark of anger at the mention of Natalie's name, but instead, she calmly nodded and took a deep breath. It was like she was mentally preparing herself for the encounter.

I went into my bedroom, where we'd set up the observation equipment. Everyone was in there and almost ready to go. Alexander was checking Natalie's earpiece to make sure she could hear him.

"All set?" I asked Natalie, placing my hands on her shoulders.

She looked nervous. "Yes. As ready as I'll ever be."

"If you need me, just say so, and I'll be there in a second."

She attempted a brave smile and then immediately walked out into the hall.

I didn't bother to sit down as we anxiously waited for Natalie to enter Becca's room. Instead, I stood by the door, ready, just in case she needed me.

Seth, who was sitting at the table, turned to look at me. "Do you think this is a good idea?"

Honestly, I didn't know, so I just replied, "It's what Natalie needs to do."

I could tell that Seth didn't quite agree with my answer, but he didn't say so. He just turned his attention back to the monitor.

Becca was still sitting up in the bed, just like I'd left her a few minutes ago. She seemed more peaceful than usual, which I thought was kind of odd. If she viewed Natalie as a threat, why didn't she seem more afraid or at least a little nervous?

The door to Becca's room opened, and Natalie slowly walked in. She stood there awkwardly, just staring at Becca.

I expected Becca to lay into Natalie with her snarky comments, like she had done with Seth and Luke, but she didn't. She just sat there, calmly keeping a watchful eye to see what Natalie would do next.

Natalie cleared her throat. "You wanted to see me?"

Becca nodded her head to a chair in the room. "Sit."

Natalie obeyed a little too eagerly, and I hoped Becca hadn't picked up on it like I had. Natalie was desperate to win Becca back over, which could easily be used against her.

"What do you want from me?" Becca asked her.

Natalie shook her head. "Nothing. Nothing at all." I could hear the emotion in her voice and hoped she could quickly get it under control. "I just want my sister back."

"And you think you're going to do that by keeping me locked in a room, tied to a bed?"

Natalie buried her face in her hands. This was too much for her.

I took a step closer to the door.

"Not yet," Alexander said, stopping me. "Give her a minute. She'll be okay."

My heart raced in my chest. My adrenaline was already starting to kick in, but I forced myself to stay where I was.

Natalie looked up at Becca, her emotions stable again.

"You tried to kill me," Natalie said firmly.

"You tried to kill me first." Becca lifted her chin. "You had me taken away from our family, from Seth."

Natalie adamantly shook her head. "*No*, I didn't. Those were all lies. Luke changed your memory of that night. And I've never attempted to kill you. I went to Charlotte to rescue Michael, but I had no idea you were even there."

Becca tilted her head, processing what Natalie had said.

"You know that Luke tricked me into kissing him, right?" Natalie continued. "You know he made me think he was Michael. That's what he did to you. He and Henley made you believe I had done all of these horrible things, but it wasn't me. Henley was the one behind it all."

I could feel my adrenaline spike higher at the thought of Luke kissing Natalie, of him touching her. The anger began to slowly sear my veins. I clenched my fists, hoping no one would notice. I definitely should have punched Luke when I'd had the chance.

I forced myself to take a deep breath. I needed to focus on what was going on in Becca's room in case Natalie needed my help.

"Then, why do I remember you helping Mr. Weber kidnap me?" Becca asked Natalie.

"I don't know ... maybe Luke somehow altered how you remembered the events," Natalie replied. "All I know is that I didn't help him do it. I didn't even know it was him at the time. I thought it was an intruder. Before I could stop him, he knocked me out. When I woke up, you were gone."

Natalie managed to hold herself together. Without a doubt, this was hard for her. She'd been carrying around so much guilt about how everything had gone down the night Becca was kidnapped. She ached for closure, but I was pretty sure she still wasn't going to get it. Not today anyway.

"Think, Becca. Try to remember," Natalie pleaded. "You have to have some memory of your life before you were kidnapped. You have to know that I would never, ever hurt you."

For the first time, I saw real emotion on Becca's face. She was thinking it through. Whether or not she believed Natalie, I had no clue, but maybe this was a start.

"I know that things could feel distorted at Henley," Natalie continued. "They hurt you so much and so often that you start to wonder what's real and what isn't. Deep down though, I think you know the truth."

I winced as the words came out of Natalie's mouth. The last thing I'd ever wanted was for her to experience that.

Raina looked over at me, sensing my distress. I gave a quick nod to let her know I was okay.

"Can I have some time to think?" Becca asked Natalie.

"Sure." Natalie stood up and gestured to the camera. "Just let us know if you need anything."

Looking more confident than when she'd entered, Natalie left Becca's room.

I stepped out into the hallway. I knew Natalie didn't like being the center of attention, and I wanted to check on her before she had to face everyone else.

Natalie slowly walked down the stairs, her mind clearly churning over the interaction. She looked up when she reached the bottom of the stairs. Her eyes lit up when she saw me waiting for her.

Without a word, she charged toward me, and I scooped her up into my arms.

Seth cringed as I heaped a big spoonful of grape jelly onto my plate. "With meatloaf? Really, bro?"

"It's so much better than tomato sauce or gravy," I insisted. "You should try it."

He shook his head. "Hard pass."

Raina shot an amused smirk at Seth as she took the spoon from me. She enjoyed freaking out our new friends.

Out of the corner of my eye, I saw Natalie fixing two plates. I walked over to her.

"Alexander thinks maybe I should bring Becca's dinner to her myself," she explained. "It'll help reinforce that I am sincere and care about her well-being."

I nodded despite the fact that I felt uneasy about it.

Natalie started up the stairs but stopped when she realized I was behind her. "What are you doing?"

"I'm going to eat in my bedroom and keep watch through the monitor, so I can be ready if you need me."

"She's tied up. I doubt she'll try anything," she said.

"I'd still prefer to keep an eye on things."

She didn't fight me on it. Instead, she just proceeded up the stairs to Becca's room.

Once inside my room, I set my plate down on the table and turned on the monitor. Natalie didn't have her earpiece in, so I couldn't talk to her. At least the microphone in Becca's room was still on, so I could hear what was going on.

I took a bite of my jelly-slathered meatloaf and waited for Natalie to appear on the monitor.

A minute later, she entered Becca's room. She set one plate on the dresser and held the other plate out, so Becca could see it. "Hungry?" she asked.

Becca skeptically eyed her and then shrugged.

Taking that as a yes, Natalie grabbed the chair and pulled it closer to Becca's bed, so she could easily feed her.

"I hope you still like meatloaf," Natalie said, and I could tell she was nervous. "I got you extra mashed potatoes with gravy too."

She scooped up a forkful of potatoes and brought the fork to Becca's mouth. Becca hesitated but then allowed Natalie to feed it to her.

"Lorena is a really good cook," Natalie said. "So, I can't take credit for these. I'd like to tell you that my cooking has gotten better since we were teenagers, but it really hasn't."

Natalie was attempting to connect with her, but so far, Becca's expression remained unmoved. Natalie pretended not to notice.

She fed Becca a bite of meatloaf.

"Thank you," Becca told her after she finished chewing and swallowed it.

Natalie looked up, clearly shocked by the acknowledgment. Then, she attempted to play it off. "Of course."

"So, what's the deal with Goldilocks?" Becca asked her.

Natalie paused for a second and then gave Becca another bite of potatoes.

"Jen?" Natalie asked. "Um, she's a good friend. When did you meet her?"

I was wondering the same thing. I couldn't recall a time when we'd sent Jen into Becca's room.

Becca shrugged. "I saw her in the other house. Seth had brought me some water, and she was waiting for him in the hall."

"Oh."

"Is she Seth's girlfriend?"

Natalie looked uncomfortable, but I saw her fighting through it. "Yes."

Becca let out a small laugh. "Figures. He always thought he was so charming. How many girls has he dated since me?"

"Well … a few … but none that were really serious until now."

"There's no way he can be serious about her," Becca said, rolling her eyes.

Natalie's brows creased. "Actually, they are engaged."

Becca's eyes snapped to Natalie in surprise. "Seriously?"

For someone who'd told Seth just the day before that she never knew what she'd seen in him, she sure seemed jealous by this new revelation.

Natalie sat there, uneasily caught in the middle. I knew she supported Seth and Jen's engagement, but she was torn between them and her loyalty to her sister.

"I never thought Seth would settle down with a bimbo like that," Becca said.

Natalie shook her head. "She's not ..." Her voice trailed off. She seemed conflicted between rightfully defending her friend and not wanting to upset Becca further.

Trying to break the tension, Natalie quickly pushed another piece of meatloaf toward Becca. I guessed she hoped that if Becca's mouth was full, she'd stop asking questions that Natalie didn't want to answer.

They sat in awkward silence for a moment.

Finally, Becca broke it. "Can I ask you for something?"

Natalie's eyes widened in anticipation. "Sure."

"After dinner, would it be possible for me to take a shower? Lorena—I think that's her name—comes in once a day to clean me up, but I still feel gross. A shower would be so nice. I can't remember the last time I had one without Tonya standing on the other side of the curtain, counting down the seconds."

I wished Natalie had her earpiece in. I would've told her to tell Becca she'd consider it, that we would wait and see how she did over the next day or so. If she continued to show consistent, genuine progress, we'd allow it.

Instead, Natalie smiled at her. "Sure. I think we can arrange that."

"There aren't any windows in the bathroom," Natalie said. "What's the worst that could happen?"

I didn't like the idea of allowing Becca out of her room. She had a half bath with a toilet adjoined to her room now, but there wasn't a shower, which meant we'd have to bring her down to the second floor. The idea of Becca knowing her way around the house made me uncomfortable. It would be too easy for her to figure out where

Natalie's room was. What if she managed to escape in the middle of the night?

"Not allowing her to bathe would be borderline inhumane," Natalie insisted.

I looked over at Alexander, confirming by the expression on his face that he didn't approve of this idea any more than I did. But still, Natalie had a right to an opinion on how we proceeded with her sister.

"Okay," Alexander finally said. "But if she tries anything, anything at all, she goes back upstairs immediately."

Natalie smiled, pleased with his response. "I think this will go a long way in me regaining her trust."

I hoped she was right.

Lorena called Alexander's name from downstairs.

"It's okay. We've got it," I assured him.

Alexander went back downstairs to see what Lorena needed, and I turned to Natalie. "Ready?"

"Yes."

I closed all of the open bedroom doors on the second floor as Natalie hurried into the bathroom to get it ready. She opened up the tiny linen closet, dug out a towel and washcloth, and laid them on the counter. I joined her, taking a quick look around the bathroom, opening cabinets and looking in the shower. I removed a pair of small scissors from one of the drawers and Jen's pink razor from the shower. Natalie gave me a questioning look.

"I know she's making progress, but I'm not going to just hand her a weapon," I explained.

Natalie must have agreed with me because she let it go. I followed her up to Becca's room.

Becca perked up when she saw us. "Really?" she asked, sounding excited.

Natalie smiled and nodded. "Yes."

I stepped forward, needing to be the voice of reason. "Look, I'm trusting you here," I told Becca. "I'm going to untie you and bring you to the bathroom, but you have to promise me you aren't going to try anything. If you do, no shower. Understand?"

Becca nodded with anticipation in her eyes.

I motioned for Natalie to wait by the door of Becca's room. I wanted to create as much distance between them as possible, just in case Becca got the idea to lunge at Natalie again.

When Natalie was safely by the door, I untied Becca's left hand. She remained perfectly still as I walked around the bed to the other side and undid the right hand. Becca shifted her legs over the side of the bed and slowly stood up. I reached down to take her arm and help her up. She didn't try to fight me at all.

"Thank you," she said quietly as I helped steady her.

Even though I was confident she was now stable enough to walk, unassisted, I held on to her arm as we went down the stairs. She was being compliant, but I wasn't going to take any chances.

When we reached the bottom of the stairs, I ushered Becca to the bathroom.

"Everything you should need is already in there," Natalie said. "But just let me know if you need anything else."

"Keep the door unlocked," I told Becca. "We'll be right outside, so just come out when you are done."

Becca nodded, and Natalie closed the door. Natalie turned to me, and I could read the happiness all over her face.

Then, I heard Natalie's stomach rumble and realized that she hadn't touched her dinner. She had been so focused on feeding Becca and trying to bond with her that she'd forgotten all about it.

"I'll wait here," I told her. "Why don't you run upstairs and grab your plate? You can eat here while Becca is in the shower."

She trotted upstairs, and I took a seat in the hallway, right across from the bathroom door. I leaned my head against the wall, carefully listening for any sign of trouble but everything was quiet.

Natalie returned with her plate of food and sat next to me on the floor. I was sure it was cold by now, but she took a bite anyway.

"Thank you for being so understanding about all of this," she said. "I really feel like we've made some progress today."

I hoped so, but I wasn't as confident as she was. I didn't quite understand how Becca's mood had shifted so quickly from an *I want you dead* rage to a civil request for a shower. It didn't add up, but I also didn't have any strong evidence to suggest otherwise. Until I was sure one way or the other, I would just err on the side of caution. If Natalie was anywhere near her, I would be there to keep an eye on things, to keep her safe.

"I didn't know what to say to her before, when she asked me about Jen," she whispered. "I didn't want to upset her, but I also didn't want to lie to her."

"I think it's good that you told her the truth. You can't control other people's reactions to things. That's up to them, not you." I was referring to her situation with Becca, but after I said it, I realized I meant it for our relationship too.

Natalie was constantly scared of hurting everyone that it often led her to take matters into her own hands. Unfortunately, that almost always resulted in her risking her own well-being.

She contemplated it for a moment as she chewed on a piece of cold meatloaf. Then, she whispered, "I still think Seth would have proposed to Jen even if he'd known Becca was still alive."

"I believe you're right." I hadn't known Seth and Becca when they dated, but I'd spent enough time around him with Jen to know that they were really in love and a great fit for each other.

We sat in silence for a second, and I started to feel nervous by how quiet it was. I leaned forward.

"What?" Natalie asked, confused. "I don't hear anything."

"Exactly."

Natalie looked away from me and to the bathroom door.

"We should hear running water by now," I told her.

Natalie slowly moved her plate from her lap to the floor.

I was about to stand up and knock on the door when we heard a loud crash come from inside the bathroom. It was the sound of breaking glass shattering against the tiled floor.

We both jumped up. Without any regard for whether or not Becca was dressed, I tried to open the door, but it was locked. I never heard her lock it.

I pounded on the door. "Becca?" I yelled.

Natalie joined me, pounding on the door and calling her name.

There was no response.

"Check the doorframes for a spare key," I told Natalie before throwing my body weight against the door.

In almost every house we'd ever rented, the owners kept spare keys to the rooms above the doorframes in the hallways in case a kid accidentally locked themselves inside.

Natalie reached above the doorframe but came up empty-handed and ran to the next door in the hallway.

"I can't find the key," she said, sounding like she was on the verge of panic. She raced to another door and searched again.

I backed up and charged at the door, throwing my shoulder in front of me. My adrenaline had picked up, and I knew before I even hit the door that it would give upon impact. I was right, and the door flew open, bouncing off the wall on the other side.

As I stormed into the bathroom, I was prepared for a fight. I was certain that Becca had broken the mirror in order to arm herself with a piece of glass to use as a weapon.

How could I have been stupid enough to agree to this?

Sure enough, the mirror was shattered, but as my eyes landed on Becca, the situation was nothing like I had anticipated. Instead of confronting Becca, I stared down at her, lifeless, in a pool of her own blood.

Nineteen

Natalie

The eerie silence that emanated from the bathroom told every instinct within me that something was terribly wrong. A knot quickly formed in my stomach. It twisted and turned violently, confirming my fears.

I raced back down the hall toward the bathroom. Michael leaped forward onto the bathroom floor, and that was when I realized Becca was down there, unconscious. Blood gushed from a wound on her neck. A large shard of sharp glass from the vanity mirror that she'd broken lay next to her hand.

I screamed and instinctively threw my hands over my mouth. I wanted to jump in, lay my hands on her, try to heal her, but I was frozen in place.

This can't be happening.

Michael quickly took action. He placed his hand on her throat, trying to heal her wound. Her blood seeped between his fingers, and I had to look away.

There is so much blood.

The sight of the blood reminded me of Henley, of them cutting into me. I remembered how the metal blade of the scalpel had felt as it glided across my abdomen. I felt nauseous.

I heard footsteps behind me and shook the thought from my head.

Alexander rushed by me, dropping to the floor beside Michael. He lifted Becca's arm, pressing his fingers to her wrist.

I held my breath as Seth stopped at my side, followed by Jen. He bent forward with his hands on his knees. The sight of Becca had literally knocked the wind out of him. Jen reached out and rubbed her hand up and down his back.

After everything we've been through to get her back, we can't lose her now.

"What do you need?" Lorena called out to Alexander from behind me.

Instead of answering Lorena, he looked at me. "Do you know her blood type?"

My mind went blank.

"Natalie?" Alexander pushed, urgency in his voice.

"A-positive," I replied as my brain remembered how to function again.

"And yours?"

"O-negative."

"Perfect." Alexander looked at Lorena. "Can you text Stan and tell him we need supplies to do a blood transfusion? Tell him *stat*."

Lorena hurried away, and Michael lifted his hand from Becca's neck. The wound had healed, but she was still unconscious.

"Let's pick her up and get her into bed. I need to check her vitals. As soon as the equipment arrives, we'll do a transfusion to replace the blood she lost," Alexander instructed.

Michael carefully lifted Becca off the floor and carried her out of the bathroom. Seth and I parted to let them pass between us.

Lorena reappeared at the top of the stairs, her cell phone in one hand and Alexander's medicine bag in the other. "The supplies will be here within the hour. Raina is downstairs, waiting for it," she told Alexander as she handed him the bag.

I turned and looked back at the bathroom. A trail of blood dripped from the countertop onto the already-large pool that had accumulated on the floor. I started to feel light-headed.

Lorena rested her hand on my shoulder. "Go with Becca. I've got this."

"Thank you," I muttered.

In a daze, I stumbled up the stairs behind Alexander. Seth came with me, but Jen remained behind to help Lorena.

Michael laid Becca down on the bed. Her pajamas were soaked in blood, which had left large splotches all over Michael's shirt. He lifted the shirt over his head and removed it. He balled the soiled shirt up in his hand. His bare chest heaved up and down as he caught his breath.

We watched in silence as Alexander examined Becca.

"You did good," Alexander told Michael. He used the stethoscope to listen to Becca's heart. "I think you got to her just in time." He stood straight up and removed the stethoscope from around his neck. "We'll do the blood transfusion, and then I think she will be okay."

"Shouldn't she be awake though?" Seth asked, looking nervously between Alexander and Michael.

"It will take her some time to heal properly. When Michael healed Natalie, she slept for several days. I think we can expect that to be a possibility here as well, given the severity of her injuries," Alexander explained. "We'll keep a close eye on her, but I have every reason to believe she will make a full recovery."

Stan came through, as always, in having the proper supplies dropped off to complete the blood transfusion. As much as I hated needles, I eagerly allowed Alexander to take as much blood as he needed from me in order to help Becca. Michael waited with me, holding the hand of my free arm until Alexander was done.

Alexander asked that I remain seated and reclined for a few minutes while I drank some apple juice and ate a few chocolate chip cookies that Jen had brought me.

Even though Becca was still unconscious, I regretted not being by her side during the transfusion. But Seth was with her, and I knew she was in good hands.

"I don't understand," I said to Michael. "She didn't seem depressed or anything. She actually seemed better. I thought she was coming around."

Michael looked at me, regret in his eyes. "I should never have agreed to her request."

I reached out and stroked his arm. "It's not your fault at all. I was the one who asked to let her do it. If it wasn't for you, she would be …" I couldn't finish the sentence. It was too painful.

"She's been through a lot," he said. "It could be more than she feels like she can handle. I want to talk to Alexander about getting her some professional therapy when she wakes up. Maybe Stan can find a psychiatrist who can be discreet about our situation."

I knew that idea was risky and not likely feasible, but I appreciated how Michael was looking out for her. Becca couldn't spend the rest of her life tied up and sedated, but without getting her real help, I didn't think we could ever trust her to be alone again. I was at a loss as to what to do with her.

"We'll figure something out," he said, as if he already knew what I was thinking.

I yawned. "I wonder what time it is."

"I'm not sure, but it might not be a bad idea to call it a night. You've been through a lot today."

I didn't put up a fight as Michael helped me up and walked me back upstairs to my room. A part of me wanted to check on Becca to see how the transfusion was going, but I decided to let Alexander do his work in peace and trust that he would send Seth down if they needed me.

Without bothering to change out of the yoga pants and T-shirt I'd been wearing all day, I crawled into bed.

"I don't want to be alone," I admitted.

Michael turned off the light, and I could see the silhouette of him taking off his jeans. Wearing only his boxers, he climbed into the bed next to me. He gathered me in his arms, and I laid my cheek against his bare chest.

We lay there in silence for a few minutes. I wasn't sure if he was asleep yet, but I was still wide awake, thinking about everything that had happened today with Becca and Luke. Henley had managed to hurt us, even outside the confines of his facility walls, and he'd used our siblings to do it.

"Are you worried about Luke?" I whispered. "I mean, I know you're worried he's going to go back to Henley and help him try to find us, but are you worried about Luke himself and what will happen to him if he does go back?"

Michael sighed thoughtfully. I knew it wasn't a question he would necessarily want to answer, but I was curious to know what he was thinking. I knew him well enough to know that even though he was angry with Luke, he still wouldn't want anything bad to happen to him. Michael wasn't that type of person.

"Luke chose this for himself a long time ago," he replied. "You don't need to feel guilty about throwing him out for what he did. If he goes back to Henley, that's his choice too."

"Can I ask you a question?"

"Of course."

"Why didn't you tell me about Luke?" I was careful to make sure the question didn't sound accusatory because it wasn't. I had Luke's side of the story and was interested to hear Michael's.

He paused, likely thinking through his answer. "I don't know. I should've told you. It's just that I don't think of him as family. We've never been close."

"Not even as kids?"

"No," he replied. "When we were kids, Henley always focused on me and my ability to heal. He spent more time testing that than Raina's telekinesis or Luke's ability to read minds. I know this is going to sound crazy, but I think Luke was jealous of the attention I received."

"Did he know that Henley was hurting you?"

"Yes … but Luke was always oddly competitive with me. Even when it came to Raina. It was like he would try to manipulate her into choosing him over me."

I thought about how Luke had shown up in my room after my argument with Michael. *Was that another one of his games to see if I would choose him over Michael?*

"Try to get some sleep," Michael said, kissing my temple. "I'll be right here if you need me."

I closed my eyes and allowed myself to feel safe in Michael's arms.

I stood inside of an abandoned warehouse. The wooden floor, splintered and broken, creaked as I took a step forward.

Graffiti adorned the brick walls, although most of it appeared in strange letters and symbols that I didn't recognize. There was, however, one word on the opposite end of the warehouse that stood out loud and clear. In white letters, the name JOSIE *was spelled out in perfect print.*

Perhaps this was the clue we'd been waiting for. Maybe my intuition was finally going to give us some insight into who Josie was. I had no choice but to approach the wall and see what else remained to be discovered.

I passed an empty red shipping container, sitting off to the side of the warehouse. Its door was partially cracked open. My pulse began to race, as I half-expected something to emerge from the ominous shadows inside it.

On the side of the shipping container was a tattered poster, caked in dirt. It was torn, and the design was hard to make out, but it looked like two green arrows pointing me forward. The arrows appeared to almost be competing with each other with one slightly in the lead.

I hesitated and waited to see if a knot would appear in my stomach, but everything seemed perfectly fine. My intuition gave no indication of imminent danger, so I decided to follow the advice of the arrows and continue toward the writing on the wall.

I passed several broken windows as I made my way to the wall. It was nighttime, so I couldn't see anything beyond the window, except darkness.

I stopped and stood directly in front of the brick wall, looking up at the JOSIE *sign. To my left, in the dark corner behind the shipping container, I heard a sniffle.*

"Is someone there?" I asked, unable to see them in the dim light.

They didn't answer, but I heard a girl whimper.

"Hello?" I tried again, keeping my voice soft.

I waited, hoping the girl would emerge.

A moment later, a small black Mary Jane shoe appeared, followed by another. The feet weren't moving toward me. Instead, the moonlight from the broken windows above me sent a trace of light across the floor and to the feet. It continued up a pair of tiny legs, which were covered in white tights. The light moved over a pewter-blue dress, like a spotlight, and up to the white collar until it finally revealed the face of a little girl. She appeared to be about six years old with dark hair and round, terrified eyes.

I knelt down in front of her. "Are you okay?"

The little girl shook from where she sat on the ground, clutching her knees to her chest. She watched me, as if I were a dangerous threat to her.

"I'm not going to hurt you," I assured her. "I'm Natalie. What's your name?"

She shook her head but said nothing.

Then, it dawned on me.

I looked up at the graffiti and then back down at her. "Are you Josie? Is that your name?"

The little girl nodded but warily eyed me.

"What are you doing here, Josie?" I asked, remembering that this was just a dream and the little girl wasn't actually here.

"Help me," she whimpered. "He's after me."

I felt a chill, cold as ice, run through my body. I didn't know who this little girl was, but I knew exactly who was after her.

"Why is he after you? Do you know?"

She looked up at me. "Because I'm like you."

I shook my head, trying to figure out how that could be true.

"I'm not going to let him get you. Where are you?"

She didn't move, but her eyes took in the wall to her left and the shipping container to her right. "Here," she replied.

She was in this warehouse, somewhere in the real world.

"Do you have any idea where this warehouse is?" I asked her.

"Close, but it's no use," she replied, sniffling. "You can't save me."

My stomach did a flip-flop, as if trying to tell me something. It was more of a jittery butterfly than a knot. Then, I remembered my prom dream and how Becca had warned me that her *death would be my fault.*

I wasn't going to let that happen.

"Stay where you are," I told her. "I'm going to come for you."

I wanted to hold on to the dream a little longer to see if I could get any more information from Josie, but I jolted awake. I sat up in a panic, trying to figure out where I was.

I felt movement next to me and realized it was Michael waking up.

I wiped the sweat from my forehead as I tried to catch my breath.

"You okay?" Michael asked, groggy but awake enough to know something was wrong. He sat up next to me, rubbing my back, trying to calm me.

I shook my head, unable to stop the overflow of emotions. I began to sob for the little girl, so alone and helpless.

He pulled me to him, gently stroking my hair. "I've got you. You're safe. Was it a nightmare about Henley?"

I shook my head again and pulled away from him, rubbing the tears from my eyes. "It was Josie."

"Josie?" he repeated, alarmed. "What do you mean?"

"She's a little girl, Michael … an innocent little girl." I felt the emotion creep back in, tightening my throat, threatening to choke me, but I managed to hold it together. "Henley is after her. I think he's going to kill her."

"We aren't going to let that happen," he assured me.

"When Becca appeared in my dream when I was at Henley, she told me, 'You're going to be responsible for her death.' That was the same dream where I overheard them talking about Project Josie. What if it's not a coincidence?"

"How long do we have to find her?"

"Not very long. I-I think she's hiding now. I told her to stay there." I shivered as I recalled how scared she'd been. "We have to save her, Michael. I don't know who she is, but we have to protect her from Henley."

It was only a little after three a.m., but one by one, Michael and I woke up everyone else in the house with the exception of Becca. As Michael started a pot of coffee, I quickly ran upstairs to check on Becca.

I cracked open the door to her room, just long enough to verify she was still sound asleep, and then locked it back in place. As Alexander had said, she would probably sleep for some time, but I'd needed to see for myself. When she woke up, I needed her to know that I was here for her.

Downstairs in the living room, Seth and Jen were snuggled together on the love seat, barely awake. They each held a fresh cup of coffee in their hands.

Raina scowled as she dropped down into the couch with an agitated thud. "This'd better be good." She folded her arms across her chest.

Lorena handed Raina a cup of coffee as she and Alexander sat down on the couch with her.

Lorena looked around apologetically. "Raina's not really a morning person."

"You say it like she's an *anytime* person," Seth mumbled.

Jen elbowed him.

Michael motioned for me to sit in the armchair, but I shook my head. I wanted to stand. For some reason, standing felt more productive. My nerves weren't going to allow me to sit.

Instead of taking the chair for himself, Michael just sat on the arm of it.

"Okay, so what's going on?" Alexander asked, giving me his full attention.

Everyone looked at me expectantly.

"I had a dream, and I have reason to believe that Josie is a little girl who has the ability to heal herself, like I do," I explained.

"Is that possible?" Lorena asked, looking between me and Alexander in shock.

Alexander creased his brows and sat up a little straighter. "I don't know, but I also didn't think it was possible for Natalie to have that ability. It doesn't seem feasible that a complete stranger would have it."

"Could it be just a regular dream? Like, from your imagination?" Jen asked.

"It could be," I admitted. "But what if it's not? If Josie is real, she's in a warehouse right now, depending on me to get to her before Henley does."

Everyone was silent, not sure what to think about it all. It did seem farfetched, I agreed, but I wasn't willing to gamble with her life.

I can't be responsible for her death.

"Do you know where this warehouse is?" Alexander asked.

I shook my head. "I don't."

Raina let out an exasperated sigh. "Can I go back to bed while you figure it out?"

Everyone ignored her.

"Can you describe it? Maybe something will come to you," Alexander suggested.

Although I never dreamed of the exterior of the warehouse, I did my best to describe the interior. I told them how it'd appeared to be abandoned, how the wooden floor was broken into splintery boards, and how most of the windows had been busted out. I described the red shipping container that had such a creepy presence.

I began to explain the old poster with the green arrows stuck to the side of the shipping container when Seth stopped me.

"Say that again," he requested.

I did my best to remember. "It was white paper, I think, but it was torn and really dirty, like it had been there forever. There were two thick green arrows, one slightly in front of the other, kind of staggered though. They were pointing me to the *JOSIE* graffiti on the wall."

Seth jumped up, patted his pajama pants where his pant pockets would normally be, and looked around. He hurried out of the room and into the kitchen. We watched in confusion as he returned and typed something into his phone.

"Is this what you saw?" he asked, thrusting his phone in front of my face.

The phone was so close that I couldn't make out anything. I took the phone from him and lowered it, so I could see what he was talking about. As soon as I laid my eyes on it, I was positive it was the same logo.

"That's it!" I said. "What is that? How did you know?"

I looked more closely at the picture, and they weren't actually just thick arrows; they were trees that were pointed horizontally, like arrows. They looked like a cross between a tree and a paper plane flying through the air.

"This is Tyler Twins Paper Company. This was their logo," he replied, taking his phone back. "We used to buy their copy paper when I worked at Clark and Weber. We switched to another brand right before I quit because they went out of business."

Michael stood up. "Any idea where their warehouses are located?"

"On it," Jen said, already searching on her phone. If anyone could find it, it would be her.

"I've never seen that logo before in my life. I don't think it was just my imagination," I said with a shiver.

If the logo was real, it probably meant that Josie was too.

"Okay," Jen announced, "there are two warehouses less than forty miles from here that used to be owned by Tyler Twins Paper Company to store and distribute their paper." She looked up from her phone. "How do we know which one it is?"

"We don't," Michael replied.

The idea of choosing the wrong one terrified me.

"What if we split up into two groups, each one going to one of the warehouses?" I suggested.

It was risky though. We would be safer if we all stuck together.

"I don't see that we have much of a choice," Alexander agreed.

"Raina and I can't be in the same group though," I blurted out without thinking of a better way to convey what I really wanted to say.

Raina looked at me, annoyance clearly written all over her face. "What's that supposed to mean?" she asked, throwing her arms up in frustration despite the fact that we all knew she wouldn't choose to be in my group anyway if given the choice.

"I didn't mean it like that," I clarified. "Hear me out. When Becca appeared in my dream, she told me that I would be responsible for her death. *Her.* She never said Josie. I just assumed that's who she meant. It would be safer for Raina if she wasn't with me during the rescue, just in case something goes wrong."

Lorena looked scared, and for a moment, I anticipated her asking Raina not to go. She didn't though, and I realized she was probably used to the idea of her family being in danger. They'd been dealing with that reality every day since rescuing Michael and Raina from Henley. It had been part of the job since she signed up to be their mother.

"It's actually not a bad plan," Alexander rationalized. "Raina and Natalie both have telekinesis, which could come in handy if there were a confrontation." No one contradicted him, so he continued, "So, we have group A with Natalie and group B with Raina."

"I'm going with Natalie," Michael immediately chimed in, and I saw Raina shoot him a dirty look.

Before I'd come along, they'd been inseparable. Now that I was in the picture, he'd chosen to leave with me instead of her on more than one occasion. As much as I wanted her to warm up to me, I also selfishly wanted to be with Michael, so I didn't push back on his declaration.

"She might need my strength. Raina has it, too, for her group," Michael explained.

"Okay, I'm going with Raina," Alexander concluded. "I don't have any unique abilities, but I can shoot."

"I'm going too," Seth insisted. "I can, um, punch people in the throats."

"Seth, that was literally one time," I challenged.

I wasn't trying to belittle him, but punching Henley's security guard was the only time I'd seen Seth punch anyone in his entire life. The truth was, I didn't want Seth anywhere near Henley ever again. He'd almost already been killed on two separate occasions.

"But it was a *good* punch," he challenged back. "I'm going. If you two are going together and you both have powers, maybe two of us regular humans can help balance out things on Raina's side."

"Or slow me down," Raina mumbled under her breath.

Jen and Lorena exchanged an awkward look, and I sensed they were trying to figure out how they could help.

"Would you stay here and keep an eye on Becca?" I asked, looking between them. "She'll probably just stay asleep, but if she does wake up, you could give her another sedative to help keep her calm. I would feel so much better, knowing you were here with her. I don't want her to be alone."

Lorena smiled kindly at me. "Of course."

I relaxed a little, knowing that Becca would be well taken care of while I was gone and also knowing that both Lorena and Jen would be safely out of harm's way.

TWENTY

NATALIE

It took us less than an hour to formulate a plan. We all knew it wasn't perfect, but if Josie really was waiting on us to save her, the clock was ticking. We had to move regardless of whether or not we'd thought through every possible scenario.

The plan was actually very simple. Both groups would leave at the samc time, heading in different directions to their warehouse. The warehouse that Raina's group was assigned to was about fifteen minutes closer, so they should reach theirs first. They'd contact me and Michael to let us know when they arrived. From there, they would have ten minutes to investigate, find Josie, and call us back.

Their call would be critical for me and Michael to know whether or not we were to proceed to our warehouse location or if we needed to turn around and provide them with backup at their location. No phone call at the ten-minute mark would automatically mean the latter.

In the best-case scenario, Raina's group would quickly find Josie and call us, and we would all regroup back at the house.

Unfortunately, there were multiple worst-case scenarios. Henley could already be at one of the two warehouses. Or we could be too late, and Josie could be gone. There was simply no way to know for sure until we got there and investigated.

"Who will have guns?" Raina asked, still sitting in her same spot on the couch. She seemed much more awake now that she was on her third cup of coffee. Each cup had been at least one-third pure sugar.

"Good question," Alexander said. He turned to Seth. "Have you ever shot a gun before?"

"Does laser tag count?" Seth asked.

Raina rolled her eyes. "The fact that you would even ask—"

"Raina," Alexander cut her off before she could finish her insult. He turned to me, his eyebrows raised.

I shook my head. "No."

"We don't have enough time today to do firearms training, so only Raina, Michael, and I will carry guns," Alexander concluded. "Natalie, you'll have to rely on your abilities as your weapons. And, Seth, you'll wait in the car while Raina and I investigate."

Seth opened his mouth to protest.

"We need a lookout and a getaway car. If something goes wrong, you need to call Michael and Natalie, so they can turn around and come help us," Alexander told him. "You're also going to be in charge of our check-in."

Jen visibly relaxed as Seth nodded. He was okay with it as long as he had a valuable part to play.

"One last thing I want to reiterate before we leave," Alexander said. "Everyone needs to remain extremely vigilant. We don't know anything about Josie. This could be a trap. She could very well have abilities like Natalie's but be on Henley's side."

"She's just a little girl," I said, shocked by the suggestion.

Alexander frowned. "There was a rumor that Henley had multiple facilities, just like the one I worked at. The rumor was, he was raising other children—like Michael, Raina, and Luke—who had been created by other scientists. At the time, I didn't think it was true, but now, we can't afford to assume anything."

That thought had never crossed my mind. I'd assumed that Michael, Raina, and Luke were the only ones since Alexander had created them himself. It never dawned on me that Henley could have other scientists working on similar projects.

"There's also the possibility that Luke could be behind all of this somehow," Raina chimed in. "If we do locate this kid, how will we even know if it's really her? It could be Luke pretending to be her to trap us."

"We won't know …" Michael replied. "But if there is a chance that this girl is real and in danger, I am willing to take that risk to save her."

No one argued with him. We all knew he was right, and we were also willing to accept the risk.

"If no one else has any questions, go get ready," Alexander said. "We will meet outside to leave in ten minutes."

We all scattered to our rooms to quickly get dressed. I threw on a pair of jeans, sneakers, and a fitted long-sleeved shirt. It was cold outside, but I didn't want to feel confined in a jacket. I pulled my hair into a ponytail to keep it out of my face.

I stepped out into the hallway to find Michael waiting on me. He was wearing jeans, a charcoal-gray T-shirt, and a black jacket.

He nodded for me to come to his room for a minute.

I followed him inside, and he closed the door behind us.

"I know Alexander said he didn't believe the rumor was true, but I do. I think there were other kids like us, being held captive at other Henley facilities," he said. "Regardless, if it wasn't true then, it's probably true now. I doubt he stopped with just the three of us."

"Okay …"

Michael put his hands on the sides of my arms, looking seriously into my eyes. "I think there's merit to what Alexander was warning us about. I need you to go in there with a full understanding that the little girl might actually be our enemy. I know that's not something that would be easy for you to comprehend in the moment. You need to prepare yourself now, so you aren't caught off guard by her if she is."

"Oh."

Even though Alexander had already warned us about the potential threat, Michael was right. I still would've had my guard down around her and wouldn't have reacted quickly if she turned on us. The reality was, if she had the powers that Michael, Raina, Luke, or I had, it would be easy for her to take us out if we weren't expecting it from her. Henley was evil enough to orchestrate something like that.

"I'll be vigilant," I assured him. When he didn't move, I realized there was more he wanted to discuss. "What is it?"

He hesitated, and I could tell he was struggling with what he wanted to say. "I need you to promise me that you are going to be cautious about everything there. No matter what happens, you must put your own safety first."

I shook my head. There was no way I would agree to that. Agreeing meant I was promising to put my own safety above his, and I would never do that. I would die before I allowed something to happen to him.

Michael closed his eyes, trying to control the frustration that I could see building inside of him. "I can't do this unless you promise." He opened his eyes and locked them with mine. "I won't be able to focus in there if I think you're going to go rogue and deliberately do something to put yourself in danger. It will get us both killed."

I reached my hand up, touching his cheek. "I know I broke your trust, but I promise you that I won't ever do anything like that again. We're really in this together. I mean it." That, I could promise him, and I hoped that he could feel my sincerity.

"Losing you would completely destroy me," he whispered as he leaned his forehead against mine and closed his eyes.

"You're not going to lose me." I moved my hand to the back of his head, threading his hair between my fingers. I stepped up onto the tips of my toes and pressed my lips to his, hoping my kiss would reassure him.

He firmly wrapped his arms around my waist. Just as his lips moved from my lips to my neck, I thought I'd heard someone call his name. He didn't stop, so I thought maybe I'd imagined it.

"Michael?" Raina called from downstairs. "Natalie?"

This time, I was positive I'd heard it.

He lifted his head and sighed as he looked down at me. "I guess our ten minutes are up."

"I guess you're right."

He loosened his grip but didn't release me. "But after we're done saving Josie's life, we are coming back here and picking up right where we left off."

I smiled up at him. "Deal."

I kept my eyes glued to the clock on the dashboard of the car as Michael drove us to the warehouse. I turned the cell phone over and over in my hands, impatiently awaiting Seth's call.

"You can call and check on him if it'll make you feel better," Michael offered. "They are probably pretty close to arriving."

"No, I can wait." I was anxious to know what was going on but wanted to stick to the plan that everyone expected.

"I've been thinking about a way to maybe help Becca remember who she was," he said, changing the subject.

"You have? What?"

"Well, do you recall me telling you about how I dreamed about you before we ever actually met?" he asked.

"Yes."

How could I forget? Those dreams were what had led him to save my life. After learning that Becca was alive, I had been certain that she was the one who'd planted them there.

"I mostly dreamed of your accident, but before that, there were also a few others. I think some of them were memories. Becca's memories."

This was news to me. He never told me specifically what any of the dreams had been about, but I'd just assumed they were all of the accident.

"Do you remember any of them?" I asked in disbelief.

He squinted, as if trying to evoke the memory. "Pieces mostly. They seem to have faded over time, like any other dream. There's one that specifically comes to mind. The one about the yellow rain boots."

I tilted my head, slightly confused.

"Does that sound familiar?" he asked.

"Well … I did have a pair of yellow rain boots, but I can't think of anything significant about them."

He glanced over at me, smiling at some memory I couldn't recollect. "That sounds about right."

"What was your dream about?" I asked, my curiosity piqued.

"I'm not sure where you were. A park maybe? You had on a rain jacket and bright yellow rain boots, but you noticed another girl who didn't have either."

"Becca and I were walking home from school," I said, reflecting back to the day.

Becca, Seth, and I used to walk home from school since both the middle and high schools were less than a mile from our houses. Before I'd moved up to high school, Becca and Seth used to wait for me at a nearby park, and we'd walk together.

On this particular day, Seth had been home sick, so it had just been me and Becca. As I reached the park to meet up with Becca, it started to pour. It had been raining that morning, so I'd worn my navy rain jacket and yellow rain boots to school. Not the best fashion move, but I always preferred practical comfort over being trendy, even back then.

"Who was the other girl?" he asked.

I shrugged. "Just some girl from my class. I don't even know her name. We weren't friends, but I'd always gotten this feeling that she didn't have a great home life. Like, maybe her parents didn't care for her properly or something."

The thought made me sad as I recalled her coming to class in day-old clothes on more than one occasion.

"What else did Becca show you?" I asked Michael.

"You ran up to her, and without hesitation, you took off your rain boots and gave them to her. You gave her your jacket too. You walked home in your socks." He looked at me again thoughtfully. "You were just being typical you."

I couldn't help but smile as I thought of how furious Mother had been when I got home. She'd yelled at me to take off my socks as I left puddles of water and mud all over her pristine wood floor. That felt like it had happened a million years ago.

"How do you think that memory can help Becca?" I asked.

"Well, if she could visit my dream and show me memories of you from her past, maybe you could do the same. Maybe you could replace the false memories she has with real ones. At some point, she's got to realize that they really happened, right?"

I nodded. "It's worth a try."

It was a great idea, although I had never tried anything like that before. I just hoped I could figure out how to do it.

"Did you see Becca in any of your dreams?" I asked, wishing Michael had gotten a chance to know the real Becca.

He shook his head. "No, I don't think so. I just saw the accident and some other memories like they were being played out on a movie screen."

The phone in my hand began to ring, and I jumped in surprise. I'd been so lost in the conversation that I'd completely forgotten what we were doing for a moment.

My fingers fumbled to answer the call.

"Seth," I eagerly greeted him.

"We just pulled in," he said. "I'm looking at the outside of the warehouse now."

"Does it look run-down at all?" I asked.

"Not really," he replied. "It's definitely vacant, but it looks well taken care of. The outside of it anyway. No one has gone inside yet."

Michael looked at me expectantly, but I just shook my head. It didn't sound like they were at the right warehouse. Even though I hadn't seen the outside of it, the inside had seemed abandoned and forgotten. Surely, he would at least see some broken windows from the outside.

"Okay, Seth, call us in ten," I told him before hanging up. I looked at Michael. "They've arrived, but I don't think they are at the correct one. What he described about the outside can't be right."

I felt relieved that they were likely walking into an empty warehouse, far away from any danger. That feeling was quickly replaced by a heightened sense of trepidation. That meant that Michael and I were probably going to arrive at the correct warehouse, and we had no idea what we would be walking into.

Michael must have been having similar thoughts because he grew quiet. He sat up straighter in his seat, as if already on high alert.

We sat in silence, counting down the minutes until Seth was supposed to call back to check in. When it got to the eight-minute mark, I started to get nervous that maybe my assumption had been wrong.

If the warehouse is empty, shouldn't they have been in and out by now?

I didn't want to vocalize it to Michael, but deep down, I was still worried about Raina and the possibility that Becca's prediction was about someone other than Josie. Even though I wasn't Raina's biggest fan, she was still Michael's sister, and losing her would be devastating to us all.

At nine minutes, the phone rang.

I let out an audible sigh of relief as I answered it. "Are you safe?"

"We're good," Seth said. "This warehouse is clear. It just took us a few minutes to figure out how to get inside. Everything was locked up really tight."

"And you're absolutely positive Josie isn't there?"

"One hundred percent," he confirmed. "Are you sure you don't want to wait on us, and we could all go to the other warehouse together?"

"No," I replied. "We're not far away, and I don't want to risk Henley getting there first. Just stick to the plan and meet us at the house."

"Okay … we're leaving the warehouse now and heading to the house," he said. "Be safe, nerd."

I did my best to silently calm my nerves as Michael drove us to the warehouse.

He turned down a desolate street that came to a dead end at the warehouse. The moment it came into sight, I knew this was it. The outside matched what I could memorize about the inside.

It was a four-story brick building that spanned both sides of the street. A walkway connected the two buildings across the second floor. At one point in time, I imagined there had been actual offices in this building as well. Each floor boasted large windows, which were mostly cracked or missing altogether. Just as I dreamed of there being graffiti spray-painted on the inside, there were similar markings on the outside.

Without a doubt, the building was abandoned. It was clear that no one had been here to care for it in quite some time. I'd actually be surprised if this location had even been open when Clark and Weber was still ordering paper from them.

Michael and I got out of the car and looked around. I could tell he was using his heightened hearing senses to listen for any hidden dangers. I listened as well, but everything seemed quiet.

The sight of the warehouse was a little intimidating. I imagined all of the rodents and bugs that probably lurked inside.

"I have a hard time believing a child would go in there," I said. "What could she even be doing all the way out here?"

There were no nearby buildings or streets that were occupied. Everything in the immediate vicinity was entirely uninhibited.

I could tell Michael was just as skeptical as I was. "Only one way to find out."

We slowly approached a door that led to the inside of the warehouse.

"Stay behind me," he said as he drew his gun. He gave the steel door a quick tug, but it didn't move. He pulled on it harder, but it wouldn't budge. "It's either locked or rusted shut."

He walked over to the nearest window, which was completely broken. It must have been smashed a long time ago because I didn't even see remaining traces of glass from the break. He peered inside, but everything seemed dark and quiet. He re-holstered his gun, and then he reached into the window frame and climbed through to the other side.

"Do you want to wait out there?" he asked me.

"No."

If he was going in, I was going with him.

He didn't fight me though. Instead, he reached out and helped me climb up and through the window.

Across the warehouse, I could make out the outline of a shipping container. The inside of the warehouse wasn't a perfect match to my dream, but the similarities were enough to make me absolutely certain that we were in the right place.

"This is definitely it," I whispered as Michael drew his gun again.

We carefully walked through the warehouse, occasionally hearing the sound of something small, like the size of a squirrel or a rat, run across the floor. Shelves that had once stored boxes of paper sat vacant and rusted.

We passed a set of metal stairs that led up to the second floor. I looked up and noticed a metal walkway that suspended from one end of the warehouse to the other. Thick spiderwebs dangled from the bottom of it.

Once we were past all of the metal shelving, I got a better view of the shipping container and saw that it was indeed red. The container sat close to the wall on the far end of the building, just like it had in my dream. If Josie hadn't moved, she would be between the container and the wall.

A knot began to form in my stomach. I reached out for Michael's arm, stopping him. He noticed me clutching my stomach. He didn't say anything, but he knew my instinct was warning us that danger was nearby.

The door to the shipping container was open. The inside looked just as threatening in person as it had in my dream.

"If she's here, she should be over there," I whispered, pointing to the wall behind the shipping container.

Michael put himself between me and the shipping container as we passed the dark opening of it. Once we were past it, I hurried to the back side, looking for Josie.

My heart sank when I realized it was empty.

Are we too late? Did Henley already find her?

With Michael at my side, I threw desperate glances around the warehouse, trying to see if maybe she'd found a new hiding spot.

That was when I looked up and saw two adult shadows standing on the metal platform above us. Michael heard me gasp and followed my gaze upward.

Michael suddenly flew backward into the wall behind us. He bounced off and hit the ground hard. His gun fell out of his hand and slid across the floor. I fought every instinct to go to him, and instead, I drew my hand upward toward the shadows. I wasn't sure which one had done it, but I was going to make them both pay.

Just as I was about to unleash my powers and push them off the platform, something sharp pierced into my leg, and I dropped to the ground. *Have I been shot?*

Michael picked himself up off the floor and dragged me behind the shipping container, out of sight from our assailants.

"Are you hit?" he asked, running his hand over my pant leg.

I expected him to find blood and a bullet wound, but instead, he retrieved a dart of some sort from my leg.

"What's that?" I asked.

He threw the dart on the ground. "I don't know, but can you stand?"

He helped me to my feet and carefully let me go. I was able to put pressure on it without a problem.

"I'm good. I can take them out," I told him.

I could tell Michael was hesitant to allow me to maneuver from behind the safety of the container, but if we were going to get out of there, he needed my help.

Just as he'd done when we escaped from my parents' house in Virginia months ago, he held out his hand, counting it down.

One.

Two.

On three, we dashed from behind the shipping container.

I set my sights on the two people on the platform and unleashed my powers on them full force while Michael grabbed his gun.

With the adrenaline strongly flowing through my body, I expected to unleash a blast big enough to knock them both off the platform, if not take down the entire platform itself. Instead though, the blast was weak, only knocking them off their feet. They landed on the platform with a metallic thud that resounded throughout the warehouse.

As our attackers scrambled back to their feet, Michael acted quickly. He fired at them, forcing them to duck down behind the railing to shield themselves from the bullets. He pushed me in front of him toward a side door in the warehouse.

Glass began to shatter from the few windows above us that hadn't already been busted out. Shards rained down all around us as we tried to run to safety.

I reached the door and pushed on it, praying it wasn't locked. It flew open, and I ran through it.

I heard Michael's breath catch in his throat right before he made it through the doorway. I quickly closed the door behind him and then looked around for a barricade of some sort. I came up empty-handed though. We were in a stairwell, and there was nothing that we could use.

Michael reached his left arm across his chest and over his right shoulder. He retrieved a dart that had hit him.

"I think that dart weakened my abilities," I told him. "I unleashed everything I had back there, and it barely did any damage." I looked down at a deep cut on my arm from the broken glass. "Look, I'm not healing either."

Michael pressed his hand to my arm, but it didn't heal.

"You're right," he agreed, removing his hand.

He quickly reloaded his gun. It was our only weapon now.

"What are we going to do?" I asked.

The stairway only went up, not outside.

"We can't go back out there," he said. "I can only provide so much cover with my gun, and it's too easy for them to knock it out of my hand, using their powers. We're going to have to go up and take our chances."

He rushed around me and started up the stairs. I followed closely behind, throwing a few anxious glances back at the door. I was terrified that they'd come down from their platform to trap us in the stairwell.

"Should we go to the third floor?" I asked as we stopped at a door on the second floor.

"If we do that, we'll really be trapped. I think we have to hurry and try to escape before they locate us on the second floor."

I held my breath as Michael opened the door. He pointed his gun, ready to fire if he spotted our attackers. We were in a section of the warehouse that must have been used for offices. It was separate from the storage area where our attackers had been.

The floor creaked as we ran across it.

"Be careful," Michael told me as he reached his arm out to stop me. He pointed to the floor, and I could see where it was sagging. "These boards are rotten underneath. They could easily give out."

A door somewhere on the second floor flew open. I could hear the reverberation of it bouncing off the office walls. Michael heard it too. He grabbed my hand as we carefully sidestepped around the rotten spot in the floor. He pulled me into one of the vacant offices, and we crouched behind a large, mildew-ridden wooden desk.

The sound of creaking boards grew closer, and I knew they were nearby. It was only a matter of time before they checked this office and found us.

Michael nudged me and pointed to a busted-out window behind us. It was our only way out.

I'll go first, he mouthed.

He quietly stood up and walked to the window. He brought one leg over and then the other. Balancing on a ledge from the outside, he held on to the windowsill and motioned for me to follow.

I stood up and took a step closer. The floor squeaked loudly beneath my feet.

"Hurry," he warned.

Our cover was blown, and I could hear the scrambling of feet outside the office. Our attackers were trying to pinpoint which office the noise had come from.

I ran to Michael and brought one leg over the windowsill. I was halfway out the window when I glanced up and locked eyes with a woman about my age with long blonde hair. She was standing just outside the office. Her blue eyes pierced into me, ready to destroy me.

I could feel Michael pulling me, trying to get me outside, but I hesitated. The girl didn't realize that she was standing by the rotten board in the floor. If she were to step a few inches forward, she'd be directly on it. If I could muster up enough strength to cause disruption to the floor, I might be able to send her crashing through.

"Natalie, come on," Michael pleaded, trying to pull me the rest of the way through the window.

Again, I hesitated. *What if there is a chance we can still defeat them?*

The fact that Henley had sent them in his place meant he knew he was no match for us on his own. He'd never be able to overpower us outside the protection of his facility walls. If we could destroy these two attackers, we'd be once step closer to taking Henley down for good.

The woman took a cautious step forward, unsure of what powers I still possessed. The tips of her toes barely grazed the top of the dip.

Maybe it's her death that I will be responsible for?

"Natalie, *please*," Michael said, desperation in his voice.

I looked at him and saw the fear in his eyes as he reached his hand out toward me. As much as I wanted to continue to fight, to take away this secret power of Henley's, I'd made a promise to Michael. He was begging me to choose him, to choose *us*.

I put my hand in his and threw my other leg over the windowsill just as the blonde-haired woman sent a blast in our direction. She barely missed me, but the blast shook the windowsill, sending Michael and me flying off the small ledge and onto the pavement below.

We each hit the ground with a painful thump.

At first, I was scared to move. I didn't have the ability to heal myself, and I was positive that I must be severely hurt from the fall.

Michael wasted no time though. Within seconds, he scrambled to his feet and was pulling me up. "Hurry," he said, towing me toward the car.

Neither of us looked back as we jumped into the car, and Michael slammed on the gas.

Twenty-One

Natalie

Michael swerved into an empty parking lot, bringing the car to a screeching halt. I looked in the rearview mirror for the hundredth time, making sure we weren't being followed.

He ripped off his jacket, and then he pulled his T-shirt over his head and took it off. Dark bruises had already begun to set in on his arms and chest. I lightly ran my hand over them. As suspected, I couldn't heal him.

"We need to apply pressure to stop the bleeding," he said as he tied the T-shirt tightly around my injured arm.

The cut didn't hurt too badly, but it was pretty deep. Alexander would likely need to stitch it up when we got home.

He reached over and placed his hands on my cheeks, searching my eyes. "Are you okay?"

I nodded. "I'm okay."

Michael narrowed his eyes, and I noticed another bruise forming on his cheekbone. "That was an ambush. My guess is, Luke was behind it."

It shouldn't have surprised me after all that Luke had done, but in a way, it did. Yes, Luke was manipulative, but setting up an ambush to kill us seemed a little out of character for him. He'd never tried to physically hurt me before.

Michael returned his hands to the steering wheel and pulled back onto the road. "Can you call Seth and let them know what happened? Alexander might want to relocate once he knows."

I wasn't sure how we were going to be able to travel with Becca, but I agreed that Alexander would likely still make that call. I pulled out my cell phone and dialed Seth.

"Hey," he greeted me. I could hear the road noise and knew they were still in the car on the way to the house. "Did you find Josie?"

"No," I replied. "It was a setup. We were attacked."

"What? Are you guys okay?" he asked. In the background, I heard him repeat what I'd said to Alexander and Raina. "I'm putting you on speaker."

"We're okay," I assured them. "Just banged up."

"You were right," Michael said loud enough, so they could hear him. "Henley has other people with powers. He sent them to the warehouse to attack us."

"Are you positive you aren't being followed?" Alexander asked.

"Yes, positive," I replied, although I checked again just to make sure.

"We're almost to the house now," Alexander said. "Meet us there. We'll contact Stan and start getting things ready. We'll need to move locations again, this time farther away."

"What about Becca?" I couldn't help but ask.

"We're just going to have to heavily sedate her and drive on through to our next destination."

Alexander was right. There was no way we could show up at a hotel in the middle of the night, dragging an unconscious girl into our room. Someone would definitely notice and call the police on us.

"Okay, we'll hurry," Michael replied, pressing harder on the gas.

When we hung up, I set the phone down on my leg and laid my head back on the headrest, trying to calm myself down.

We have a process, and as long as we follow that process, we should stay safe, I tried to reassure myself.

I uncomfortably shifted in the seat as my body started to ache from the impact of the fall. I was going to be really sore tomorrow.

"Can I ask you something?" Michael asked me after a few minutes.

"Sure. Anything."

He looked at me cautiously. "What happened back there at the warehouse? Why did you hesitate to leave?"

"I was contemplating trying to take out the girl," I replied honestly.

His brows creased together. "Without your powers?"

"Yeah," I admitted. "I thought there was a chance I could let out another small burst, enough maybe to make the floor give out beneath her."

"But you chose not to do it. What made you change your mind?"

I looked over at him. *Doesn't he know?*

"There was a chance that it wouldn't work, and if it hadn't, she'd have likely killed me." I reached over and took his hand in mine. "I meant what I said to you earlier. I wanted to keep my promise."

He lifted my hand and kissed it.

The phone began to ring. I looked down and saw that it was Seth. He was probably at the house and calling to see how far away we were. I let go of Michael's hand and answered it.

"Hi, Seth," I said, shooting Michael a quick smile.

I heard nothing.

"Seth?" My heart began to race, and my stomach twisted.

Silence.

"Seth?" I practically shouted into the phone.

"Natalie … help!" Seth yelled, but he sounded far away from the phone.

I could hear a lot of talking and commotion in the background, but I couldn't make out what anyone was saying.

My mind began to race with possibilities. *Did Henley go to the house? Was he just distracting us by setting up the ambush? Did he go after Becca?*

"Nooo," Seth cried in torment before the phone went dead.

"Seth?" I yelled even though I knew the line was disconnected.

Michael pressed on the gas again. We were now flying twice the speed limit down the road.

I attempted to call Seth back, but it just rang and went to voice mail.

"Try Alexander. Try Raina," Michael told me. His voice was calm, but I could tell by how tightly he was gripping the steering wheel that he was just as worried as I was.

I dialed Alexander and got his voice mail. I called Raina, but the same thing happened. Next, I tried Lorena and then Jen. Every call went to voice mail.

"Where are they?" I cried, feeling the hot, anxious tears begin to spill out of my eyes.

Why can't we reach anyone? What's happening?

It felt like an eternity had passed before we were near the house. The tires on the car squealed as Michael rounded the final corner to turn down our street. We barreled into the driveway, pulling in next to Alexander's car. The car came to a stop, and Michael threw it in park, but he didn't even bother to turn it off.

We bolted out of the car and up the front steps of the house. Michael drew his gun again. I had no weapon, but I didn't care. I would fight to the death with my bare hands to protect our family.

The front door was partially open, and Michael entered first. He came to an abrupt stop in front of me, and I almost bumped into him from behind. I moved to his side and stood there in shock.

The inside of the house looked like a bomb had gone off. Furniture had been overturned, the curtains in the living room had been pulled from the rods, and there was a giant hole in the wall, exposing the kitchen in the next room.

It took me a moment to register that everyone else was on the floor. To the left of the living room, Lorena lay on the floor, unconscious. She was bleeding from a wound to her head, and Raina had her hand pressed to it, uselessly trying to stop the bleeding. Alexander sat on the other side of Lorena, digging into his medical bag.

My eyes shifted to the right side of the room, where I found Jen lying on the floor. Seth was trying to wake her up.

Did the two assailants make it to the house before we did? Or are there others that we don't know about? Are they still in the house?

Michael ran to Lorena, and I rushed to Jen. I dropped to the floor, next to Seth.

"What happened?" Michael asked Alexander.

"We don't know," Alexander replied, and I could tell he was trying his best to remain calm. "We found them like this."

I looked down at Jen. She wasn't moving.

"Please heal her," Seth begged me, his voice tight. "She won't wake up."

Jen's arm was bent strangely and swollen, obviously broken. I reached down and gently rested my hand on it, willing it to heal. Nothing happened.

Jen had the start of a black eye. I moved my hands to cup the sides of her face. Still, she remained the same.

The dart. I can't heal her.

"Why isn't it working?" Seth asked.

"I … I don't have my powers."

"I don't think she's breathing," Seth said, moving to the other side of her. He quickly checked her pulse and then started to perform CPR.

I looked over at Michael. He had the same look of shock and helplessness that I knew mirrored my own horror. We were useless to aid them.

Michael fumbled in his pocket and pulled out his phone. He was resorting to calling 911—something we *never* did.

"Come on, baby," Seth said as he administered compressions to Jen. "Please don't leave me."

I stood up, feeling like I was in the center of a bad dream. I blinked, hoping that maybe I could wake up from this nightmare, the way I had always been able to wake up from senseless dreams in the past.

I closed my eyes, trying to find my way out of this strange world. *This isn't real. This can't be happening.*

"You're going to be responsible for her death, you know." I heard Becca's voice echo in my mind. *"How are you going to live with yourself?"*

My eyes snapped open. All this time, I'd thought she meant Josie's death, but I'd misunderstood.

I looked between Lorena and Jen. Lorena was the mother of the man I loved and had been like a mother to me since we left Charlotte. Then, I looked at Jen, one of my dearest friends and the fiancée of my best friend. The thought of losing either of them was unimaginable.

The knot took hold of me once again, and I knew I was right. One of them was going to die, if not both of them.

In a failed attempt to keep them safe, I was the one who'd asked them to stay behind, to look after Becca. *This is my fault.*

My eyes trailed up the stairs, and I wondered if there was any chance that Becca was still up there, unharmed and asleep in her bed. I knew that was unlikely though. Whoever had done this must have been there to retrieve her. Henley must have planned this whole thing to leave her unguarded, so he could take her back without a fight.

The knot twisted again, and it felt like it was pulling me up the stairs. The inkling concerned me. Without a doubt, Becca knew a lot about the inner workings of Henley's facility, and that would pose a threat to Henley himself if she were to remember who she really was.

What if Henley had decided to kill her instead of reclaiming her?

I wanted to sprint up the stairs, but my legs felt heavy, and my brain was in a haze. I slowly moved up the stairs, terrified that I would find my sister dead.

In the background, I could hear Michael on the phone with the 911 operator. Seth remained at Jen's side, performing CPR. Alexander was saying something to Raina, but I couldn't make out the words.

I made it to the second story of the house and felt almost relieved to be out of the chaos, to hear only muffled noises coming from downstairs.

The feeling, however, was only short-lived.

Parts of a door lay scattered in the middle of the hallway. The hinges were still attached to one piece of it. I looked at each of the bedrooms on the second floor. All of the doors were open and intact. The broken door must have come from upstairs—from Becca's room.

From the hallway, I could see that each room on the second floor was in complete disarray. Furniture had been thrown around the rooms and broken apart. Piles of clothes had spilled out of the dressers and onto the floor.

I started up the stairs to the third floor to Becca's room, terrified of what I would find when I got there. Halfway up the stairs, I confirmed that it had in fact been her bedroom door. Wood from the doorframe drew outward in pointed spikes. The walls surrounding the stairs showed large holes and indentions from where they'd sustained substantial impact. The door had been blown off, but it had occurred from *inside* the room. This, I hadn't expected.

As much as I wanted to turn around and run back downstairs, my intuition urged me forward. It insisted that I go upstairs to her room. It whispered to me an awful truth that I didn't want to hear.

When I reached the doorway to Becca's bedroom, I saw that her room had been completely devastated, but she was nowhere to be found. The knot began to release, but I still felt an overwhelming sense of dread as I took in the sight of Becca's headboard split into two separate pieces.

The sound of a bloodcurdling scream resonated throughout the house from downstairs. It was Raina—and that could only mean one thing.

Lorena is dead.

I heard feet pounding up the stairs, but I couldn't move. My eyes shifted from the headboard, to the shattered dresser drawers on the floor, to the pile of ripped sheets that used to cover Becca's bed. Next to them were the shredded remains of the scarves that had once restrained her.

I knew it was Michael behind me. I could feel his presence.

I gathered the courage to turn around and face him. His eyes were questioning, searching the room as I had, looking for answers. I watched helplessly as he realized what had really happened.

We'd blamed Luke for the ambush, but in reality, this hadn't been about Luke at all. It had been about Becca and her plans to escape.

Becca must have heard me and Michael talking in the car about how I'd gotten my powers after he saved me. Her suicide attempt had really been a ploy to get Michael to heal her. She had known he loved me, and because of that, he wouldn't let her die.

Becca had somehow used her dream-visitation abilities to make me believe Josie was real and in danger. Despite thinking I was a threat to her, Becca knew deep down that I would never allow a little girl to suffer the same nightmare I'd lived through at Henley. She'd set it up, so we'd all leave the house to rescue Josie, and that was when she'd planned to make her move.

Michael looked at me, his eyes full of hurt and shock. It had never occurred to either of us that Becca could inherit his powers the way I had.

I turned back to face the room and the grim reality of our future. There was no going back to the way things had been before. Things could never be normal again.

My sister was now a murderer. She was dangerous and powerful and posed a threat to us all.

She was a monster that Henley had created and that we had unknowingly fed.

And now, she is a monster that must be stopped.

THE END

ACKNOWLEDGMENTS

Thank you to my fun, sweet, and supportive husband, Dran. I love you more than anything.

Mom, thank you for not only being my mom, but also my friend, shopping buddy, non-paid therapist, and biggest cheerleader.

Brande and Melissa, I could never thank you enough. Your faith in my writing is what pushed me to believe I could actually do this.

Pam, thank you for not only being an amazing sister in law and a dear friend, but for also agreeing to lend me your medical expertise for this book.

A special thanks to Mary, for always believing in me.

Jovana, you are amazing. I'm not kidding when I tell you that you are an editing genius. I'm so thankful that I get to work with you.

Tim, thank you again for creating another amazing cover for my novel. Your work is truly remarkable.

Thank you to all of my friends and family who have loved and supported me on this journey. I will never be able to express to you how grateful I am to have you all in my corner!

And thank you to everyone who has taken the time to read *The Unveiling* and now *The Deceiving*.

About the Author

Laurie Harrison graduated from the University of Central Florida with a degree in Interdisciplinary Studies, majoring in both Letters and Modern Languages, and Social Sciences. She has since found her niche, writing young adult and new adult fiction. When she's not writing, Laurie enjoys spending time with her husband, traveling, and getting lost in a good book. You can visit her website at www.laurieharrisonauthor.com.

Other Books by Laurie Harrison

The Unveiling

The Deceiving

Made in the USA
Columbia, SC
28 June 2025